I0548858

# Dick in the Everglades

## A. W. Dimock

**Dick in the Everglades**

Copyright © 2014 by Bibliotech Press
All rights reserved.

Contact:
BibliotechPress@gmail.com

The present edition is a reproduction of 1909 publication of this work. Minor typographical errors may have been corrected without note, however, for an authentic reading experience the spelling, punctuation, and capitalization have been retained from the original text.

ISBN: 978-1-61895-190-8

To Raymond Firestone

Dear Raymond,

I hope you will like these dream children of mine, as well as I knew they would like you

Affectionately yours

The Happy Vale
Peekamose ny
May 7, 1917.

iii

# PREFACE

Dick in the Everglades is a true story. All that imagination had to do with it was to find names for the boys and arrange a sequence of events. Other characters, white and Indian, appear under names similar to, or identical with their own. Any old alligator hunter, familiar with the swamps and the Ten Thousand Islands, can follow the course of the explorers from the text of the story. It would be possible for two fearless boys, imbued with a love of Nature and the wilderness, to repeat, incident by incident, the feats of the explorers in the identical places mentioned in the story.

Many of the stories are understatements, seldom is one exaggerated. I have been asked if it were possible for a boy to handle a manatee in the water as one of the boys was represented as doing. I have done it myself three times with manatees three times the size of these in the story. In the story the manatees escaped. Two of those which I captured were sent to the New York Aquarium, where one of them lived for twenty months. The crocodiles which the boys sent to the Zoological Park may be seen to-day, alive and well in the reptile house. The frequent swamping of canoes and skiffs by porpoises, or dolphins, tarpon and manatees are all experiences of my own.

Aside from the Government charts which give the coast line only, the existing maps of the scene of the story are worse than useless. In them a hundred square miles are given to Ponce de Leon Bay, which doesn't exist, unless the little depression in the coast which is called Shark River Bight is accounted a bay. Rivers are omitted; one with a mouth fifty feet wide is represented as a mile broad. A little stream four miles long is sent wandering over a hundred and forty miles of imaginary territory. I have sailed and paddled for days at a time over the watercourses of South Florida, with a compass before me and a pad at hand on which every change of course was noted and distances estimated, and although no attempt at accurate charting has ever been made, I am quite sure that none of the natural features or products of the country traversed by the young explorers have been misrepresented in the book.

The pictures are from photographs taken on the scene of the incidents they illustrate. They show more conclusively than can any words of mine, how beautiful is the region traversed by the boy

iv

explorers and what interesting and exciting adventures they enjoyed.

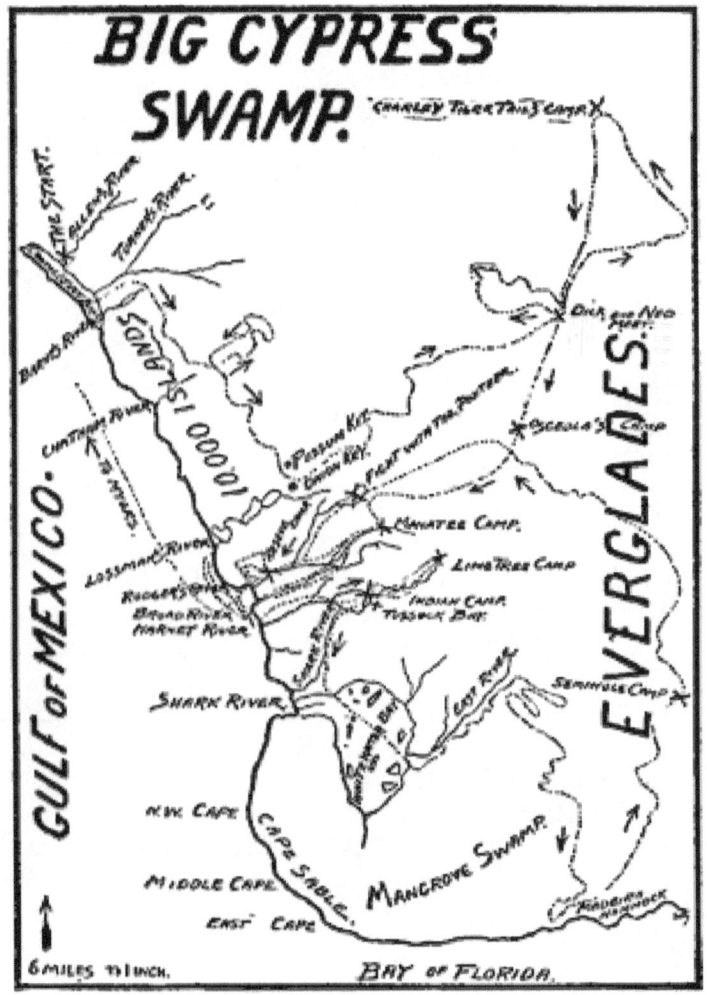

MAP SHOWING DICK'S CRUISE IN A CANOE

v

# CONTENTS

# CHAPTER I

## THE CHUMS

"Come in!"

The doctor's voice had a note of sternness which was not lost on the two boys waiting outside his study door. The taller of the two, Ned Barstow, turned the handle and stepped into the study, followed immediately by Dick Williams. The doctor, sitting behind his desk, looked decidedly uncompromising as he said:

"Now, Barstow and Williams, you were absent from your room last night. Where were you?"

"Camping in Farmer Field's woods, sir," replied Ned Barstow.

"How often has this happened before?"

"Twice, sir."

"Was any one else with you?"

"Only last night, sir. Another boy was with us then," said Ned.

"Who was he?" "I can't tell you, sir."

"Williams, you may go now. I will see you later."

After the door had closed on Williams, the doctor turned again to Barstow, and said:

"Barstow, I have always felt that I could rely upon your influence with the younger boys being for good. Now, I find you aiding to upset the whole discipline of the school by this camping affair. I hope there has been nothing worse. You know I never insist on tale-bearing regarding mere boyish escapades, but I would like to know if there was any other reason for your refusing to give up your companion's name."

"Yes, sir, there was. We had a chicken for supper, that was taken from Farmer Field's poultry-house."

"Did you or Williams steal that chicken, Barstow?"

"No, sir, but we knew about it and helped eat it, and are just as much to blame as the boy who took it."

"And, now, you mean to protect the thief?"

"Well, you see, Doctor, a good many fellows don't look at hooking apples, or nuts, or chickens as real stealing."

"What do you think about it?" asked the doctor.

"I think it was wrong and I am very sorry it happened. It won't occur again."

"I have no fear that it will. But it is too serious an offence to be

1

lightly passed over. In the first place you and Williams must see Farmer Field, tell him what you have done and pay for the chicken that was—taken. After that I will talk with you. Now send Williams to me."

When Dick Williams came in the doctor began:

"Williams, how much do you love your mother?"

"Why, more than anyone else in the world, sir."

"She is keeping you here at considerable expense. Don't you think you owe it to her to pay more attention to your studies?"

"Yes, Doctor, and I am going to do better hereafter."

"How will your mother feel when she hears of this chicken-stealing episode?"

"Oh! Doctor; she mustn't hear of it that way. We didn't think of it as stealing last night, but this morning Ned and I talked about it and we are going to see Farmer Field and tell him what we did and pay for the chicken."

"Do you mean, Dick," and the good doctor's voice shook a little as he asked the question, "that you and Ned decided to tell Farmer Field about the taking of his chicken, before you knew that I had heard of your camping out?"

"Why, yes, sir. I supposed Ned had told you."

"Your friend Ned is rather a curious boy, but when you are in doubt about the right and wrong of anything, you might do worse than ask his advice."

"Oh! I get enough of that without asking for it," said Dick.

And the doctor laughed, but he soon looked pretty serious again, and said:

"Dick, I think no one will tell your mother and she need never know, but I hope you will tell her all about it of your own accord."

"Sure!" said Dick, "I couldn't keep that or anythink else away from Mumsey for five minutes after I saw her."

There was a significant pause, during which the doctor stroked his chin meditatively before asking:

"Now, what in the world made you two boys go on that camping escapade? I want you to tell me that, Dick."

The boy hesitated a moment and then said:

"Why, I really don't know, Doctor—we just wanted to. You see, there are so many things to see and listen to at night that way. Birds and animals, I mean. Ned and I are going to be explorers some day, you know."

"Hum!" said the doctor.

"Well, that will do for the present, Williams. I hope you understand that you are escaping serious trouble very easily and

2

that you mean to be as good as you can for the rest of the time you are at the school."

Fanner Field received Ned and Dick with an air of gruffness that was belied by twinkling blue eyes and, when Ned had finished telling his story and offered to pay for the chicken, said:

"Did you take that chicken out of my poultry-house?"

"Not exactly, but it's the same thing. We knew about it and helped eat it."

"Was it tender?" asked the farmer.

"No, sir, it was the toughest thing I ever put in my mouth."

"I thought so. Why, that rooster was a regular antique. He must have been a hundred years old. Next time you want a chicken for a late supper, better let me choose it for you. Who helped you eat that rooster?"

"Please don't ask us that. We'll tell you anything about ourselves, but we can't give him away."

"Wouldn't think much of you if you did. No need of it anyhow. I know who it was."

"He must have told you then, for we haven't told anybody."

"Do you remember that while you were cooking that rooster out in my woods, Steve Daly, your companion, said he heard somebody in the bushes and you said it was only a dog?"

"Yes, I remember it. I did say that."

"Well, I was that dog!"

"And you never told on us?" asked Dick. "Then you've been mighty kind and I'm ashamed to look you in the face."

"Never be ashamed to look anyone in the face, my boy. It isn't good to take even a little thing that doesn't belong to you, but that won't happen again to you. But weren't you playing truant when you had that tough supper in my woods? Doesn't your conscience trouble you at all about that?"

"Not a bit," said Dick; "that wasn't mean."

It was fortunate for Dick's peace of mind that his conscience wasn't troubled by mischief, for he was never out of it and was at the root of about all the purely mischievous happenings at the school.

Even the lesson of the camping incident and the doctor's kindly talk wore off in a fortnight. Yet he was popular with teachers as well as pupils. His head was crowned with a mass of sandy hair and his impertinent face plastered with freckles. The boy was quick and full of grace as a wildcat and so well built and lithe that he was a terror on the football team.

Dick was often too busy to attend to his studies and fell behind in his lessons, until the good doctor sent for him and gave

3

him an earnest but understanding talk which sent the boy back to his books, filled with remorse and determined to get to the head of his class in a hurry. One of these resolves was usually effective for about a week. After which Dick generally suffered a severe relapse.

During his last winter at school, he frequently took long tramps in the woods in the hours when he should have been at his books, and was finally taken to task by his chum for the bad example he was setting the younger boys by playing truant.

"But, Ned," said Dick, "I just can't keep away from the woods, and they do me good, I know they do. I am a whole lot better every way after a good long tramp by myself through the thickest woods I can find. I'd like to camp out in them to-night and I believe I will."

"That's all right, Dick. I'll camp with you; only we've got to have Doc's permission. He trusts us a lot, and we can't go back on him."

"Nice chance we've got of getting that. Maybe he'd camp with us!" said Dick satirically.

"Shouldn't wonder if he would. You don't understand Doc. Did you ever know him to refuse a fellow anything he squarely asked for, unless he simply had to do it? Come along."

And the boys walked together to the study.

"Doctor," said Ned, "Dick and I want to camp out to-night in Farmer Field's woods, if you have no objection."

"Want to camp out? Well, so do I, only I am afraid I might be needed here. Do you know how to camp? What do you expect to take with you and how will you keep warm?"

"We thought of taking a hatchet, a blanket for each of us and some potatoes to roast. Then we will make a bed of hemlock boughs, build a fire near it and roll up in our blankets."

"Well, you may go, and I will help out your commissariat with a loaf of bread and a chicken. But be sure you have plenty of fuel ready before dark. It will be a cold night and you will have to replenish your fire three or four times before morning."

"Thank you, Doctor. You don't know how much obliged we are to you for your kindness."

"And you don't know how much trouble I am in for, when the rest of the boys hear of this escapade of yours."

But after the study door closed the doctor smiled quietly to himself and said under his breath:

"Just like myself at their age—have the woods instinct."

Ned and Dick slept little that night. There was about a foot of snow on the ground and they scraped bare a place for their camp-fire beside a big stump and gathered enough fuel from windfalls for

4

the night. Then they rolled a log beside the fire for a seat and built a soft bed with fragrant branches of hemlock and spruce. They roasted the chicken over a thick bed of glowing coals and baked potatoes in the ashes of the fire. The chicken was carved with their pocket knives and they got along without forks or plates. By using bark gathered from a birch and softening it over their fire they made cups with which they brought water from a nearby brook. When supper was finished the boys rolled up in their blankets and lying on the bed they had built on the snow, inhaled its fragrance as they watched the eddying smoke of their camp-fire and the stars that shone through the spreading branches above them and listened to the voices of the night, from the distant cry of an owl to the whish of falling snow, shaken from evergreen boughs by the breeze. They had visions of camps, scattered from the equator to the poles, some of which were destined to be realized. Ned formed a plan that night, of which he wrote to his father, but of which he said nothing at the time to his chum.

But as Dick stood beside Ned in their last hour at Belleville, and the sadness of parting was in the face and eyes from which fun usually bubbled, Ned said:

"My father owns a tract of land in the Big Cypress Swamp of Florida. There is a lot of fine timber on it and he intends to set up a lumber mill in the swamp and perhaps build a railroad from Fort Myers to some part of it. A surveyor with a guide is going into the swamp this fall to locate the best timber and I'm going with them. You know how we have planned to do real camping and exploring together. Well, here's our chance. I've written to Dad and he invites you to go with me. We can start any time. When can you be ready, Dick?"

"Ned, I'd give all I have in the world to go with you, but I can't—I can't. Mother has spent more than she could afford to keep me at this school and sometimes I'm ashamed when I think how I've wasted my time. Now I don't mean to be an expense to her or anyone else hereafter. I won't take a penny that I don't earn, from anybody, and I won't go on any trip, even with you, until I can pay my own way, every cent of it."

"But, Dick, your companionship and the work you can do will be worth all it costs, twice over, to me and to Dad and he will feel just that way about it."

"It's like you, Ned, to say all that, but it's no use and you know it. You've been mighty good to me ever since I came to this school and I'm going to keep your good opinion by not accepting your offer to go with you now. Some time, when I can keep up my end, I'll be with you bigger than an Injun. If you ever find strange footprints down in those Everglades, better foller 'em up. They'll likely be mine. Good-bye, Ned."

The boys clasped hands and as Dick walked away tears rolled down his freckled cheeks.

Four months after the parting of the two friends, at Belleville, Dick received a letter postmarked "Immokalee, Florida," which was headed:

Big Cypress Swamp,
20 miles from anywhere,
October 10th.

DEAR CHUM:

Here I am! on a prairie inside the Big Cypress Swamp, about which we used to talk and where we planned to camp some day. Well, it's bigger than anything we ever dreamed of and every foot of it is alive. Sometimes I sleep in a tent, but more often under the stars. Last night I heard the scream of a panther, so near that it made me shiver, and the next minute a frog dropped from the branch of a tree over my head and fell on my face. I must have screamed louder than the panther, for I scared Chris Meyer, the surveyor, who is camping with me, pretty badly. The guide we expected didn't come, so we are guiding for ourselves. I hope Chris knows where we are, for I am sure I don't. We measure the big cypress trees with a tape line and Chris calculates the number of feet of lumber in each tree. Then we estimate the trees in an acre and guess at the number of acres. At least that's the way the business looks to me. Sometimes the walking is easy, but to-day we had to wade through mud waist-deep and the moccasins were pretty thick. I watched out for the ugly things and it kept me on the jump, but Chris marched straight ahead and paid no attention to them, excepting once when a big cotton-mouth that was coiled on top of a stump struck at him. Then he fell over backward into the mud, and I had a good laugh at him—afterwards. Chris killed that snake. It was a short, thick snake and about as pretty as a Bologna sausage, but its mouth opened five inches and its long, needle-like fangs were dripping with venom. I am hungry all the time and enjoy our bill of fare very much, although it is only bacon, grits and coffee, morning, noon and night. We are traveling light, for we carry all our baggage on our backs. We see deer and wild turkey every day and it's pretty hard to keep my hands off my rifle, but I promised Dad not to shoot anything out of season. In three weeks the law will be off and then it will be bad for the first buck I meet. Chris says it's good for me to see a lot of deer before I shoot at any. He says I won't be so likely to miss or only wound them when I really hunt them. I guess he's about right, for when I first saw a deer—it was a big buck and only twenty yards away—I had a regular attack of buck ague and I couldn't have hit the side of a house even if I'd been inside it. Now I can look at one, point a stick at him and say bang, with my nerves just as quiet as if it were a cow. I have seen a few bears, but they are very shy. We'll turn loose on them, too, when we get round to hunting, but in the mean time we are sticking to our timber job for all there is in it.

An old alligator hunter is camping beside us to-night. He is bound for Boat Landing, with a lot of alligator hides and otter skins, and I am finishing up this letter to send by him. Just as soon as this surveying business is over I am going to have a glorious hunt. If only you were here we would start out by our lonesomes and have all the adventures we ever talked about. Probably Chris will go with me. I haven't quite the pluck to try it alone, as I know you would do in my place. I may brace up to it, though. Dad has given me permission to do just as I please. He says he trusts me not to be foolish or foolhardy and to keep him informed of my plans. Isn't he a good Dad? Come if you can. Come when you can.
Always and forever your chum,

NED

Dick's mother read Ned's letter and was quiet and sad all the rest of the day. After Dick had gone to bed she went into his room, sat down on the bed beside him, kissed him and said:

"Dicky boy, mother wants you to take a good, long vacation. You've worked hard and been a great comfort to her since you left school and now she's going to send you to your chum Ned, down in Florida where she knows your heart is. Now—don't speak yet— mother knows what you want to say. dear, but she can perfectly well afford to send you and you will hurt her feelings if you don't let her."

Dick put his arms around his mothers' neck and as soon as he could speak, half sobbed out:

"Oh, Mumsey, I can't take your money. You've got so little."

"But mother wants you to, so much."

Dick held his mother's face close to his own for a minute and then said, very slowly:

"Mumsey, I'll go—and it's really and truly because you want me to—but I won't take any of your money. Hush, now! Don't you say a word, or I'll—disown you. I've got a ten-dollar bill of my own

7

and I'll keep that in my pocket just so you won't worry for fear I'm hungry; and I will bet you ten dollars I'll bring that same bill back to you and I won't go hungry one day either."

"But, Dick—"

"Not one word, Mumsey, except to say you'll take that bet. I can get a ride to New York on a boat, any day. Then I'll go to the Mallory Line and work my way to Key West on one of their boats; and from Key West I can find a fishing boat that will land me on the west coast of Florida somewhere within a hundred miles of Ned, and I'd walk that far just for the fun of surprising him."

# CHAPTER II

## DICK GOES TO SEA

Three days after Dick's talk with his mother, he boarded a Key West steamer just as it was leaving its New York pier. He sat on the deck and watched busy ferry-boats in the river, fussy tugs and chug-chugging launches in the harbor, and the white-winged yachts and great ocean steamers in the lower bay. He looked back from the Narrows upon the receding city, to the east upon Coney Island with its pleasure palaces, and to the southwest upon the great curve of Sandy Hook. Every step upon the deck near him brought his heart into his mouth in dread of what he knew he had to face. When the steamer was opposite Long Branch and there was small chance that he could be sent back, he inquired for the captain, whom he found talking to some young girls among the passengers. This somewhat reassured Billy, for he felt that the captain wouldn't eat him up in the presence of the young ladies, and he stood waiting with his cap in his hand until the captain spoke to him.

"Do you want to see me, my boy?"

"If you are Captain Anderson, I do, sir."

"All right, go ahead."

"I want you to set me to work, sir."

"Why should I set you to work? Do you belong on the boat?"

"Not yet, but you see it's this way. I had to get to Key West and I thought I'd work my passage with you."

"Why didn't you ask me before we left the dock?"

8

"Because I was afraid you wouldn't take me, if you could help it, and I had to go."

"You cheeky little devil, I believe I'll chuck you overboard."

"Oh!" said a brown-eyed girl who stood beside the captain, "you mustn't do that!"

The captain laughed and said to Dick:

"I hope you understand that you owe your life to this young lady. Now, go and report yourself to the cook and tell him to put you on the worst job he's got."

"Thank you very much, Captain, but couldn't you make it the engineer instead of the cook? I'd rather work than wash dishes."

"I'd like to oblige so modest a boy. Report to the chief engineer, give him my compliments and tell him you are to have the hottest berth on the boat. He'll probably set you to shoveling coal."

Dick thanked him again; then looking into the face of the girl, he said:

"Thank you, Miss Brown-Eyes, for saving my life," and, bowing low, turned away.

"Captain, couldn't you see that he was a gentleman? What made you give him such hard work?" asked the girl.

"Because he was such a cheeky gentleman that if I let him stay on deck he would take command of the boat by to-morrow and all you young ladies who helped him would be guilty of mutiny and would have to be executed."

Dick was put to work in the engine-room, oiling the machinery. Some of the work was easy and safe, some of it was easy but not safe. Oil cups had to be filled as they flew back and forth, bearings must be oiled after great steel rods had flashed by and before they returned. The swift, silent play of the great piston and the steady motion of the resistless, revolving shaft, half hypnotized the boy and he stood, dazed and in danger, until called down by the sharp rebuff of the engineer.

"'Tend to your business, there. Don't watch that shaft or you'll go dotty."

On the second day of the trip there was trouble in the fire-room. The steamer had started on the trip short of firemen and now a fireman who had fallen in the furnace-room, striking his head on the steel floor, was lying unconscious in his berth. The pointer on the steam-gauge fell back, the engine slowed down, crisp commands came from pilot-house to engine-room, sharper messages passed between engine and fire rooms, while overworked men grew sullen and threatened to throw down their shovels.

9

Dick offered to do the work of a fireman, but the engineer shook his head and said:

"That's a man's work, boy."

"Give me a shovel and a chance."

And they were given him. He soon learned to throw the coal evenly and feed the furnaces like a fireman, but his unseasoned body shrank from the fierce heat; he staggered back from the hot blast every time he swung open a great furnace door and, until the clang of its closing, he could scarcely draw a breath. He threw off his jumper and his white skin fairly gleamed in that grimy place. The other firemen looked curiously at that slight, boyish form which was doing a man's work like a man and there was no more shirking in front of those furnaces. The fireman nearest the boy often pushed him aside and spread shovelfuls of coal over his grates, rushing back to his own work that it might not fall behind. A strong beam wind sprang up and the boat rolled badly, while Dick, with his hands blistered, fought fiercely to keep off seasickness and to keep up his fire.

Up in the main saloon and around the deck a young girl wandered as if she wanted something without quite knowing what it was. She climbed stairs under the sign "passengers not allowed," went in and out of the pilot-house and, meeting the captain, asked if she couldn't go wherever she wished on the boat. He replied:

"Yes, Miss. I appoint you third mate, with power to give any orders you please and go wherever you wish."

A little later, with a dark waterproof drawn tightly over her light dress, she opened the door leading to the engine-room, and clinging to the heavy brass rail, climbed slowly down the narrow, greasy iron stairway till she stood beside the mighty engine. The engineer hastened to her side.

"It's against the rules and very dangerous, Miss, for a passenger to come into this room."

"But the captain told me I could come."

"All right, but please be very careful and hold tight to that rail. I am afraid I haven't any right to let you stay, anyhow."

"Thank you very much and I'll be very careful."

The girl watched the engine for some time and then crept slowly along a steel bridge that looked like a spider's web, from which she could look into the furnace-room, with its roaring fires, scorching heat and constantly clanging iron doors. For some minutes she gazed silently, then turning quickly, hurried across the bridge, up the greasy stairs and on to the main saloon where she found her father in a big arm-chair, buried in a book. The girl first

10

pulled the book out of her father's hands, then, sitting on the arm of his chair, clasped her hands on his shoulder and whispered eagerly into his ear.

"Daddy, I want you to get that boy out of that hot place down in the bottom of the boat where he is at work. I know he's sick, for I saw him lean up against the wall and shut his eyes and he was just as white—"

"Why, Molly, where have you been to see all this?"

"First, I went where the big engine is, then I went a little farther and saw—Oh! Daddy, hurry, please; if you don't I know he'll die."

"So you want me to get this boy up in the saloon to play with you?"

"I don't mean that at all, Daddy. I should think you'd hate to see anybody worked to death down in that hot hole."

"Well, I'll see the captain about it as soon as I have finished my book."

"Don't you think you'd better see him now? I'm quite sure you won't enjoy your book while I'm here and I've decided to stay with you for the present."

"All right, Molly, come along," and they hunted up the captain, whom they found sitting near the pilot-house.

"Captain, I have taken an interest in that stowaway of yours. Is there any objection to having his name put on the cabin list, at my expense, of course?"

"No kick coming from me," said the captain, "though we are short-handed in the fire-room and the boy has been doing a man's work there. I don't believe he will accept your offer, for he's an independent little cub and, as I have put him to work, I can't insist upon it."

The captain sent a deck-hand for Dick, and the boy appeared on deck in overalls and jumper, cap in hand.

"Dick," said the captain, "this gentleman has put your name on the passenger list. The purser will give you a room and a seat at the table."

"Oh, Captain, please don't take me from my work. I know I've got to leave it if you say so, but—"

"No, you haven't," interrupted the captain; "you are on the pay-roll and can hang on to your job as long as you do your work."

Dick's face was still troubled as he turned toward Molly and her father, meeting a reproachful look from the girl, which made him wonder if he had seemed ungrateful for the kindness shown him, and said:

11

"I want to thank you a thousand times for your kindness and I will come to the cabin if you think I—Have you any boy of your own, sir?"

"Yes, I have a boy of about your age."

"If he were here, in my place, what would you like to have him do?"

"I'd be proud of him if he did just what you're doing, my boy."

Tears were in Dick's voice as he said:

"Thank you very much, sir," then, turning to Molly, a roguish smile lit up his face as he bowed to her, saying:

"Thank you again, Miss Brown-Eyes."

The next day when Dick was off duty, instead of going to his bunk, he dressed himself carefully and went up on the promenade deck. It was quite contrary to the rules, but the officers only smiled and looked away, while many of the passengers spoke to him, for the story of his having refused cabin passage was pretty well known on the boat. He walked about restlessly, as if in search of something or somebody, until he caught sight of a girl in the extreme bow of the boat, looking down upon the water twenty feet below her. Dick suddenly discovered that he wanted to look over the bow, too. A minute later he was leaning on the rail behind the girl, looking down upon a school of porpoises, or herring hogs, which were playing about the boat. A jet of water and spray curled upward from the cutwater of the steamer, which was running at high speed, but the graceful little creatures kept abreast of her without apparent effort. There were twenty or thirty of them, gliding in and out as gracefully as if they were moving to the measure of a waltz. Sometimes one touched the prow or side of the boat; usually they kept pace with the steamer as evenly as if they were a part of it; but occasionally one darted ahead at a speed which left the boat behind as if it were standing still. At last the girl, long conscious that some one was standing beside her, putting out her hand to that somebody, said:

"Aren't they dears? Oh!" she added, as her hand was taken and she looked around, "I thought it was Daddy. Please excuse me."

Dick looked as if he might be persuaded to forgive her, and for some minutes they stood in silence, leaning over the rail and looking at the playful porpoises beneath them, when he said:

"I hope you don't think I didn't appreciate your father's lovely offer. You will never know how grateful I really was to him—and to somebody else, too, who, I think, had something to do with it."

"Of course I don't think you were ungrateful, but I did hate to see you at work down in that hot place and I don't see why you

12

couldn't have come up in the cabin and been comfortable and not had to wear such greasy clothes."

"How did you know where I was at work?"

"I happened to be looking at the big engine and I walked along a little way and saw you way, way down near the bottom of the boat in front of a hot furnace, shoveling coal into it."

"Now I know where that offer came from," said Dick, "and I want you to see why I couldn't accept it. I wanted very, very much to get to Key West and I was very glad of the chance to work my passage. Perhaps it was wrong to come aboard the way I did. I guess it was. But Captain Anderson gave me a job and made it all right. Now I'm not ashamed to look anyone in the face, even when I have on my fireman's clothes, while if I gave up my work and let a stranger give me what I could earn myself I would feel like a charity scholar and I don't think I'd have the cheek to speak to you or any one else on board."

Molly told her father of her talk with Dick and he said:

"I can use that kind of a boy in my business. I'll have a talk with him when we get to Key West."

Three days later the great steamer lay beside her wharf in Key West. Dick was paid the full wages of a fireman for the trip and when he said he wasn't worth so much, was good-naturedly told to shut up and advised that if he refused to take money that was offered him in that town he was likely to be caught and exhibited as a freak. He shed his jumper and overalls and exchanged hearty good-byes with the whole crew of the steamer. He walked through the saloons, but it was early, most of the passengers were yet in their berths and neither Molly nor her father was to be seen. Dick went out on the dock to inquire for a boat to Chokoloskee, Caxambas or Marco. He was referred to a Captain Wilson, who told him that the boat for Chokoloskee had just sailed, was beyond hailing distance and wouldn't leave again for a week, and that there was no Caxambas or Marco boat in port. Dick found the captain so genial and friendly that he told him something of his story.

"I'll fix you out," said Captain Wilson. "I own a sponging outfit and am just starting out on a cruise, but I'm one man short. So you come in his place. It will be a short trip, not over four weeks. You'll make good wages and I'll find you a chance to get to Chokoloskee when we get back. You can live on board till I find it. If you stay here you are bound to lose a week and your board anyhow."

"I'd like to go first rate, but I don't know anything about sponging."

"You'll learn fast enough. Can you scull?"

13

"A little. I can row better."

"Have to scull in sponging, but you'll pick that up. Can you come aboard now? I want to be off."

"I need some clothes and would like to say 'good-bye' to some friends on the steamer."

"I can fit you out on board with all the clothes you will need on the cruise, so hurry up and see your friends. I'll wait here for you."

But Molly and her father had left the steamer and Dick went with Captain Wilson aboard his sloop, which sailed at once.

The captain hunted up some clothes for Dick to wear while sponging and as the boy came on deck after putting them on, his first glance fell on the white sails of a schooner yacht which had just passed them, but was then two hundred yards away. The beauty of the boat appealed to Dick and his eyes rested lingeringly upon her. How much greater would have been his interest had he known that the two forms which he could see on the deck of the yacht, near the companionway, were the Molly of whom he was thinking at that moment, and her father, and that they were talking of him. What a pity that he couldn't have known that Key West had been searched for him and that Molly's father had offered a reward for his name and address! Had Dick come on deck two minutes sooner the bow of the yacht Gypsey would have been thrown up in the wind and that tiny launch lowered from the boat's davits in less time than it takes to tell of it. And then, had Molly's father known Dick's name, he would have taken the boy to his yacht, if he had had to tie him to do it, but if Dick had once heard the name of Molly's father it would not have been necessary to tie him. However, if either had known the name of the other this story would not have been written.

## CHAPTER III

### LIFE ON A SPONGER

The yacht sailed on and Dick, walking up to Captain Wilson, who stood at the wheel, said, as he lifted his cap:

"I beg to report for duty, sir." The captain grinned, as he replied:

"I hope you'll always be as polite. You'll sure be a curiosity on

14

this coast. I'll put you in with Pedro. He doesn't know much English, but you can talk enough for both. There he is, that black-mustached fellow, with little rings in his ears. He will let you know what your duties are."

A string of four dingies trailed behind the sponger and as many poles, each thirty feet long, with a sponge-hook at one end, lay upon the deck. Pedro was examining one of these poles when Billy went to him and said:

"Pedro, I am to go in your boat. What do I have to do?"

"You scull where I tell you—slow—I look in glass—see sponge—take up pole—you stop still—then you scull where pole go—you work good or I keek you."

"Pedro, if you ever keek me, you'll go overboard queek and don't you forget it."

The sponger lay at anchor on the sponging ground for nearly a week before the water was clear enough for work. Dick spent most of his time sculling his dingy and soon learned to throw his weight on the big sculling oar to the best advantage without going overboard very often. One day while Pedro sat in the bow, they saw a 400-pound loggerhead turtle lying asleep on the water. Pedro motioned to Dick to scull up to the turtle and when the dingy was within three feet of the creature he jumped on its back and seized the edge of its shell just behind the head, with both hands. Pedro's weight was so far aft on the turtle's deck that the bow pointed upward and the reptile's struggles only served to keep its head above water and thus carry the man comfortably on its back. Soon Pedro shifted his right hand to the tail-end of the turtle and thereafter navigated his living craft with ease. Dick sculled the dingy beside the turtle and, while trying to make fast the boat's painter around the creature, fell overboard. Pedro didn't know enough English to express his feelings fully, and so talked Spanish for a while. Dick thought he could get the rope around the turtle more easily if he stayed in the water, and he finally succeeded, though the reptile got one of the sleeves of his shirt while he was doing it. Then the boy and Pedro got into the boat and pulled the turtle beside it. In rolling the reptile aboard they shipped a lot of water and as the turtle dropped suddenly to the bottom of the dingy Dick fell backwards out of the boat. Pedro began to express himself in Spanish again, and, as the sponger was less than two hundred yards distant, Dick swam to it, leaving his companion to bail out the dingy and scull it to the big boat. The boat's tackle was required to hoist the turtle aboard, where it was turned over to the Cook, who butchered it on deck. The heart of the reptile continued to beat for

15

hours after it had been removed from the body, so strongly that its throbbing could not be restrained by the grip of the most powerful hand. Pedro said that the heart would beat till the sun went down, and it did.

For days Dick hunted all the turtles he saw lying on the water. At last he got near enough to one to grab him before he dove. But he got hold too far back, the reptile's head was already turned downward and his flippers forced him rapidly forward. Dick hung on as well as he could, which wasn't for long, for the strong rush of the water and its great pressure as the reptile made for the bottom quickly compelled the boy to let go. Yet he was under water so long that when he came to the surface Captain Wilson was in a dingy sculling like mad to reach him. The captain gave the boy a kindly warning, which affected him so much that in ten minutes he was off after another turtle, which he saw asleep. The creature began his dive just as Dick jumped for him, and the boy got hold of his tail-end as it was lifted above the water, in time to get a sharp slap in the face from the heavy hind flipper of the turtle. Dick sculled for an hour without seeing another turtle, when, as he was returning to the boat and within a hundred yards of it, one rose beside the dingy so near that the boy was on its back before it could go under the surface. He soon had his charger in fair control, but the science of riding a big loggerhead turtle isn't picked up in a minute. One of the crew came out in a dingy to help, but Dick asked him to pick up his boat and oar and take them to the sponger and said that he would ride back on the turtle. Sometimes his steed was manageable, and once he got within a few yards of the big boat, when it broke loose and carried him fifty yards away. Then, as Dick tried to check the reptile, he pulled its head too far and tipped it over on its back on top of himself, with his own head so near the parrot-like jaws of the loggerhead that when they were snapped in his face they missed his nose by about an inch. The turtle was as anxious to turn over as the boy, and, by favoring his motions, Dick soon had the creature right side up, while he again rode triumphantly on his back. In another hour the halyards were fast to the turtle and Billy had made good his promise to ride it back to the boat.

When the water became clear the dingies were sent out with two men in each, one of whom sculled while the other sat with his face in a water-glass watching the bottom for sponges. The water-glass is a bucket with a glass bottom which so smooths the surface of the water as to produce the effect of a perfect calm to one who is looking through it. The first day of sponging was like a dream to Dick. The water was smooth as a mirror and no water-glass was

16

needed. He sculled slowly over water so clear that he seemed to be floating in the air. Beneath him was fairyland, filled with waving sea-feathers and anemones, paved with curious shells, strangely beautiful forms of coral and sponges of various kinds, and alive with fish of many varieties. Sometimes there floated on the surface of the water Portuguese men-of-war, most beautiful of created things, like iridescent bubbles, with long silken filaments, delicately lined in pink, purple and entrancing blue. Lighter than thistledown, fitted to drift with the merest zephyr, they can nevertheless force their way against a breeze. Harmless as a soap-bubble in appearance, each of them is charged with virulent poison, and when Dick touched one with his hand he received a shock that made him wonder if a bunch of hornets had hidden in that innocent-looking bubble.

Sometimes schools of little fish gliding beneath the dingy began to dash wildly about, and a moment later a group of jackfish or Spanish mackerel could be seen darting around and picking up stragglers from the little school, which often huddled for protection close beside and beneath the dingy. Dick like all brave boys, was on the side of the under dog, and he laughed with glee when a quick-moving mackerel shark appeared among the pursuers of the little fish and picked up a few of them for his breakfast as he drove the rest away. As Dick sculled easily with one hand, he kept an eye upon Pedro, and obeyed the signals of his hand, to go to the right, the left, or stop, as sponges were seen. Then from time to time the long pole with the claw at the end was lowered to the bottom and a sponge torn loose.

Sometimes Dick changed places with Pedro, and manipulated the long pole with the claw, while Pedro handled the sculling oar. Then Dick began to learn the difference between coarse grass and common cup sponges, and the finer fibred glove and choice sheep's wool varieties. For when he was clumsy with the pole, Pedro only swore softly in Spanish, but when he brought up a worthless grass sponge, the big oar was lifted, and the boy might have been knocked overboard but for the iron claw which he held high, while a purpose gleamed in his eye which made Pedro peaceful. But Dick felt that Pedro was half right and he set to work studying sponges until he knew them almost as well as his teacher. His strength and skill with the sponge hook were less than the Spaniard's, but his eye was quicker and Pedro's chronic growls were often changed to grunts of approval. When the surface of the water was ruffled by a breeze it was needful to use the water-glass. Then Pedro sat with his head in the bucket, studying the bottom, and when he took up the heavy pole which lay on the thwarts of the dingy and dipped it vertically in

17

the water, it was the duty of Dick to stop sculling at once. But once while Dick was sculling and looking for sponges he saw gliding beneath the dingy, a whip-ray, the most beautiful member of the ray family. Shaped like a butterfly, its back is covered with small, light rings on a black background. Its long, slim tail is like the lash of a coach-whip and at its base is a row of little spears with many barbs, which are capable of inflicting exceedingly painful wounds. The roof of the mouth and the tongue of the fish are hard as ivory and shell-fish are ground between them as rock is pulverized by the jaws of a quartz-crusher. As Billy watched the graceful swaying of the body of the whip-ray under the impulse of its wings, a wandering shark came upon it. In its first rush the tiger of the sea almost caught the beautiful creature, which fluttered for a hundred yards upon the surface of the water, with the jaws of its pursuer opening and closing within a few inches of its body.

Dick was so busy watching the chase and so earnest in his sympathy with the frightened, fleeing whip-ray that he quite forgot his duties. He was reminded of them when Pedro, who had been frantically signaling him, took his head from the bucket and made a speech in Spanish to Dick that must have used up all the bad adjectives in that language. Dick's conscience hampered him so much that he was quite unable to reply fittingly, and the battle of words was won by Pedro. The dingy drifted so far during the discussion that they were unable to find the sheep's wool sponge that Pedro had seen, and which he now described as the finest one ever found.

Each day the spongers in the dingies worked farther from the sloop and each day more time was lost when the sloop made its round to pick up the spongers for dinner. There were too few sponges to please Captain Wilson, who sailed over the ground whenever the water was smooth, studying the bottom with practiced eye and throwing out little floats, with anchors attached, wherever a sponge was seen.

"I'm going to the 'Lake,'" said the captain, one afternoon at the end of a day of little success. "It's a feast or a famine there. You get rich or go broke."

"What is there at the 'Lake'?" asked Dick.

"Sponge, all sponge, the bottom lined with sponge. If the weather is just right we'll pile the deck with sponges in a week till you can't see over them. If the weather isn't exactly right we won't get a sponge. On one cruise there, the men on this sloop averaged twenty-five dollars a day apiece. I've been there five times since without ever making enough to pay for our salt."

18

A week later the captain said to the boy:

"Dick, you are a mascot. You've brought us big luck. We never had such weather here but once and I don't care now how soon it comes on to blow. I reckon it'll begin to-night from the looks and we'll hike for Key West to-morrow."

Dick was glad to go. The week had been a hard one, the work incessant and each night he felt as if his back were broken. He was used to the fresh, sweet air of his country home and the sloop he was in was arranged like most of the sponging craft, with quarters sufficient for half the crew it carried. The deck of the sponger was piled with the result of the work of the week. The sponge of commerce, the one you buy at the drug store, is the skeleton of the creature; the thing taken from the water is its corpse. Not until this body has rotted away is it pleasant to live with. Day by day the stench, like that of a charnel house, became more unbearable to Dick. The crew seemed never to notice it, which caused the boy much wonderment that noses had ever been given them. He was glad when a strong wind came and swept some of the smell away instead of leaving it to settle in chunks in every nook and cranny on the boat.

At Key West most of the crew went to their homes, but Dick was invited to live on the sloop till he found a boat for the coast he wanted to reach.

Cargoes sent to Key West for a market are almost always sold at auction and the auction houses in the early morning are busy marts. Cargoes of sponge, fruit, vegetables, lumber and other goods are sold in lots to suit purchasers, who range from the dealer who buys by the cargo, or the small merchant who takes a few boxes of pines, oranges, grape-fruit, or tomatoes, to the housewife who wants a watermelon or a bunch of bananas. On the day following their arrival at Key West Captain Wilson handed Dick a roll of bills containing a hundred dollars, saying to him:

"That's about your share in the cruise, Dick. The sponge hasn't been sold yet, but you are in a hurry to get off and I reckon that's about right."

Dick was dazed as he took the roll, but a moment later he handed it back to the captain, saying:

"I can't take that, Captain Wilson. It is ten times as much as I have earned. You took me on as a boy and I want you to pay me just what you would have paid any other boy."

"Put that money in your pocket, Dick. You've done a man's work and now you've got a man's pay and that's all there is to it. Lucky for you, though, that the weather was good at the Lake. If it

19

hadn't been you wouldn't have got anything but your board. Now come ashore and we'll hunt up a boat for Marco or Chokoloskee."

They stopped at an auction room in Key West for a minute, when Captain Wilson sang out to a boy who was passing:

"Hi, Johnny! Where's the Etta?"

"Same old place, off the end of the dock."

"Thought yesterday was your sailing day."

"So it was, but Cap'n's in the calaboose. Got drunk yest'd'y and had a fight. I got ter raise th' cash ter git him out."

"Why don't the boss bounce him? He's drunk most of the time."

"Boss says Cap'n Tom's a better sailor when he's drunk than any of th' others when they're sober."

"Well, I'll get Tom out of limbo for you and charge it to the boss. Only you must take this friend of mine with you to Chokoloskee."

"Sure! What's his name?"

"Name's Dick. Can you make an alligator-hunter of him?"

"Reckon I kin, or kill him tryin'."

## CHAPTER IV

### CAUGHT IN A WATERSPOUT

The next morning the Etta, with Dick on board, started for Chokoloskee. The weather was bad, with a succession of squalls from the southwest, and the captain kept in the lee of the line of keys instead of taking the straight course across the Gulf. But he carried all sail till the rotten main-sheet parted at the boom, and when he came up in the wind to lower the sail the main throat halyard refused to unreeve. Before an order was given Dick was half way up the mast and soon came riding down to the deck on the gaff. When reefs had been taken in the sails, the sheet replaced, and the boat was again under way, the captain said to Dick:

"Who taught you sailoring?"

"Captain Wilson taught me some, and—"

"That's enough. You don't need to mention anybody else. What Wilson doesn't know about sailing, sponging and fishing isn't worth knowing."

20

By noon they were about twenty miles southwest of North-West Cape and, as the wind had moderated, the reefs were shaken out and the bow of the Etta pointed due north, straight for Sand-Fly Pass. The breeze grew less and less, and in two hours had died away entirely. From the northeast a black, threatening cloud was moving slowly toward them, while the sails flapped idly as the Etta rolled to a heavy ground swell. The cloud came nearer and grew blacker, while swirling little tails dropped from it, almost touching the water, and then suddenly returned to the black mass above.

"What a funny cloud," said Dick to Captain Tom. "Does it mean a hurricane?"

"No. This is the hurricane month, but hurricanes always give a day or two's warning through the barometer and that hasn't changed a tenth in a week. But this is worse than a hurricane if it hits us. Those are waterspouts in the making, that you see dropping from the big cloud, and when one of them gets a good hold on the water you will see something that you won't forget as long as you live, which won't be a great while if it hits us," said the captain.

Almost as he spoke a great inverted cone of cloud settled down from the mass above and touching the surface of the water set it whirling furiously. The water from the Gulf was lifted skyward, in a column which constantly grew broader at the base while its pointed top, mingling with the almost equally solid cloud, gave hour-glass form to the huge, swirling, threatening mass that bore down on the Etta, within a half mile now. Suddenly the waterspout separated from the great cloud mass and moved rapidly eastward. For ten minutes the crew of the Etta watched it until, when more than a mile distant, the waterspout collapsed more suddenly than it had formed and from the foam-covered water a great wave rolled outward, spreading until the Etta rocked in its path.

"Thank goodness, that trouble's over," said Dick to the captain.

"Yes, but how about this one?" replied Captain Tom, as he pointed to the big cloud which was now within two hundred yards of them and more threatening than ever. Another waterspout was forming and soon its roar filled their ears, while a towering mass seemed to spread over their heads, ready to fall upon and crush them. Already, spiteful patches of wind, torn from the revolving cyclone, slapped the sails of the Etta as if to tear them from the mast.

"Shan't I take in sail?" asked Johnny of the captain.

"No use," was the reply. "When that thing strikes us nothing

21

will make any difference and a bit of breeze in the next minute might pull us out."

For a long minute they watched the approaching demon which was now within a hundred yards and its tremendous suction was already disturbing the water about them when the captain shouted:

"Launch the dingy and get aboard; leave the oars to me!"

In an instant the little dingy had been slid overboard and the boys were sitting in the stern; then Captain Tom stepped aboard and was soon pulling mightily away from the Ella and across the line of progress of the waterspout. But it was all too late. The dingy was less than two hundred feet from the Etta when she began to toss, lifting her bow high and then plunging it deep beneath the surface. The first touch of the waterspout carried away mast and sails and swept clear the deck. In another instant the schooner was engulfed, but her bulk broke the back of the waterspout and it began to sway; its straight, smooth column began to kink up and break, and many hundred tons of water fell crashing into the Gulf. When the great column fell the dingy was within three hundred feet and, as Captain Tom threw his weight on the oars in a last effort to increase the distance, one of the oars snapped and the captain fell on his back in the bow of the boat, striking his head on the gunwale with a force that stunned him. At this moment the outflowing wave from the falling water swept over the skiff, rolling it upside down. Dick, who was a regular water-dog, saw the big wave coming and, as it rolled the dingy over, he sank for a moment beneath the surface till the wave had passed, then came up with all his senses alert. He swam to the capsized dingy, which was near him, and was soon joined by Johnny.

"Where's the captain?" shouted Dick. "We've got to find him. Look everywhere, Johnny."

The broken water was now tossing madly and it seemed an age to Dick before he caught a glimpse of the captain's head on the crest of a wave two boat's lengths distant. He swam to the place, and searched the water above and below, diving until he was exhausted. He was losing hope when once more the captain's body came to the surface and Dick seized it. He started for the dingy with his burden, but was fearing he would never make it, when he found Johnny beside him, saying:

"Here, you're played out. Put your hand on my shoulder. I can take care of the cap'n, too."

"All right, you take care of the captain. I can get back to the dingy."

When they reached the dingy the water had become so much smoother that they were able to rest while clinging to the side of the dingy and holding the captain's face out of water.

"Don't 'spose Cap'n's dead, do yer?" said Johnny.

"Don't think so, but we've got to get this dingy bailed out and get him in it, mighty soon. Then I know what to do to bring him to, if there's life in him. Lend me your cap and I'll bail out the dingy."

"That ain't the way we bail boats down here," said Johnny, who got into the dingy and began to rock it. In about a minute he had rocked it nearly dry and finished the job with his cap. Dick then climbed into the dingy and the boys pulled the body of the captain beside it and, bearing down on the gunwale until water began to come in, dragged it aboard, half filling the dingy as they did it. As Johnny began to bail again a feeble voice beside him whispered:

"What you fellers doin'?"

The captain soon got stronger, and said he was all right but for a headache which was splitting his skull. He tried to rise, but fell back in a faint, and Dick told him he must lie still and give orders, which Johnny and he would obey. Then Dick stood on a thwart and studied the water as far as he could see, hoping to find an oar. He saw a mast, a hatch cover and some broken fragments from the Etta and at last the blade from the oar which the captain had broken. Johnny and he paddled with their hands until they recovered the oar blade. As a light breeze had sprung up from the south, which was causing them to drift northward, they headed south, paddling and watching by turns, until they found the lost oar. Then Dick, resting the oar in the sculling hole, called on the captain for orders.

"Better strike out due east and make for Nor'-West Cape. That's the nearest land and we're liable to be struck by a squall 'most any minute. Then there's a cocoanut grove at the Cape and you'll be thirsty by the time you get there."

"Gee!" said Dick, "I'm thirsty now. Wish you hadn't spoken of it."

Dick put his weight on the oar and as he swung back and forth on it the captain called out:

"You sure can scull, boy, but take it easy; you've got over a dozen miles of it to the Cape and near fifty more up the coast, after that."

"Where do I come in?" said Johnny.

"Go 'way, child, this is man's work," replied Dick, as he swung easily on his oar, but with a vim that drove the dingy through the water at good speed.

Johnny begged for his turn, but didn't get it for two hours, by which time the tops of the cocoa palms could be seen. Then Captain Tom began to feel better and talked of doing his share of the work, upon which Dick whistled a few bars of "Go 'Way Back and Sit Down," which the captain seemed to understand, for he gave no more trouble.

It was nearly dark when they landed on a beach at the border of a forest of cocoa palms and in a few minutes Johnny had a dozen young nuts on the ground and was hacking at the tough husk of one with his knife. When the ape-faced end of the nut had been laid bare and the eye cut out with a pen-knife blade, he gave the nut to Dick, who was soon absorbing the most delicious drink of his life. There was about a pint of milk in each nut, and it took a round dozen to quench the thirst of the three. They broke open half-grown or custard nuts and ate their pulpy meat and they tried some of the hard flesh of the mature nut.

The castaways built a fire on the beach for cheer and warmth and piled up fallen leaves of the palm to soften their beds on the sand. Captain Tom told the boys that the plantation house was not occupied, and that the next house down the coast was a number of miles distant and just opposite to the course they wanted to take. He then added that he was no more captain now than his companions and would give no orders, but he advised that they start up the coast before sun-up and do a lot of their sculling in the cool of the morning. The boys collected a couple of dozen of nuts to keep down their thirst and when the sun rose they were several miles up the coast.

About nine o'clock Dick said to the captain:

"I wish it was breakfast time. I'm starving."

"Have your breakfast any time you want it."

"Want it now."

"All right," said the captain, who was sculling, and he headed the dingy for shore, where it struck on a reef at the mouth of a stream.

"Now, if you boys will rustle some wood I'll have your breakfast ready."

"I don't see anything to eat round here," said Dick.

"How would an oyster roast strike you?" asked the captain.

"My, but wouldn't an oyster taste good? Do you s'pose there is one within ten miles?"

Johnny laughed and said:

"What you standin' on? Must be a hundred barrels on 'em."

Dick looked down and was amazed to see that the whole reef

24

was composed of oysters—oysters of all sizes, oysters single, in small bunches and in great masses.

"Woods are full of 'em," said the captain, and he pointed to the mangrove trees that lined the stream, the lower branches of which were burdened with bunches of oysters bigger than Dick's head. A fire was made and branches of these trees containing bunches of oysters were thrown on it. A few minutes later the branches were taken off of the fire, with shells bursting open showing hot, steaming oysters ready for the sharp sticks which took the place of forks with the castaways. After Dick had filled himself with roast oysters, he ate a few dozen raw, by way of a change, and then went back to his roasting, until he was so full that he told Johnny that he never wanted to eat again as long as he lived, at which Johnny grinned. Only three hours later, as Johnny was sculling over a shallow bank, he stopped work and began to thump the bottom with his oar.

"What is it?" asked Dick.

"Bottom covered with clams. Reckon I'll pick up a few for Cap'n and me. You said you didn't want to eat again, ever," replied Johnny.

But both of the boys went overboard and in a few minutes had put more clams aboard the dingy than the whole party could have eaten in a week.

The castaways camped on their second night at the mouth of Lossman's River, where they had a famous clam-roast. They found a fisherman's house where they got fresh water and a can to hold it, also some cornmeal, with which Johnny made an ash-cake, or, as Dick called it, Johnny-cake. The captain said it was the best thing he had ever eaten, and Dick engaged him on the spot as a camping companion on his hunt for his chum.

The next morning the boys slept till the sun had risen and the captain awoke them to look upon a gorgeous picture seldom to be seen. The unclouded sun was shining brilliantly and the eastern sky clear and bright, but in the west a storm was gathering. There were snow-clad peaks brilliant with sunshine, thunder-heads black as midnight from which lightning was playing, while above and beneath them all shone a perfect double rainbow and an equally perfect reflection of it from the mirror-like surface of the Gulf. So perfect a double-circled rainbow the captain had never before seen, and, though he lived near the coast, Johnny had never seen one at all. By the time they had finished their breakfast of roast clams and ash-cake the rainbow had melted away and the storm-clouds were nearer, but Dick wanted to start on up the coast. The captain shook his head and Johnny recited:

"Rainbow in the mornin', sailors take warnin'."

Half an hour later all hands were glad to run to the fisherman's house, from the doorway of which they looked out upon storm-driven sheets of rain that shut out the Gulf and fell in hissing masses upon the palmetto roof that covered them, while the continuous blaze of lightning and crash of thunder gave Dick his first taste of a tropical thunderstorm. Half an hour later the sky was cloudless, the sun more brilliant than ever, and the only reminder of the storm that had passed was the sullen roar of the surf as the big waves broke on the beach.

When Johnny proposed to renew their voyage and the captain assented, it was Dick who held back.

"What can we do out there?" said he, waving his hand toward the white-capped waves that were sweeping in and sending their foam high up the beach. Johnny only laughed in reply, but the captain and he dragged the dingy, in which two poles had been placed, out into the surf until the waves rolled waist deep past them.

"Tumble aboard, both of you," ordered the captain, as he stood by the stern of the craft, holding its bow squarely against the incoming waves. The boys climbed aboard, and Dick, following Johnny's example, seized a pole and together they held the boat against the sweep of the surf until the captain was aboard with the oar in his hands. It was exciting work and as they pushed on and out, with each new wave tossing the bow of the boat in the air and spilling its crest of water and foam over the gunwales, Dick exclaimed:

"Isn't it glorious? I never had such fun," and even the captain smiled assent.

They pushed on until outside of the breakers and among the smooth-rolling waves, where the deepening water made poling difficult and they resumed their sculling. The captain took the first trick, while Johnny bailed out, with his cap, the water that the waves had spilled aboard.

Everything went smoothly and there was no more excitement on the trip until in the afternoon, when Dick was working the sculling oar. He was swinging it slowly, as he looked down into the water, when there appeared suddenly, just under the dingy, a great black creature, broader than the boat was long. As it rose nearer to the surface, almost touching the craft, he saw a great open mouth, three feet across, with a heavy black horn on each side of it, which looked quite equal to disposing of Dick and his boat at a single bite.

26

The sight was so frightful that Dick impulsively thrust his oar against the creature, and was instantly thrown from his feet as the stern of the dingy was tossed in the air and a column of water fell upon and around him. When the commotion was over and Johnny had crawled back into the submerged boat and was rocking it dry, Dick said to Captain Tom, who was swimming beside him:

"I believe I'll swim the rest of the way. I'm getting tired of being pitched overboard every few minutes."

After they were all aboard and Dick had resumed his work with the oar, he asked the captain:

"What was that thing that looked like a devil, that I hit and that hit back?"

"That was a devil-fish. They are perfectly harmless," said the captain, adding, reflectively, "unless you punch 'em."

The tide favored the castaways at Sand-Fly Pass and they reached Chokoloskee Bay without further adventure, but then came the painful part of the trip: telling the owner of the Etta of its destruction by a waterspout. All the comment Mr. Streeter made was:

"Glad none of you went down with the boat."

The captain and Johnny went to their homes, while Dick accepted Mr. Streeter's invitation to stay with him.


## CHAPTER V

### OUTFITTING FOR THE HUNT

The Streeter home was on the bank of a little river that emptied into Chokoloskee Bay, and Dick, for the first time, saw oranges and grape-fruit growing and tasted the delicious alligator pear and the guava.

After supper Mr. Streeter said to Dick:

"Johnny tells me you have got a friend lying around loose somewhere in the Big Cypress Swamp, or the Everglades, and that you and he are going to take a day off to look him up."

"That's about the size of it, only of course I don't expect to find him in a day or a week. I had some hope that a month would do. I suppose it all seems very silly to you?"

"Not a bit, not a bit. The Big Swamp isn't a bad place, if you've sand and sense, and I reckon you have both or you wouldn't have got as far as you have. I suppose it's Ned Barstow you're looking for?"

"Who in the world could have told you? I haven't spoken his name since I left home."

"Nobody told me, but last week Chris Meyer, the surveyor, was here and, as we are old friends, we talked half the night. He told me of his work for Mr. Barstow, the big lumber man, and said that Ned Barstow, his son, had been out in the swamp with him as surveyor's assistant for 'most a month, Chris told me that when he left, Ned was arranging to go on a hunting trip with Billy Tommy, a Seminole Indian. He thought the plan was to hunt slowly through the swamp to Tommy's canoe, which he had left somewhere between Boat Landing and Charley Tiger's. Ned expected then to work down through the Everglades to Cape Sable if possible."

"Is there any chance of my finding him in that great wilderness, Mr. Streeter? It looks so much bigger than it did from up north. How is it possible to keep from getting lost?"

"Don't have to. Soon as you begin to worry because you don't know where you are, trouble begins. More than one man in this country has gone crazy and killed himself because he thought he was lost. Why, you can't be really lost. If you're worried just start for the North Star. You'll hit somebody before you strike the North Pole. But it's a heap easier to keep from worrying if you've got company. Lordy, the picnic you and Johnny are going to have! I wish I was as young as you and going with you. Your best way to find Ned will not be to follow his trail, but to head him off somewhere in the Glades. That's easier than you think. I could pretty nearly figure out to a mile where he is this minute. You see, he's with Billy Tommy, and I know that Injun. Couldn't make him hurry if he tried, and he won't try. He'll be so busy shootin' things and skinnin' 'em and fussin' 'round camp that they'll get ahead mighty slow. Shouldn't wonder if it took 'em a week from the time they started to get to where Tommy left his canoe. Then they will put out in the Glades and head straight for Charley Tiger's camp."

"How do you know that?"

"Because I know Tommy and because it's the only Injun camp 'round there where he'd be sure to find whyome—that's whisky, or rum, or anything that'll make drunk come."

"But suppose Ned wouldn't go that way?"

"Oh, Tommy'd fix that. He'd point to the west and say, 'Big Swamp, canoe no can take!' Then he'd wave his hand to the east, 'No trail, oko suchescha (water all gone), saw-grass ojus (heaps)!' No,

28

they never got past Tiger's camp without stopping. Then Tommy got drunk and Ned couldn't move him under four days. It's an even chance that they are right there now."

"How far from here is Tiger's camp?" asked Dick.

"Less than forty miles, but you'd think it was four hundred before you got there, if you tried to cross the swamp to reach it. Besides, they would certainly be gone before you could possibly get to the camp. Then you couldn't take a boat, and you've got to have one to follow your friend."

"Can I buy or hire a skiff, here?"

"You can do a lot better. One of your Northern tourists left a little beauty of a canoe with me, to be sold first chance I got. It cost seventy dollars, delivered here, and you can have it for twenty. It's only fifteen feet long and about two feet wide amidships, but it weighs only forty pounds and when there isn't water enough for the canoe to carry you, why, you can carry the canoe. Then a few little traps go with it which you may find useful. There's a broken fly-rod, which you can fix all right, and a little single-barrel shot-gun, not worth much, but you can always pick up a supper with it. There are also a pair of grains, a light harpoon, and a cast-net which is torn some, but Johnny can fix it. Johnny's got a rifle and all the camp kit two tough boys will need.

"Better take a piece of light, waterproofed canvas big enough to keep off some of the rain when it storms, an axe, a bag of salt to save the hides of the alligators you will be sure to kill if Johnny goes with you, and some grits and bacon. Oh! you may need a mosquito-bar, and if you do want it you're likely to want it bad. Make it of cheese-cloth; that'll keep out sand-flies, too. Some of my folks will run it up on the machine for you in a few minutes. There may be some other little things that you'll need, but you can trust Johnny to think of 'em. Now, Dick, you don't have to pay for any of these things till you get good and ready. I'm used to giving long credits and this time I'm glad to do it."

"Oh, Mr. Streeter, you don't know how grateful I am to you for all you are doing for me. The money is the least part of it and I can fix that all right. You wouldn't think I was a capitalist to look at me, would you?" said Dick, laughingly. "Since I left home I've rolled up quite a fortune as a fireman and a sponger and I can pay my little bills and have money to burn besides. How soon do you think we can get off?"

"You ought to start to-morrow. You can get ready in an hour. Know anything about canoeing?"

"Not much, but I've rowed some in a shell."

29

"That'll help you a little, but it leaves you something to learn. The man whose canoe you have bought was cruising down here with his family and he told me that every time one of 'em stepped in that canoe he went overboard. He said he had to choose between the canoe and his family and had concluded to let the canoe go. One of my boys owns a little Indian canoe in which Johnny and he have poled around a good deal, so I reckon Johnny can keep inside of your canoe, but you'd better spend the forenoon to-morrow practicing in it with a paddle, then you can get off right after dinner and your clothes will be dry before you make camp at night."

"Does Johnny know the course we ought to take from here?"

"Not far, but I can help you some and you'll find out the rest for yourselves. You'll have to. Then Johnny savvies Injun talk pretty well and you're sure to run across them or their camps. And he'll likely know them, and if Ned's anywhere in their country or has been there they'll sure know it. You will leave this bay by way of Turner's River, which will take you into the most tangled up part of the Ten Thousand Islands. You will go through rivers and bays, around keys, along twisting channels and up narrow, crooked creeks. You'll be lost from the start, but you don't want to think of that. Just make your course average southeast for the first fifty miles, which you ought to cover in three days. Then hunt for some creek coming from the east. It will be a little one, you will have to drag your canoe, perhaps for miles, under branches that close over the creek and you may have to carry your canoe and pack your dunnage over prairie land. In a day you ought to strike the Everglades. Then turn to the north and look for Indian trails, which you want to follow whenever they lead anywhere near where you are trying to go. They will help you to dodge the worst of the saw-grass which is likely to be your greatest trouble.

"Keep along the border line between the Everglades and the cypress country and you will probably hit Osceola's camp. He's about the whitest Seminole in the State and he'll help you all he can. Remember, when in an Indian camp, that their brand of politeness is different from a white man's, though it may be just as sincere. If you're hungry, and don't see a spoon lying around, just dip your hand in the family pot, if you can eat that way. If you want to sleep lie down on the nearest unoccupied bunk. If you make a mistake they won't tell you of it.

"Now, remember above all things, that you mustn't get rattled. That's the biggest risk you'll run in this country. If you get separated from Johnny and think about being lost and get excited and begin to walk fast, or run, stop right there and sit down and don't go on till you're perfectly cool, not if you have to camp right where you are for a night, or a day, or both. Just as soon as you have taught yourself that when you get excited you have got to sit still for an hour or two, you'll stop getting excited. There is mighty little real danger where you are going. There are bear and panther, but the only thing on earth that's a bigger coward than a bear is a panther. People from your country think the alligator is a dangerous brute. I have lived among them, killed them, dealt in their hides, of which I have shipped north the biggest consignments sent from this coast, since before you were born, and I never knew of a human being having been harmed by one. This deep river running in front of my door used to be full of them, and there are some there now, but my whole family of children swim in it almost every day without thought of danger. Only two weeks ago Johnny killed a ten-foot 'gator right in front of my house and within a hundred feet of it. Any of our hunters will wade into a pond where there are fifty alligators, to drag out one they have shot; many of them will tackle, with nothing but a stick, any 'gator under six feet that they can catch on a prairie or asleep on a bank, and a few of the boys will wade bare-footed and bare-handed into a pond on the prairie and bring out little alligators. Johnny is a dabster at that. Likely you'll see him do it before many days.

"Of course rattlesnakes are bad, but they always give warning, usually a good long one. I've killed hundreds, perhaps thousands of them and never been bitten. Cotton-mouth moccasins are poisonous, but they are sluggish and not so very plenty. You'll have to get used to the smaller moccasins. You will find lots of them. I've kicked them out of my path on the prairies and in the marshes for a good many years without having been bitten by one.

"Sharks have a bad name, and Florida waters are full of them, but there is no authentic instance on record of their having killed a man, woman, or child in this country. There are convicts and other outlaws in the Ten Thousand Islands. They may steal something from your camp, but they won't harm you. Some of them are bad men, and when they kill their own kind, people here don't mind it, but the outlaws know that the community wouldn't stand for their hurting any of you boys."

Dick was ashamed when he got up to breakfast to find that Mr. Streeter and Johnny had been at work for an hour and had got everything ready for a start, even to the mosquito-bar, which one of the family had already made.

The outfit consisted of a fly-rod, with reel, line and flies; rifle and shot-gun, with fifty cartridges for each; pair grains, harpoon,

31

line and pole; cast-net, fish hooks and lines; forks, tin-cups and plates, two each; light axe, saucepan and frying-pan; piece of waterproofed canvas, six by eight feet; lantern, kerosene, and bag of salt; white bacon, hominy and corn meal, five lbs. each; canoe, two paddles and one long oar; five gallon can of water, and bucket; waterproof box filled with matches.

Each of the boys carried a clasp knife and a pocket, watertight match safe.

Nothing had been loaded on the canoe, as Mr. Streeter wanted to be sure that Dick could stay in it, before he filled it with goods that water might harm. He was soon satisfied on this point, for although Dick got into the canoe with exceeding care, he kept his balance perfectly, and after the first few strokes appeared perfectly at home in the craft. He paddled for a few minutes kneeling on the bottom of the boat, then sitting on a thwart, and finally came back to the dock sitting on the stern, while the bow of the canoe tilted up in the air. Then Johnny got in with him and the boys maneuvered the craft until Mr. Streeter called out to them:

"You kids are all right and don't need to waste any more time. Better pack up and be off, and save half a day." They loaded the canoe carefully and took their positions, Dick in the stern and Johnny in the bow. Then lifting their caps to the family, who had come down to the dock to see them off, the boys dipped their paddles together in the river and began Dick's hunt for his chum.

## CHAPTER VI

### DICK'S HUNT FOR HIS CHUM

An hour's paddling brought Dick and Johnny to the mouth of Turner's River, up which they headed the canoe. A strong tide setting up the river nearly doubled their speed.

"Lucky for us that the tide is running our way," said Dick.

"Not much luck about it. Mr. Streeter knew about the tide. That's why he hurried us off 'fore dinner. Tide'll be other way this evenin'," replied Johnny.

"Isn't Mr. Streeter a brick?"

"He's all that. Lots o' people 'd have hard times 'f he moved away. He helps th' Injuns, too, when they're in hard luck."

The first fork in the river was a mile from its mouth and Dick, who was steering, took the right branch, which led southeast, although it was much the smaller stream. At the next parting of the stream one branch led to the east and the other due south. Fortunately Johnny knew which fork to take, and for a mile or two there was no trouble. Then the river opened out into a broad shallow bay, filled with little keys, but nothing to tell Dick which way to steer. He tried to keep to a southeast course, but ran into shallows which soon ended in a pocket from which they had to back out. Often they followed a good channel for a mile, only to have it end in an oyster reef, and again they had to turn back. A pair of dolphins lifted their heads above the surface in front of the canoe and with a sniff of fright started away across the bay like an express train. They were great creatures, nearly nine feet long, and were followed in their flight by a baby dolphin less than half their size, which rose within reach of Dick's paddle, sniffed impertinently in his face and skittered away after his mother as fast as he could wiggle his funny flat tail.

"Better foller them porpoises," said Johnny; "they know the channel."

The dolphin is so uniformly miscalled porpoise, on the west coast and everywhere else, that the creature will soon come to think that it really is a porpoise.

Dick followed the dolphins as long as he could see them and was led into a deep channel which opened out into a series of broad bays through which they paddled until, among the sunken lands of the flooded mangrove keys, they came upon a shell mound, the site of an old abandoned plantation. Dick's aching muscles and Johnny's clamorous stomach had long been pleading for a rest, and the boys landed on the mound for a picnic dinner. They opened a box which Mrs. Streeter had given them as they started from her home, and found a bountiful lunch of cold venison, baked sweet potatoes, boiled eggs, bread, butter, orange marmalade and two pineapples.

"Gee!" said Dick. "Are we going to live this way, Johnny?" but Johnny only grinned.

After the boys had eaten, as only boys can eat, they crawled through the vines and among the thorns of the overgrown plantation. They found stalks of sugar-cane and bunches of bananas; wide-spreading guava and lime trees, loaded with fruit; and tall Avocado pear trees from which hung purpling globes of that great, creamy, most delicious fruit, commonly called alligator pear. They filled with fruit the shirts they wore, till they bulged like St. Nicholas, and made many trips between the trees and their canoe.

33

As Dick was standing beside a lime tree, he heard a sound near him like the whirring of a big locust. Dick had never before heard the angry jarring of the rattles of the great king of snakes, but he didn't need to be told the meaning of the blood-curdling sound, which seemed to come from all directions at once. He gazed about him for a moment, with every muscle tense, until he caught sight of the head of the reptile waving slowly to and fro above the irregular coils of his body. The snake seemed to be within striking distance and the unnerved boy sprang suddenly away from it, landing among the thorn-bearing branches of a big lime tree. Dick soon recovered his nerve, and hunting up a big stick, went cautiously in search of the reptile, which he found still coiled. He broke the creature's back with his first blow and had struck several more when Johnny came crawling through the undergrowth, and called out:

"Want to save his skin?"

"Sure," replied Dick, who hadn't thought of it before.

"Then don't smash him any more and I'll show you how to round-skin him. He's dead enough, now. A feller from New York showed me how. He skinned 'em for a livin'. Birds, too. Said he'd give me ten dollars if I'd get him the skin of one of these fork-tailed kites. He wanted the nest and eggs, too. Say, but he could skin things. Skin a bird without losin' a feather or gettin' a drop o' blood on it. Said the best way to skin snakes was 'fore they was dead."

As Johnny began cutting the skin free from the jaws of the reptile, the long, needle-like fangs dripped yellow venom and Dick, looking on with a white face, half whispered:

"Suppose you happened to touch those fangs?"

"Ain't a-goin' to touch 'em. Wish I had my pliers here, to pull 'em out. You oughter save 'em, and the skull, too. The feller I was tellin' yer about always did."

"I don't want them; makes me sick to look at them," said Dick, who looked mightily relieved when, the head having been skinned, it was cut off and thrown into the bay. After that he became interested and helped Johnny with his work until he held in his hand the beautiful skin of a diamondback rattlesnake, over six feet long.

In the afternoon the boys entered a big bay that seemed to have no other outlet. They followed its shore for an hour, exploring every little bay that looked big enough to hide the smallest creek. They sounded the depth of the water with their paddles and traced a little channel to a clump of bushes that overhung the water from the shore. Johnny pulled the bow of the canoe under the overhanging branches and found a little creek through which the water was

34

flowing. They dragged the canoe into the stream and found water deep enough to float it, but branches and vines obstructed them above, while logs and snags troubled them below. They used their knives and the axe more than they did their paddles. At times they lay down in the canoe and dragged it under branches and at others got overboard, and standing in water and mud, lifted it over logs. They were in the deep gloom of a jungle from which the thick growth above shut out nearly all the light. As they pushed the canoe forward, unseen vines seized their throats in a garroting clutch, while solid masses of spider-webs stuck to their faces and spiders the size of a saucer ran over them. As Johnny sat in the bow, he collected the most spiders, since Dick only got those which his companion managed to dodge, but then Johnny was used to the critters and didn't mind them, while Dick wasn't, and did.

"What kind of snakes are these swimming round my legs?" asked Dick, as he stood nearly waist-deep in mud and water and helped lift the canoe over the biggest log they had struck.

"Speckle-belly moccasins. Mustn't get scared o' them, if you're goin' to hunt in this country. They ain't likely to bite if yer don't step on 'em and they won't kill yer, nohow," said Johnny.

The stream was so crooked that the boys had to travel three miles to gain one and as the troubles in their path seemed to increase they talked of turning back. But as it was already too late to get out of the creek before dark, they decided to keep on. As it was, darkness overtook them while they were yet in the creek. Among their stores was a lantern, by the light of which they progressed for a little while, when Johnny proposed making camp.

"But we can't camp here. I'm not a merman, to sleep in the water," said Dick.

"You can stretch out in the canoe, if we tie it so it won't tip over, and I'll build a brush bed good enough for me in ten minutes," said Johnny, who took the axe, and cut a short pole, which he rested on the branches of two trees which grew side by side, so that the stick lay parallel to a fallen tree trunk which lay about five feet distant. Then he cut a number of inch saplings into six-foot lengths, with which he made a platform from the pole to the tree, and spreading his blanket on this elastic couch announced that his bed was ready. The boys made a hearty supper from the fragments that were left from the bountiful provision that Mrs. Streeter had made for their dinner. Dick's bed in the canoe was probably softer than Johnny's bed, but he didn't sleep as well. The sides of his canoe were only five inches above the water which contained the moccasins, and Dick was sure he could feel their tongues touch his face as the reptiles searched for a soft place to strike. Then the snarling from a tree beside him would have been less terrifying if he had known that instead of being, as he supposed, two wildcats quarreling for the first bite at him, it was merely a friendly family discussion between two 'coons.

Things looked more cheerful by daylight, and when Johnny asked whether they should go on or turn back, Dick replied:

"Go on just as long as the creek runs." But the creek became choked with brush and turned back on its course, until Johnny said:

"If this crik gits any crookeder it'll fetch us back home."

The boys had to cut away two trees which had fallen across the creek where the growth was so thick that to cut a path around would have been more work than to clear away the logs. The trees were large, their axe a little one, and when the boys came to three trees lying near together across the stream Dick was so dismayed that he said to Johnny:

"Let's get back out of this creek. We must be on the wrong track, Mr. Streeter said Indians and hunters got through this country, but they never got through this way. What do you think?"

"Hate to go back, but s'pose we've got ter."

Dick's spirits ran low during the return trip through the creek. They were going in the wrong direction, and each hour was taking him farther away from where he supposed Ned was. Many times he wished they had kept on and fought their way through the creek. After reaching the bay they had left the day before they turned to the east and north as they followed labyrinthic channels that led around big and little keys in that part of the ten times Ten Thousand Islands. The work became confusing, the waterways they followed led them toward every point in the compass. Sometimes a narrowing stream made them think they had struck a creek which flowed from the mainland, but always it opened into some small bay filled with little keys. Late in the afternoon they found a point of land high enough for a camp, where they spent the night. After they had eaten their supper, Dick said:

"Johnny, do you know where we are?"

"Nope; bin goin' 'round so fast I've got dizzy."

"You mean we are lost?"

"Yep; but that's nothin' s' long's we don't stay lost."

"What shall we do, and where shall we go?"

"Go anywhere, only stick to it. Got ter do sumpthin; fresh water's 'most gone. Reckon we'd better go 'bout sou'west. We kin find a river that'll take us t' the coast, 'nd I kin find a way that'll take us where you wanter go."

36

An hour's paddling brought the boys to a bay in which were several pretty keys, on one of which Dick saw a number of beautiful white birds.

"What are those?" he asked.

"Egrets," said Johnny. "Want ter shoot 'em?"

"Of course not," replied Dick. "It's against the law, and wicked, besides. They are the loveliest birds there are and never ought to be killed just for fun."

"We never kill 'em for fun. Only tourists do that. If you Northern fellers didn't pay us ter git plumes we'd never kill 'em. D'ye remember that key over there?"

"No. What about it?"

"See that crik by the palmetter 'nd the big stump? Know it now?"

"What! Isn't that the creek we slept in night before last?"

"Sure! 'nd that's where we wanter go now. Them trees that we stopped fer was cut by our fellers to keep off the Lossman River plume hunters. We've got ter cut 'em out, er git 'round 'em if 't takes a week."

"How about water?"

"Find it t'other side o' the crik. I'd rather go without than go back t' anybody's house fer it."

"But that old shack where we killed the rattler isn't far off, and I saw a water-barrel under the caves."

"So did I, 'nd a possum floatin' in it, too. That's why I didn't fill up there. We'll go slow on what we got 'nd do without a day 'r two, 'nd we'll find some by then if we stick t' anything."

"We're going to stick to things hereafter, Johnny. It was plumb foolish to lay down just because a tree got in our way, and it was my fault, too. It isn't going to happen again, though. Let's get through that creek to-night, if we have to work by the light of the lantern."

"Ain't you 'fraid o' the snakes?" said Johnny.

"No. I'm too ashamed of myself for backing out of that creek to be afraid of anything, except doing it again."

When the boys got back to the trees which lay across the creek, they took turns with the little axe, which was not much heavier than a hatchet, until they had cleared an opening for the canoe. They found other trees in their way, but they kept on. Once they unloaded the canoe on stumps and logs until they could lift it over a log that lay so deep in the water that it was hard to cut. Five minutes later, and within a hundred yards of where they had turned back on the previous day, the boys reached the end of the creek, where it opened into a bay which seemed to Dick as beautiful as a dream. It was dotted with little islands, on some of which were picturesque groups of palmettos, and on others big trees filled with white-plumaged birds. Two black dots on the surface of the water a hundred yards from the canoe moved slowly across its bow. Johnny stopped paddling and said:

"There's a 'gator. D'ye want him?"

"I don't see him."

"See them two black knobs on the water? The little one's his nose 'nd the big one's his eye. He's turnin' 'round 'nd showin' both eyes, now. Shoot him in the eye if yer want t' kill him. It'll take some time t' skin him, though, 'nd mebbe ye're in a hurry to get along."

"I sure am," replied Dick, and as the paddles dipped together in the water, the alligator, suspicious of them, slowly sank from their sight.

At the end of the bay the boys found a deep, narrow river with a current which Dick supposed was tidal, but which Johnny thought came from the Glades. Dick tasted the water and was surprised to find that instead of being salt it had the sweetish taste of merely brackish water. There were birds of many kinds in the trees on the banks of the river, and as the boys paddled against the current Johnny saw a brace of ducks swimming ahead of the canoe. He took in his paddle and picked up the shotgun, which, with much forethought, he had placed beside himself in the canoe before starting out. Dick paddled very slowly and quietly toward the ducks until they were within easy range. Johnny had been told that if he wanted to be a real sportsman he must never fire at birds with a shotgun unless they were flying. So he waited until the ducks rose before firing at them. The next instant a bird fell heavily on the water a few yards ahead of the canoe.

"Why, that bird fell out of this tree!" said the astonished Dick. "I didn't know you fired up in a tree."

"I didn't," replied Johnny. "That was a water-turkey, and he isn't hurt a bit. They often act so when they're scared. Watch out for him under the bank."

In a minute or two Dick saw a long, snake-like head and neck thrust out of the water by the bank. The head twisted about with a quick, jerky motion till the bird's eyes rested on the canoe, when it disappeared as suddenly as it had appeared.

"What became of the ducks?" said Dick.

"Reckon we'll find one of 'em 'round that p'int. The other got away." Johnny was right, and the duck was found just around the point.

38

At some places the river narrowed into deep creeks and at others broadened out into wide, shallow bays, where the boys were puzzled to find the inlet they wanted. It was nearly noon when they struck a stream of quite a different sort from anything they had previously seen. Its mouth lay between banks that were high for Florida, and through it flowed a stream of crystal-clear water, which, to the great relief and delight of the boys, was fresh as a mountain brook The bed of the stream looked like sand to Dick, but when he thumped it with his paddle he found it was coral rock. Suddenly Johnny called to him:

"Watch out fur the boat," and resting his hands on the sides of the craft leaped into the water without disturbing in the least the balance of the canoe.

As Johnny swam rapidly under water, close to the white coral bottom of the creek, Dick saw that he was chasing a turtle which was skurrying toward the bank for protection. It got there all right, but the bank didn't protect it, and soon Johnny came to the surface hugging to his breast with his left hand a wildly flapping turtle, while with his right he struck out for the canoe. Getting into the canoe would have been a ticklish job, so Johnny handed the turtle to his companion and swam to the bank while Dick followed with the canoe. By the time Johnny had butchered the turtle, Dick had constructed a very creditable camp-fire under a palmetto, in the shade of which the boys rested while they waited for the turtle stew to be ready for them. Their breakfast had been a cold one, consisting entirely of fruit, and they had decided that for dinner they would begin with turtle stew and end with broiled duck. When the stew had been finished, Johnny inquired:

"Want that duck cooked now?"

"No, I don't. If I ate another mouthful I'd bust. Let's have the duck next week."

Yet each of the boys managed to eat about a hatful of wild grapes, which they found growing a short distance from their camp-fire.

Just as the boys were starting out again, Dick saw a turtle, and, laying down his paddle, said:

"Johnny, if you can catch turtles, I can. See me go for that one."

"Hold on," shouted Johnny, as Dick was about to jump overboard. "That's an alligator turtle. Bites worse'n a bulldog, and ain't good fur much t' eat, nohow."

As they kept on up the creek, its banks came nearer together, trees were more numerous, and the bushes thicker. Soon these

39

began to close overhead, while the stream itself broke up into several smaller ones. As these twisted about, forming a labyrinth of little channels bounded by hundreds of tiny keys, all cohered by an interlaced canopy of leaves and branches, Dick wondered if ever they could find their way out. But he had resolved that morning that never again would he turn back in his exploring so long as it was possible to go on. The little streams continued to become smaller and the turns shorter, until to get around the bends the axe was in constant use to clear a path, while the boys waded and often dragged or carried the canoe. It was wearing work, and they frequently sat down to rest. On one of these occasions Johnny inquired:

"How long you want ter keep this up? This ain't the right creek, not the one Mr. Streeter told about."

"I know that. The creek he spoke of must be away south of this, but this will probably take us to the Everglades, or near them. So we had better keep on till the brook gives out and then travel to the east, toting the canoe till we get to the Glades. We may be away north of Osceola's camp, but there will likely be a trail that will help us to find it, and anyhow we will be near the line that Mr. Streeter thinks Ned and the Indian will follow. Don't you like the plan?"

"Me? Sure! I don't want any better fun than t' keep on t' the Atlantic Ocean, only 'fraid it'd be too hard fer you."

Night found the toys in a narrow stream, scarcely more than the width of the canoe, with bushes around them so thick that they found it hard to clear a place big enough to sleep on. They were tired enough to sleep soundly, in spite of the occasional cries of the birds and beasts of the forest.

They made an early start in the morning, and, although the creek was crooked and they had to cut away many small trees, they were encouraged to find the bushes becoming less abundant as the water grew more shallow, and by dark they were on the border of an open prairie, where they made camp for the night.

# CHAPTER VII

## THE MEETING IN THE GLADES

"The Everglades at last!" said Dick the next morning as the rays of the rising sun fell on the waters of the Everglades in the distance and lit up the clumps of cypress and groups of palmettos that dotted the prairie before him. A little to the north and extending into the Glades was a row of willows which Johnny visited and found that it marked the course of a slough that crossed the prairie and extended far out into the Glades.

They were soon afloat in this slough, paddling toward the Everglades, but the channel which they followed was crooked and it was an hour before they reached them. The boys made their camp beside a little group of palmettos on a bit of dry ground which had often been used for that purpose. Johnny pointed to a faint line in the grass of the Glades and told Dick that it was an Indian trail. Dick was excited at the thought that the chum he had come so far to meet might even now be in sight. When, far to the north, he saw what Johnny said was an Indian canoe with two people poling it, he could scarcely restrain himself from paddling out to meet it. The canoe came on rapidly, and Dick's excitement increased until he began to fancy that in one of the faces that showed above the grass he could make out the features of his chum, when Johnny dashed his hopes to the ground by saying:

"Them's Injuns. Squaws, too. B'lieve I know 'em."

Then as the approaching faces showed more clearly through the tall grass:

"Sure thing. It's Miami Billy's girls. They'll savvy where Charley Tommy is."

The Indian girls were poling past the canoe without appearing to see it, when Johnny spoke to them. Then the girls, who were clothed in the brightest of prints, with masses of beads on their necks, sat down in their canoe and had a pow-wow with Johnny that was altogether unintelligible to Dick. When the girls had gone, Johnny explained:

"Squaws say: 'Think so Charley Tommy not been Osceola Camp, two moons. Been Big Cypress; hunt 'gator. Maybe so hunt with white man. Not been Charley Tiger camp this moon.' The girls left that camp day 'fore yesterday. Only other trail from Tiger's camp goes t' Miami. We c'n camp right here 'nd ketch 'em sure."

Johnny proposed that while waiting they do some alligator

41

hunting. They got out their canvas and rigged up a regular camp. Dick wrote a few lines on a scrap of paper, addressed it "Mr. Edward Barstow," and fastened it on a palmetto tree, in such a way that no one passing along the trail could fail to see it. The boys then unpacked the canoe, and turning it upside down on a bit of dry land stowed their stores under it. They gathered a lot of grass for their beds, arranged for an early start in the morning, and slept dreamlessly till morning came. The hunt was to be on foot, and Johnny insisted that Dick carry the rifle, while he made up a light pack for himself of axe, frying-pan, forks and a little bacon, corn meal, bait and matches. When Dick saw Johnny's pack, he said to him:

"Won't we get back to-night?"

"Mebbe so, but you can't allers tell. We might get to follerin' sumthin and be gone two or three days. I don't reckon we're goin' to get lost, though we may be bothered some."

"If there's a chance of that we haven't got enough to eat."

"Got plenty. All we really want is a rifle, matches and salt. They'd be good for a month."

"What do you do for bread?"

"Cut the bud out of a cabbage tree."

The boys tramped across the prairie to a belt of cypress, where Johnny stopped for some minutes, looking back to study the landscape and take note of every clump of trees and bit of water in sight.

"I thought you were not afraid of getting lost," said Dick.

"I ain't afraid. I could alters git home all right, but I'd hate to lose the canoe."

The cypress strand was swampy, and they crossed it by stepping from root to root, excepting that once, when Dick was looking at a moccasin, he made a misstep and landed in the mud, where he sank to his waist. The woods were narrow, and beyond them was a broad prairie with clumps of trees and pools of water scattered through it. As they walked and waded they crossed the tracks of many animals and birds, to most of which Johnny could give names. There were plenty of 'coons, a few wildcats, some deer, and one bear, while between the little ponds alligators had worn regular paths.

"What's that?" said Dick as a lizard-like creature scuttled through the grass some fifty yards in front of him.

"'Gator! Shoot quick, 'fore he gits t' that pond!"

Dick fired, and his bullet spattered the mud over the reptile's back as it slid into the water.

42

Dick was very much chagrined at missing his quarry, but Johnny consoled him.

"I'll git ye another shot at him. I'll call him out o' the water, and if he don't come I'll take a stick an' go in there an' run him out."

Johnny stood beside the pond and grunted in imitation of a young alligator. In a few minutes two black dots appeared on the surface of the water, and, slowly rising, disclosed the eyes and the point of the nose of an alligator. Johnny grunted again, and the big mouth opened wide to take in the baby 'gator which the reptile thought he heard. Then the horny ridges of the back began to appear, and soon the whole body of the reptile lay on the surface. Johnny whispered to Dick:

"Shoot him in that hump behind his eyes." Dick took careful aim and fired. The alligator rolled slowly over, with its yellow belly on top and its four paws uplifted. Johnny waded into the pond and dragged out the body of the reptile, which Dick helped him skin. When this had been done Johnny cut from the creature a round strip of white flesh, about a foot long, beginning at the hind leg and running toward the tail.

"What's that for?" said Dick.

"Fur dinner. I told ye we'd find 'nuff t' eat."

"Do yon s'pose I'm going to eat that?"

"Sure! 'nd yer goin' ter like it."

"Then I wish I hadn't helped skin it."

Just as the boys were leaving the pond they heard a little grunt, and turning around saw a baby alligator, less than two feet long, lying on the surface.

"Want ter ketch that alive?" asked Johnny.

"Can you do it?"

"I'll show' yer."

And Johnny took off his shoes and waded into the pond. He waded about the pond, feeling in the mud with his toes until he felt the reptile, when, slipping his toes under it he lifted his foot suddenly and brought the alligator near enough to the surface to be able to seize him. Dick was delighted with the captive, but was frank enough to say:

"Johnny, I said once that I could learn to do anything that you could. I take that back. I couldn't learn to do what you did then in a thousand years."

Johnny laughed and said:

"You'd do it this afternoon, and I'll bet on it."

Johnny tied a string around the jaws of their little pet and handed it to Dick, who carried the wiggly thing so awkwardly that

43

Johnny took it back and, opening the bosom of his shirt, put the alligator where he would have a soft bed and plenty of room to prowl around.

"That's another thing I'd be scared to do," said Dick.

Johnny led the way to a clump of palmettos beside a clear little spring and a nice shady bit of ground, where they made a camp-fire, after driving away a family of moccasins that seemed to own the place. A slice of alligator steak, nicely browned, was served on a palmetto fan to Dick, who nibbled squeamishly at the delicate morsel at first, but soon handed back his leafy plate for another helping.

"Wouldn't have believed it," said Dick, "but I never tasted any better meat."

"Wait till I cook ye a rattler. That beats fried chicken."

"No, thank you. I draw the line at snakes."

"You drawed it at 'gators this mornin'. Want some more?"

And Dick shamelessly passed up his plate.

The boys walked and waded several miles, until they were near a heavily wooded tract, which Johnny said was cypress swamp. It was late in the day, and they were about to turn back when Dick saw a turkey, which was holding her head half as high as his own, step silently into the cover of the woods, followed by half a dozen of her half-grown brood. Johnny saw the birds almost as soon as Dick, and exclaimed excitedly:

"We've got ter have one of them young turks if it takes all night."

They entered the swamp and got sight of one of the turkeys as he ran along a log, and they walked to where they saw the bird, only to get another glimpse at about the same distance. Again they followed the birds, this time as cautiously as if they had been stalking hostile Indians. Often they saw one or more of the turkeys, but never within easy range.

"Better try a long shot. They're gettin' wild," said Johnny.

"No, you try 'em, Johnny; you're used to the rifle and you're a better shot than I, anyhow."

Johnny took the weapon, and his chance came soon. One of the young birds lit on a stump within long range of him and remained there until he had taken a careful sight and fired. The bird fell, and the rest of the brood flew into the depths of the swamp. When the boys were ready to start back to camp, Dick discovered to his chagrin that he had no idea of the direction in which they should travel. Johnny, too, was in some doubt, and as it was already

44

growing dark and they had been traveling in the swamp for an hour or two, he proposed that they camp right where they were.

"How can we camp here? Water's knee-deep, there's no place for a fire, and I'd starve to death before morning. Don't you expect to have anything to eat until to-morrow?"

"Bet yer I do! What's the matter with young turkey?"

"Young turkey's bully, but raw turkey's bum."

Johnny laughed and waded to where a fallen tree had left a level place among its upturned roots. A few minutes' work with the hatchet, which Johnny always carried when hunting, cleared out a good foundation for a fire.

"Bully for you! I'll dress the turkey while you build a fire," said Dick.

By the time the bird was ready for the frying-pan, Johnny had not only built the fire, but had cut a lot of poles and rigged up a rough cot between the fallen tree and a rotten log that lay near it. Johnny cut some thin slices of bacon for the frying-pan and then filled it with thick slices and chunks of turkey. When this had been cooked and disposed of, Dick still looked hungry, and another panful of the bird was fried. Dick slept some during the night, but complained that he had a map of his bunk on his back, which had been printed deeply. When breakfast was over and the last bone of the turkey had been picked, the boys turned their faces to the east and started for their camp. They soon reached an open glade, which was quite unfamiliar to them, and were about to enter it, when Johnny, who was ahead, slipped behind a tree and held up his hand warningly to Dick, who promptly got behind another. Two deer were in the opening, about a hundred yards to windward of the boys, toward whom they were slowly feeding. Dick was excited and was nervously raising his rifle, when Johnny whispered:

"Don't hurry. Got lots o' time."

Dick was ashamed of his nervousness, and determined to conquer it, even if he didn't fire at all. One of the deer was a buck with fine antlers, and Dick watched his slow advance, as he looked around for a moment and then browsed for a minute or two, until the boy felt that his nerves were steady once more. The buck was within fifty yards when Dick lifted the rifle to his shoulder and let his cheek rest upon its stock. In another instant the hunted deer had caught sight of the hunter, but it was too late. The beautiful creature stood motionless for half a minute, while Dick wondered if he could have missed, and then sank slowly to the ground, dead. At the report of the rifle the other deer, which was a doe, scampered a few yards, then, turning back her head, gazed with wondering eyes upon

45

her fallen mate. Johnny took from his pocket a cartridge, and, holding it between thumb and finger, looked inquiringly at Dick. Dick shook his head, and in another instant the doe had scampered out of danger. Dick helped Johnny skin and dress the deer, and learned a lot while doing so, but he seemed less happy than a boy should be after killing his first deer.

"Johnny, I wish that buck hadn't looked at me out of his big eyes just when I was killing him. If I had waited a second I believe I wouldn't have fired."

"Glad ye didn't wait, then. Why didn't yer worry about th' 'gator? 'Gators has fine eyes."

When the boys started on again they counted their loads light, but after they had crossed the glade and waded and wallowed through a mile or two of swamp they were of a different opinion. When at last they had crossed the swamp and only a bit of prairie lay between them and the Everglades, they were glad enough to throw down their packs for a long rest. The Everglades were before them, but where was their camp? In that open country they could have seen it for three, perhaps four, miles. Johnny had studied the country around the camp when they left it the day before, but could see nothing familiar now. However, the boy wasn't worried.

"Reckon we're too fur north. Better go south a few miles, 'nd if we don't find it we'll turn 'round 'nd go t'other way. All we got ter do is t' stick t' the saw-grass," said he.

For a quarter of a mile the tramp was an easy one. Then the boys struck a hit of boggy ground, in which they sank over their knees at every step. When the ground became firmer the water got deeper, and after wading half a mile without a chance to lay down his pack and rest, Dick said:

"Johnny, I always heard that Florida deer were small, but this one must have weighed a ton. Wonder if your half is as heavy as mine. I've got to sit down on that hummock and rest."

Dick waded to the hummock and sat down on it, wondering what Johnny was laughing at. The next minute he understood, for the hummock gave a heave and Dick rolled off into the water, while a scared alligator scurried away through the water and mud of the prairie. The hummock was only a pile of loose grass such as alligators often collect and under which they live in the Everglades and the submerged prairies about them. Soon the boys found dryer ground, and after a brisk tramp of half an hour were cheered by the sight of their camp. There was no sign of life about it, to the great disappointment of Dick, who had been hoping that Ned had found

46

it. Before reaching their camp they had to cross a slough that was wide and deep.

"Reckon we've got ter swim," said Johnny as he found a dry place on the bank for his pack and his rifle before wading into the stream. But the bottom was of coral and hard, the water reached only to his arm-pits, and the boys crossed without trouble, carrying their packs on their heads. Dick decided to wait for Ned at the camp, and Johnny collected wood and proceeded to smoke their venison. For two days they stayed by the camp, watching the trail and keeping the buzzards away from the venison by day and listening to the cries of the wild creatures in the woods near-by at night, when Dick's patience gave out.

"Johnny," said he on the morning of the third day, "we've got to find Ned Barstow. Do you s'pose if he knew that I was within fifty miles of him he'd loaf in camp for a week expecting me to run over him? Not much he wouldn't. He'd be sky-hootin' from daylight till dark over the whole country till he lit on me. Mr. Streeter said Charley Tommy couldn't get past Tiger Tail's camp under four days. Now, what's the matter with our meeting him there? Can't you follow the trail of those squaws bade to Tiger's camp?"

"I kin try. Mebbe 'tain't so easy's you think, though."

"What risk do we run in trying it?"

"Nothin', 'cept we may miss your man. We're all right 'nd could live anywhere in this country for a year on what we've got and could pick up."

"Then let's hike out. I can't keep still any longer."

The boys followed the trail by which the squaws had come without difficulty for a few miles. Then came a stretch of open water, where their eyes failed to catch the faint traces of the passing canoes among the few scattering blades of grass that appeared on the surface. Several times they picked up the trail after they had lost it, but at last they missed it for miles. They decided not to go back, and kept on, hoping to find it again. They kept in the light grass as much as they could, but in avoiding the strands of the heavy saw-grass of the Glades they were forced farther and farther to the east, until night found them in the open Everglades with no hope of a place to camp.

They made their way to a flooded key of sweet-bay, myrtle and cocoa plums, and Johnny piled up brush on which he tried to sleep, while Dick lay in the canoe, which had been lashed between two little trees. They were awakened by a deluge of rain, and in a few minutes there wasn't a dry rag between them. They used their canvas to protect guns, ammunition and such things as had to be

47

kept dry. A cold wind chilled them to the bone, and they had to sit down in the water to get warm. It was a short-lived storm, and when the rain ceased and the stars came out Dick said to his companion:

"It's no use trying to sleep to-night; let's pull out for Tiger Tail's."

When morning came the boys saw, far to the northwest, an Indian camp which they knew must belong to Charley Tiger Tail. But between them and the camp was an almost impassable barrier of saw-grass. They paddled to the east, keeping on the southern border of the saw-grass strand, and whenever an opening appeared they followed it until turned back by grass too heavy for them to force their way through. They worked until noon and were out of sight of the Indian camp when they saw, a mile north of them, a couple of Indians poling their canoe. Johnny waved his hand to the Indians, who stopped poling and waited for the boys to get to them. He was soon pow-wowing with them, and translating to Dick as he talked.

"These Injuns, Charley Jumper and Cypress Tiger. This Miami trail. Goes Tiger Tail's camp, 'bout six mile. Hooray! Charley Tommy 'nd your man there. No, went away this mornin'. They say think so on Osceola trail. That's the trail the squaws was on, 'nd we lost it."

"Can't we cut across to that trail and head them off, or catch up with them?"

"I asked 'em. They say: 'No good, trail bad, trail to Charley Tiger good, then go Osceola trail. Maybe so Charley Tommy stop Osceola camp, maybe Miami Billy camp, maybe so not stop anywhere.' They say they sick ojus, want whyome. That means they're awful sick and want whisky, but all Injuns is that. These is good Injuns. Better do what they say."

The trail to the Indian's camp was a crooked one, but Johnny followed it without trouble, although it was nearly dark when they reached the camp. They slept on one of the high tables which the Seminoles use for their beds, and found Charley Tiger Tail quite a civilized Indian, who spoke a little English, sold whisky and dealt in the contraband plumes of the egret.

The boys were up and off at daylight, for they had agreed to do two days' work in every twenty-four hours till they caught the canoe they were chasing. Johnny had talked with Tiger about the Osceola trail, until he felt he could follow it blind-folded, and little time was lost in studying as they poled and paddled that day.

Soon after their start in the morning Dick had said, as he threw his weight on the paddle, which he was using as a pole:

48

"Are you game, Johnny, to camp to-night where we jerked the venison?"

"I kin stand it if you kin. Them squaws took two days, though, 'nd I ain't lookin' ter beat Injuns much with a canoe."

It is doubtful if the boys could have made the camp, for darkness came before they were in sight of it, had not Dick said:

"Johnny, isn't that a light over there toward the land? I've seen it two or three times. Do you s'pose it's a fire in the woods?"

"Don't see it," said Johnny. "Yes, I do, now," adding excitedly an instant later: "Don't you 'member th' big bend in th' trail jest after we left th' camp we're lookin' fer? That fire ain't in th' woods. It's at our old camp, 'nd Charley Tommy built that fire, sure as shootin'."

Dick was faint with excitement, and could scarcely hold his paddle.

"We must get there soon as we can," said he.

"Sure!" said Johnny. "Only let's go quiet 'nd s'prise 'em."

If Charley Tommy had been a white man the plan would probably have been successful. As the boys approached the camp they moved more and more slowly, until Dick laid down his paddle and Johnny did all the work. There was not a sound that Dick could hear, and when the canoe was within a hundred feet of the fire he could see Ned Barstow resting his elbow on a log near it, while the Indian lay beside a palmetto, apparently asleep. But as the canoe continued to approach, Charley Tommy lifted his head, took a swift look around, and, half rising, gazed keenly out over the water toward the boys in the canoe. Further concealment was impossible, and Dick called out:

"Hello, the camp!"

Ned sprang to his feet, and looking across the water in the direction from which the dream voice seemed to have come, was silent until he saw the shadowy outline of a canoe, when he spoke in a voice that trembled with emotion:

"Dicky boy, is that you?"

"Yes, Neddy!" And soon the reunited chums had grabbed and hugged one another till both were breathless. Then they began asking and answering questions, sometimes by turns and sometimes together, till they were breathless again.

"How did you come to recognize my voice so quickly?" asked Dick.

"Because I was thinking of you, Dick, and wondering when we could take the trips we planned in that camp in the North. Now those wonderful dreams have come true!"

49

# CHAPTER VIII

## OLD DREAMS REALIZED

There was a long council around the camp-fire that night, and it was settled that Ned and Dick were to take the light canoe with their own stores and start off by themselves on the hunting and exploring tour of which they had dreamed for years. Johnny was to go on an alligator hunt with Charley Tommy. Johnny thought the Indian could stand the work about two months, after which they would go to Chokoloskee and sell the hides. Ned paid the Indian for his time and made him a present, in addition, of an outfit of clothing from hat to shoes, without any objection from Charley. But when Dick came to settle with Johnny there was trouble. For Johnny refused to take any pay and said that if Dick paid him for coming to where Ned was he would have to pay Dick for carrying him to where Charley was. Ned had to chip in before Johnny could be persuaded to take the pay he had earned. Ned had a better equipment than Dick and a much larger lot of stores. These he shared with Johnny, so that the boy was provided with more luxuries than are often carried on an alligator hunt.

When the boys were about to start away in the morning, Johnny told them that Tommy wanted to go to Osceola's camp for a day or two, and he proposed that the boys come with them. Johnny said that if they went to the Indian camp with Tommy the Indians would talk and the boys could learn a lot of Seminole in two or three days, enough to pull them through in their visits to other camps. The chance was too good to be lost, and the long, heavy Indian canoe was followed down the Glades by the light Canadian canoe of the boys.

Ned and Dick were pretty husky youths, and as their canoe didn't weigh more than one-fourth that of the one just ahead of them, they thought they were in for a picnic. Very soon they changed their minds. Sometimes they could paddle, but generally they used their paddles as poles. They had one oar for pushing, which helped them a little. A light push sent the canoe forward, but when the push ended so did the motion. It took a stronger push to start the Seminole canoe, but the stroke was much longer, and when the stroke ended the motion continued. The boys were game and wouldn't admit that it tired them to keep up. But when a strand of heavy saw-grass had to be crossed they found trouble to burn. The round, heavy wooden cylinder of Seminole make slid slowly through the tall, stiff, saw-edged mass. But the light canoe was thrown back

50

from each stroke by the elastic grass. Dick never liked to be beaten, so he went overboard and floundered along the trail ahead of the canoe, dragging it by the painter, while Ned got out and pushed from behind the stern. The sharp, serrated edges of the grass cut their faces and lacerated their hands. No air was stirring at the foot of those tall spears, and Dick thought of his hours in the fire room of the Southern steamer. Sometimes a big, deadly cotton-mouth, the ugliest snake in the world, swam in front of Dick as he struggled forward, but though his flesh quivered he said nothing lest he make Ned nervous. Then occasionally a poisonous brown moccasin rose out of the mud which the canoe stirred up, and, with uplifted head and open mouth, threatened Ned as he stumbled behind the craft, but he was silent about it lest he worry the chum who was new to the country. The saw-grass strand was only two hundred yards across, although it seemed a mile to the boys, who made light of it when they reached the other canoe, but their bleeding hands, torn by the terrible grass, told another story.

The canoes and cargoes arrived at Osceola's late in the afternoon, and Ned and Dick saw their second Seminole camp. It was the best camp in the Everglades, as Osceola himself was perhaps the best specimen of the Florida Seminole.

The three buildings which constituted the camp consisted merely of high roofs, beautifully constructed of palmetto, which came within four feet of the ground at their outer edges. Below this they were entirely open. These buildings were nearly filled with tables, about four feet high, on which the Indians slept at night and occupied as a floor during the day. The buildings were placed about a round shed, under which the cooking for the whole camp was done. The fire was built in the usual Seminole fashion. Logs of wood were arranged like the spokes of a wheel, and the fire built at the hub. When the cooking was finished the logs were drawn back a few inches and the fire went down to coals, but continued to smolder. When the logs were brought together again the fire blazed up.

Ned and Johnny made their bed on one of the tables and slept well, but they kicked at dipping their hands in the family stew, and broiled their venison and made their coffee over the common fire. It was a good-natured camp, but the boys made life a burden to the Indians for two days by their incessant attempts at conversation in the Indian tongue. Some of the old Indians were sociable, and the boys got along very well with them, but the younger ones were shy and refused to talk until, having put on the white man's clothes that Ned had given him, Tommy took several of the young squaws and pickaninnies out in an Indian canoe. The young Indians laughed so

51

much at Tommy that they began to forget their shyness, and when Tommy bought for Ned a bright-colored Indian shirt that a squaw had just made and the boy put it on, the Indians gathered around him and made fun, very much as white children would have done. One of the squaws brought him a red handkerchief, such as many of the Indians wore, and when Ned nodded and tied it around his neck they all laughed. Another squaw motioned at Ned's hat, and then at several Indians who were bareheaded. Ned nodded again and tossed his hat aside. Then as a squaw pointed at his trousers and afterwards at the bare-legged Indians about him, Ned shook his head vigorously, and even the older Indians joined in the laughter.

The children of the camp were shy things, and peeped out at the strangers from behind trees and out of hiding-places, but Dick was fond of all wild creatures and few of them could resist his friendly advances. Soon every pickaninny in the place was tagging after him. The older ones took him out in canoes, which soon were capsized, and all hands swam back, each accusing the other of having upset the craft.

When the boys went to the Osceola camp of Seminoles with Tommy they found a people as stolid and taciturn as those of any Indian tribe of which they had read. After four days, during which all hospitality was extended to them, they left behind them a kindly group of untaught native Americans, who went out of their way to show friendliness to their guests. Johnny nearly cried over the parting, and would have bartered his hopes of the hereafter to have been allowed to accompany the boys, while Tommy, clothed again in his native costume and in his right mind, preceded them for two miles in his canoe to show them a blind, side trail which they were to take. When they turned to take their last look at him, the Seminole was standing in his canoe, leaning on his long pole and looking fixedly at them.

For a few miles the trail was easy, but then became too dry for paddles, and Dick pushed with an oar, while Ned used a pole which he had brought along for use with a harpoon. As the trail grew dryer, it became impossible to pole the canoe, and Ned took the painter and, stepping into the nearly dry ditch in front of the canoe, dragged the craft, while Billy got overboard and pushed from behind. Sometimes Ned stopped to kick something out of his path, and at last Dick called to him:

"What are you kicking, Ned?"

"Nothing but yellow-bellies and once in a while a brown moccasin. I used to worry myself half sick over them, but after seeing Chris Meyer wade through bunches of them in the Big

52

Cypress without paying any attention to them, I got ashamed of being afraid, and now I don't mind moccasins much unless they are cotton-mouths."

"But they have all got fangs, are all poisonous, and all seem anxious to bite," said Dick.

"But their bite isn't fatal. Tommy told me that he had been bitten six times, and when I asked if the bites made him sick, he said: 'Lilly bit, one moon.' I asked him about rattlesnake bites, and he said: 'Make sick ojus (heap), think so big sleep come pretty quick.' He told me that the moccasins bit him while he was pushing his canoe and stepped on them."

"Neddy, Johnny used to talk just as you do, and Mr. Streeter said a lot more, but it makes me sick to hear it. I can feel the little squirmy beasts under my feet every step I take."

About noon the boys struck a creek, where their paddles came into play, and very glad they both were. For a time grass troubled them, and their progress was slow, but the stream gradually broadened and deepened, while its banks became covered with trees and vines, and the very sound of their paddles dipping into the clear water was a joy to them. Again the brook widened, this time into a shallow bay, but a narrow, deep channel remained, which soon led the boys into a tidal river.

They were about to follow the current of the river when the head of some strange animal was lifted above the surface of the water near them, followed by a mass of water thrown high in the air by a big tail, which flashed in sight for a moment. A line of great swirls, like those made by the propeller of a steamboat, led out in the bay and marked the course of the fleeing creature. Ned and Dick forgot that they were tired, and paddled furiously on the trail until they reached the end of it. Another line of swirls showed where the creature had gone, and once more they followed him. Again and again they were led on until they had traveled a couple of miles, when they lost the trail completely. While they were trying to find it Dick saw the head of the thing lifted for an instant, some two hundred yards away, at the mouth of a little cove. When they reached the cove they found the water clear and deep, and while drifting quietly on its surface they saw resting on the bottom near them a curious creature about ten feet long, with flippers like a seal and a big, powerful tail set crosswise like that of a dolphin.

"I know what that is," said Ned excitedly. "I've been reading about the fauna of Florida lately, and this isn't a fish. It's a very rare mammal, a manatee, or sea-cow. It's perfectly harmless. I wonder if

53

we could catch it. Let's try it. I'll fix a lasso and throw it over the manatee's head when it comes up to breathe."

"S'pose you get your rope over its head, what will happen next to the canoe—and to us?"

"That's what I want to find out. Please paddle a little nearer very quietly. He is beginning to rise," said Ned, who had made a noose in the end of a harpoon line and was standing in the bow of the canoe, ready to throw it the instant the creature's nose reached the surface.

"I see our finish," said Dick as he held his paddle ready to steady the canoe, which was already endangered by Ned's standing up in it. The next instant the manatee came to the surface, and as the creature lifted its head Ned threw his lasso over it. An upward stroke of the big tail of the manatee sent a column of water in the air which half filled the canoe and nearly capsized it, in spite of Dick's best efforts. When the commotion subsided Ned had disappeared. Dick looked wildly over the surface and then into the water, and was just going overboard to search the bottom when Ned's head appeared on the surface. At first the boy seemed confused and swam away from the canoe, but turned when Dick called to him. The canoe was half full of water, and as it would have been difficult for Ned to get aboard without capsizing it, he swam to the nearest key, while Dick paddled the canoe to the shoal water beside it. As the boys stood in the water bailing out the canoe and examining its cargo, Dick said to Ned:

"What did your book say about the manatee being a perfectly harmless animal? I'd sure hate to be spanked by that harmless tail."

"So it is harmless, and if we can tire one out I'm not afraid to go overboard and tackle him in the water."

"Neither am I afraid, and I'll go overboard with you, only I'm afraid that by the time we've tired one of those things I won't be able to swim at all."

Late that afternoon, as the boys were paddling through a long narrow bay of many keys, they became anxious, because for hours they had not seen a bit of ground on which they could camp.

"Looks as if we've got to sleep in the water," said Dick. "If Johnny were here he would fix up a camp anywhere, and I'll do the best I can. Let's keep on to that point where the palmettos are. If we don't find land there we'll camp on mangrove roots."

The boys were in luck, for under the palmettos on the point was a regular Indian camping-ground, with logs for the camp-fire in place and poles ready for stretching a canvas covering, or rigging up mosquito bars.

It was the boys' first real camp together, the very camp of which they had talked and dreamed for years in that far-off Belleville, now more than a thousand miles away. Never before was there so wonderful a supper as the boys enjoyed that night. There was venison, superbly broiled by Ned; a perfect ash-cake, built and baked by Dick, and a pot of gorgeous coffee, for which both claimed credit. They lingered long over their supper, and then talked for half the night as they lay on their bed of palmetto leaves and watched the stars that looked down upon them through the tops of the trees. From the deep water that flowed past the point on which they were encamped came the occasional snort of a dolphin, the crash of a whip-ray as he struck the water after a leap high in the air, and the splashing of fish as they pursued others or were pursued by them. From the thicket behind their camp came the snarling of wildcats, while in the more distant woods the curdling cry of the panther, or mountain lion, could be heard from time to time. A long roar that rose and fell and seemed to come from all sides at once was recognized by Ned as the bellowing of an alligator. Sometimes they heard the beating of invisible wings as flocks of birds flew over them, while the "Hoo! hoo hoo! hoo hoo!" of talkative owls as they conversed lasted throughout the night.

Ned was so anxious for another chance at a manatee that the boys decided to camp where they were and hunt the creature regularly.

"We'll leave all our stores in camp," said Ned, "because we might get capsized."

"Oh, yes! We might get capsized! Is there a chance on earth that we might not get capsized? We'll leave everything in camp excepting the paddles and that lasso of yours which did you so much good yesterday."

"You like to talk, Dick, but you know you wouldn't miss that manatee hunt for a farm. We will have to put it off a day or two, though, until we kill a deer and jerk the venison. We've just eaten the last scrap of meat in camp. There's a trail running back into the bushes that must lead to a meadow where we can walk and probably find deer."

"All right. You'll take your rifle and I'll tag on with the shotgun, just to see that you keep out of mischief."

The trail which the boys followed did lead to a meadow where there were plenty of deer tracks, but no deer. They waded and tramped through the meadow to its farther side, where they entered a wooded swamp. Here they started up a deer, at which Ned took two snap-shots as the creature ran away. They traveled in the

55

swamp for an hour, when they came to another meadow, on the farther side of which two deer were feeding. The wind must have carried a hostile scent to the quarry, for they slipped quietly into the swamp, and when the boys entered it were not to be seen. Again the young hunters sought their game through the swamp. They worked their way through thickets, among tangles of roots and vines, and wallowed through moccasin-infested pools of water and mud. In the excitement of the chase the boys took no note of time or of the direction in which they were traveling. It was late in the day when, with clothing muddied and torn, the boys, exhausted and discouraged, sat on a log in a swamp and decided to give up the hunt and go back to camp. They turned back and Ned led the way while Dick followed until they brought up against an impassable mangrove swamp. Ned looked to the right and the left, and then turning to Billy asked if he knew where camp was.

"No," said Dick.

"Then we're lost."

"Of course. You're always lost in a swamp. Mr. Streeter says so. He says you may lose your boat or your camp, but with a rifle, matches and a little salt you can travel over all South Florida.".

Ned looked so unhappy over their prospects that Dick took the lead, saying:

"If we don't get out of this swamp pretty soon we'll have to camp in it, and we'll need some daylight to fix up in."

At this moment a night heron lit on a branch near Dick, who raised his gun and shot it.

"That's our supper, Ned. I wouldn't shoot a bird sitting unless I was starving. Don't the woods look lighter over there?" In a few minutes the boys were in an open prairie, where Dick produced a waterproof match-box, which was well filled, and a small bag of salt. A fire was soon built, the heron dressed, broiled and eaten with only fingers for forks. The boys washed down their dinners with water from a pool, which they first examined for moccasins by the light of a burning palmetto fan.

Ned slept with his rifle by his side, and Dick was awakened in the morning by its discharge. He saw Ned sitting beside him with the rifle in his hand, while a hundred yards away, on the edge of the clearing, a buck lay on his back kicking. While the boys were hoisting the carcass to the branch of a tree, Ned said to Dick:

"I was in a blue funk yesterday afternoon. I want you to promise to kick me if I get scared that way again."

Dick laughed and replied:

56

"That would be all right, Ned, if I felt sure what you would be doing while I was kicking you."

After breakfast, which consisted of venison, Dick suggested that they go to work systematically to find their lost camp, and proceeded to climb a tall palmetto that stood in the clearing to take an observation. When half way up the tree he slid back to the ground looking like a chimney-sweep. For the outside of the palmetto, like most of those that grow on prairies, had been turned into charcoal by the burning of the prairie grass.

"Ned," said Dick, when the former had stopped laughing at the blackamoor before him because he was out of breath, "I guess it's your turn to kick me. Do you see that trail where I stopped last night to build our camp-fire because I didn't know the way to camp?"

"See it now. Didn't know it was there before, though."

"No more did I; but I saw it yesterday morning, and I took special notice of this palmetto and made sure that I'd never forget this prairie. Why, Ned, this is our own camping-ground, and I could throw a biscuit from this prairie to our canoe. Now you can kick."

After the boys had carried their venison to their camp, Ned said:

"Dick, do you know how to jerk venison?"

"I've seen Johnny smoke it. Is that the same thing?"

"Sure! So while you're skinning the buck I'll lam into that black mangrove log and build a fire under the little scaffold of small poles there, which you hadn't seen, but which was built to cure venison. Say, Dick, don't you want to hire out as a scout?"

Dick grinned, but made no other reply, and they began the work of jerking the venison. They cut it in thin strips and hung it over the fire of the black mangrove, which is one of the smokiest woods on earth. All day long they fed the fire and watched the venison, while scores of buzzards sat around on the trees and overlooked the work. Far into the night the boys lay beside the fire, watched its curling smoke, and talked of that camp in the snow in the North of the long ago.

# CHAPTER IX

## THE CAPTURE OF THE MANATEE

The manatee hunt began as soon as the venison had been cured. The boys explored the waters about their camp, making each day a longer trip and taking careful note of all the waters they explored. They usually hunted through the forenoon, and after dinner Ned mapped out the course they had taken while Dick took a walk with the shot-gun and picked up an Indian hen, or limp-kin, or a brace of ducks for supper. Within a week Ned had made a good working chart of the country about them, both land and water, and the boys had come to know their surroundings as if they had been born among them. Nearly every day they found and chased a manatee. Sometimes they found three or four in a day, but the creatures always swam faster than their pursuers and were still frisky when the boys were worn to frazzles.

One morning a big manatee which they were chasing happened to come up beside the canoe to breathe, when Ned splashed it with his paddle and drove it under water before it could catch its breath. The sea-cow had to come up again in a few seconds and was once more driven below the surface by Ned. Almost instantly the creature lifted its head so far above the surface that Ned dropped his paddle and seized the soft nose of the manatee with both hands.

"Look out!" yelled Dick, but he was the one to have looked out. For, as the sea-cow threw down its head and tail, Ned was dragged out of the canoe onto his upward-arching back. Then the animal's back was curved downward and the flat tail thrown violently upward into the air. As the stern of the canoe was over the tail and Dick was in the stern of the canoe, both boy and canoe went suddenly in the air with a few barrels of water over and around them. When Dick came to the surface he saw his companion being savagely tossed about by an angry monster that seemed to be holding him between his jaws. Dick was terribly frightened and swam as swiftly as possible to Ned's help, but before he could reach him the boy had been tossed aside and the manatee had disappeared.

"Are you hurt?" said Dick, as soon as he got enough breath to speak.

"Course not! Manatees are harmless. Told you so before. But, say, Dicky boy, why didn't you get there a minute sooner and grab a flipper? He'd be our manatee now, if you had."

58

"More likely he'd have had us, Neddy. You didn't see what he did to me with just one slap of his tail."

The boys collected their paddles and swam with the canoe to shoal water, where they lifted it, poured out the water and got aboard.

On their next hunt the boys put a number of chunks of wood in the canoe and when a manatee was started they paddled quietly and tried not to frighten the creature by going too near it at first. Then Ned took in his paddle and armed himself with chunks of wood, while Dick paddled toward the quarry. When the sea-cow lifted its nose out of water, for air, it was hit or splashed by a chunk. The frightened animal dove quickly, but came up again almost immediately for the air it had to have. Another chunk hit its nose, but, confused and half strangled, the manatee hardly moved until Dick had driven the canoe beside it and Ned had landed on its back. Ned failed to grasp the creature's nose with his right hand, but caught the manatee by the flipper with his left and clung to it, although tossed off of the back of the animal. But Dick was in the river a second after his companion and was clutching the right flipper of the manatee with one hand and reaching for its nose with the other. The sea-cow threw its tail high in the air, then lashing it downward, plunged, head-foremost, deep in the water. The boys went under but hung on to the flippers, and Dick got a grip on the creature's nose. Both of the boys were expert swimmers and divers, and were prepared to stay under water as much as a minute rather than release their quarry, but within half that time the animal wanted to breathe and rose to the surface. After that the boys had little trouble, and the manatee, which was a small one, became almost tame. They swam with it to a shoal place where, standing in water a little more than waist deep, they petted and soothed their prize until it seemed quite friendly. Suddenly, Dick exclaimed:

"What's become of the canoe? I capsized it when I went overboard and haven't thought of it since."

"I'd forgotten it, too. It must have floated with the tide a good ways down the river by this time. I'll swim down stream and hunt it up, if you will stay here and take care of the manatee, unless you think we had better turn it loose and both go for the canoe. We will be in a bad fix if we lose it. If you can take care of the manatee I can find the canoe." And Ned swam away down the river.

Helped by the current he had swum a mile when the stream spread out into a bay that was a mile long and nearly as wide, which was filled with eel-grass and covered with moss. He soon found one of the paddles, but in getting it became entangled in the long grass,

59

until he was in great danger of drowning. By lying lengthways on the paddle, keeping his legs extended and swimming with long overhand strokes, he got out of the tangle. He had been pretty well frightened, and swimming to the shore, climbed up on some mangrove roots. After looking for a long time, Ned made out the bow of the submerged little canoe sticking out from a bunch of moss in the eel-grass. It was about an eighth of a mile away and he started for it, swimming along the edge of the field of grass, but sheering away constantly, as the treacherous current seemed striving to sweep him within the clinging clutch of the swaying blades of the rope-like grass.

When Ned got opposite the canoe he found that it was forty feet within the field of grass. He dreaded to put himself again within that deadly grasp, but the thought of Dick waiting for him, alone with that strange beast, nerved him to make the plunge. Again he lay on the paddle, keeping his feet quiet and making his way slowly with his hands toward the canoe. At last he reached the craft, but could do nothing with it. He could not pull it and it refused to be pushed. He could touch the bottom with his feet, but it was of soft mud and the thick grass tangled him worse than ever. He got into the canoe and lay on his back under the thwarts, with only part of his head out of water. By rocking the canoe, with a short, jerky motion, he got rid of some of the water and finished the bailing with his hat. It was not easy to paddle out through the grass and moss to the open water, but Ned accomplished it. Standing up in the canoe, he searched for the other paddle and soon saw and recovered it. He had now more than a mile to paddle against a tide that was still strong, and he saw, to his alarm, that it was nearly sunset. It was about midday when they tackled the manatee, and Dick must have been alone with it for a good many hours. Ned was so anxious that he paddled furiously and was glad enough when he found Dick standing in water shoulder deep, hanging on to the flipper of the manatee, and occasionally patting its nose with his hand.

"Oh, Ned! I'm glad to see you," was Dick's greeting to his chum. "A hundred times, I've almost let this beast go so that I could swim down the river and look for you. If I hadn't heard you coming a few minutes ago I'd have been off by now, anyhow."

"What could you have done, swimming down a big river like this, in the dark?"

"What could I have done here, or back in camp, without you, Ned?"

Ned gave an amusing account of his adventures and made fun of his fears.

60

"Now tell me what happened to you, in those long hours. Did you get scared, too, Dick?"

"Most of my scare was about you, though I did have one or two little troubles of my own. For a good while after you swam away the baby behaved like a cherub. He let me put my arm around him, as far as it would go, and when I rubbed his soft mouth with my hand he seemed to like it. Then, suddenly he lashed out with his tail, threw me off my feet and carried me out into deep water. I don't quite know how I managed to turn him around and get back with him into shoal water. I know I was under water a good deal and got very much out of breath. I guess, though, from the grip I kept on that baby's nose, that he was short of wind himself. Anyhow, when we got back and I let go, he lifted his head out of water and sniffed and snorted like a cow with the consumption. Then, just as I was feeling pretty good and thinking what a nice nurse for a manatee baby I was and what an easy job it seemed, I got a terrible jar.

"Something punched me gently in the back, and when I turned my head I saw a monster that must have been twelve feet long, and weighed a ton or two. It was Baby's ma! She poked her nose all over him and even rubbed it against my arm, which was around him, but I never flinched, though there ought to be some stronger word than scared to fully express my feelings, when I felt that big mouth against my arm. The great manatee mother didn't seem to mind me a bit, as she swam around us two or three times, but I squirmed a good deal when that tremendous tail, which was moving so slowly, came opposite me, and I wondered if it was going to mash me as flat as a sheet of paper, or only knock me over the tops of the mangroves. But that scare was nothing to the next one. After Ma Manatee had gone, Baby and I had a quiet hour or so and I was getting pretty tired and beginning to worry a lot about you, when something happened to set me to worrying about myself. This is a big, deep river, and there was enough going on to amuse me, dolphins, turtles and tarpon coming up to blow as they passed and small fish jumping out of the water most of the time.

"Sometimes a splash and the scattering of little fish when a big one got after them startled me for a minute, but I got over minding it much, when a big, big splash came and there was a long struggle in the river near me. Perhaps I wouldn't have minded it so much, but Baby got crazy again and I couldn't soothe him. Next minute I didn't blame him, for I was 'most crazy myself. Out from all the ruction in the water, there came, swimming slowly toward us, a great leopard shark. I knew him from the spots which covered his body, for he was so near that I could have counted them. He was

61

certainly over ten feet long and looked as if he had plenty of room in his stomach for both the baby and me. I remembered that Mr. Streeter had told me that no shark in this country had ever attacked a human being, so I braced up a little and pulled that splashing manatee baby out toward the shark, and I splashed some myself and acted as if I wanted to eat that Tiger of the Sea. Would you believe it? He was scared silly and, though I was in a blue funk myself, I laughed so that you might have heard me if you had been listening. For behind that shark was a wake such as a big motor boat would have made. After the shark had gone, I had another worrying fit. You had been gone a long time, and the thought kept coming to me that you might have met that shark. Neddy boy, next time you go off alone on a long swim, I'm going with you. Now what shall we do with the baby? The tide will turn before long and I s'pose we could get him to camp. He'd go along all right, but it would be a mile swim, though we could take turns at it."

"I'd rather swim all the way," said Ned, "than to climb into this canoe once, from the river. But what's the use? There's no grass at the camp and the water is too deep for an infant like Baby. Why not tie him here for to-night? Then to-morrow we will take him down to that big bay and make a nursery for him in a shallow little cove that I saw there. It's full of nice manatee grass and we can put stakes across the mouth, or pasture Baby at the end of a rope. But what are we going to do with him, after that?"

"Don't borrow trouble, Ned. That question will come up later. The next thing for us to do is to tie this little beast. So trot out that harpoon line."

Dick untied the harpoon line, which was kept lashed to a thwart in the canoe, and, after getting overboard, carefully fastened the painter of the canoe to a mangrove root. The boys made a harness for the little manatee of one end of the line, by making one loop around the body of the baby, just behind his flippers, another around his tail and then connecting the two. The other end of the harpoon line was then fastened to a mangrove tree on the bank and the baby was turned loose. Dick steadied the canoe while Ned climbed aboard, but when Ned tried to steady it for Dick to get in it, there was a capsize. Dick apologized for his clumsiness and Ned complained that he hated to get wet. The next attempt was successful and the boys were soon eating venison and drinking coffee at their camp. They were tired and talkative when they lay down for the night, and both went to sleep in the middle of a sentence.

The boys hurried through their breakfast the next morning,

anxious to see their captive, which they found where they left him, quite friendly and almost unafraid. Dick took the line in the stern of the canoe, while Ned paddled from the bow. Baby was tractable and allowed himself to be towed, even swimming himself. He behaved best when his head was brought beside the canoe and seemed to like the petting that Dick gave him. When the baby had been tied in the little cove that Ned had discovered, in such a way that he could range over the whole of his nursery, the boys decided not to put a row of poles across the mouth of it. Dick thought it was too much work and Ned said it was no use, because Ma Manatee would knock the whole business over the tree-tops with one gentle little whack of her tail.

They paddled back to their camp and hunted over the prairies behind it all the afternoon. Ned shot another buck, this time in a very boggy swamp. It was not a big buck, but before they got out of the swamp with it the boys had learned several ways in which a deer should not be carried. First, one took the carcass by the tail-end and the other by the head. The middle of the body sagged down in the mud and pulled the boys after it. Then the creature was slung on a pole, which they took on their shoulders. This was better, but every time one stumbled, which was most of the time, both landed in the bog. Then Ned remembered what all boys should know, and the legs of the buck were skinned up to the knee joints. With these loose ends of skin, the legs were so tied together in pairs as to form a loop through which the arms could be thrust and the whole body of the deer worn like a coat.

By taking turns at toting the thing, the boys got their venison to camp without very much trouble. While jerking it they were very glad to lie around camp and rest, and gossip. But their talk always came around to one subject—what to do with their captive. Ned wanted to send him North to some aquarium, but didn't quite see how to do it. Dick offered to swim him down the rivers to the Gulf of Mexico if Ned would sail him up the coast to Marco or Myers, for shipment by water or rail.

"I'm really in earnest about this, Dick, because I know father would like it so much. He is always looking out for curiosities to send to museums or his collecting friends, and this would be such a rare thing."

"Would your father stand for a good big bill to get Baby north?"

"He'd stand for anything! What's in your noddle, Dick?"

"It can be done, easy. We're not many miles from the coast, and I've been wrecked on that coast, Neddy, so I remember it. We

63

will paddle down this river, and as many more as are necessary, until we get to the Gulf. Then we'll paddle along the coast to the shack of a fisherman whom I know. He's got a sloop and all you've got to do is to offer him enough, to make him hustle around for lumber and make a water-tight box big enough for Baby to travel in. Then we will help him get the infant aboard, start him for the railroad and go back to our hunt. Has your father an agent in Myers who'd take your word for the bill? Coz if he didn't the account would likely be settled with a shot-gun."

"Agent? Why, dad will be there himself by that time. And if he isn't, the agent is there all right, all right. So if your pirate settles with me with a shot-gun, I'll settle with that agent, same way."

As soon as the meat was cured, the boys started for the coast in their canoe. On the way they stopped at the nursery and found Baby almost glad to see them, and when Ned put half a banana in his mouth, the little manatee seemed really grateful. Ned even thought that when he pressed the baby's flipper good-bye, the pressure was returned, at least that is what he told Dick. The canoeists had trouble in avoiding the grass and moss of the big bay, but two hours of paddling carried them to the coast, where a strong on-shore wind was sending long rollers up on the beach. Dick knew where they were, and said that they had come down Broad River, and that the fisherman's ranch was only six or seven miles up the coast.

"We can walk up the beach to it and save time. The water is too rough for the canoe," said Ned.

"I don't know about that. I've lived on the water some and I've seen curious things done with canoes. Let's try it."

"Better try the waves with an empty canoe first. Then I'll be with you."

The canoe was unloaded on a quiet bit of the beach which lay behind a shoal and the boys by turns got into the canoe and paddled out among the breakers. Then they went out together and through it all the canoe rose to the waves like a duck. Then they reloaded their canoe and started up the beach. At times the wind was stronger and the waves bigger, but always the canoe rode them with a gait like a rocking-chair. They paddled easily, "taking the waves on the bias," as Dick observed, heading a little off-shore to balance the push of the wind and the waves.

The fisherman was at home, and Ned soon closed a contract with him to carry Baby Manatee to Myers at Ned's cost and risk, payment to be made in Myers by Mr. Barstow or his agent. The man had just got in some lumber to build a skiff. This would serve to build the box, and the charge for it would be five dollars. The fisherman said he would need the help of his son; that the charge for the two would be four dollars a day, and he "reckoned" it would take eight days, so the contract was closed for thirty-seven dollars. He was ready to start right off and catch the evening tide up Broad River.

"Don't you want to make the box first?" said Ned.

"Reckon not. 'Druther see the manatee 'fore I spile good lumber. Manatees is mighty scurse in this country."

Dick flared up, and said to the fisherman:

"Do you mean that we've been lying about a manatee?"

"Course not, not lyin'; manatee's all right, only you ain't much ust to 'em and it may be bigger'n you think, 'nd I'd hate to make th' box too little."

The lumber was taken on board, the canoe unloaded and laid on the deck of the sloop, the sails reefed and with her skiff drawn close up under her stern the craft was soon flying down the coast. When she reached the river the reefs were shaken out and in little more than an hour anchor was dropped beside the manatee cove. It was nearly dark and work was to begin the next morning, but all hands wanted a look at the little manatee. The fisherman and his son went in their own skiff while Ned and Dick led the way in the canoe.

"Now I'll show you something worth seeing," said Ned, as he took hold of the end of the line and pulled it all easily in. As Ned sat looking at the broken end of the line, half stupefied by the greatness of his surprise, the fisherman laughed and said: "That sure was worth seem', 'nd I reckon I've saved you five dollars by not makin' that box till I got here 'nd saw the critter."

"I'll keep the contract. It isn't your fault that the manatee has got away."

"No, I reckon 'twan't anybody's fault, much. All I want out o' you is four dollars for one day's work," and the fisherman laughed again, adding a moment afterward:

"I'm 'most ashamed to take that much, but I reckon the joke's been wuth it ter you."

Ned paid the four dollars and the boys paddled back to their old camp for the night. On the way back Ned stopped paddling, and turning back, said to Dick:

"Did that old fellow mean that he didn't believe we had caught a manatee at all?"

"If I thought he did, I'd go back and punch his head."

"No, you wouldn't. He isn't to blame. He only thought what

65

everybody who hears of it and don't know us will think. I hope he won't tell about it in Myers, so that it will get to Dad's ears."

"I shouldn't think you'd care for that," said Dick.

"Well, Dad enjoys a joke and I would likely hear of 'Ned's manatee' pretty frequent for some time."

# CHAPTER X

## HARPOONING FROM A CANOE

Do you want to go for any more manatees?" asked Dick, the next morning.

"Guess not. We're pretty well acquainted with the critters already and if we tackled another it would likely be a bigger one, and the sample we had was about all we could manage. But the bay here is full of big fish. Suppose we get out the little harpoon and pick up some drum-fish, channel-bass or a whip-ray?"

When the boys started out for a day of harpooning, Dick sat high up on the stern of the canoe with the paddle, while Ned stood in the bow with the harpoon.

"Hadn't you better sit down in the bottom of the canoe to paddle? The canoe feels wobbly to me," said Ned.

"What's the matter with your nerves, Neddy? I'm not going to capsize you. S'pose I practiced half a day with that papoose for nothing?"

"Most of that practice was swimming, wasn't it? I don't want any of that in mine to-day."

Ned harpooned several large drum-fish, and finally got a channel-bass, after missing several.

"We've got a lot more fish than we can eat now. Let's go for something big and have some fun. Hit that shark over there."

"That shark could bite this canoe in two and then swallow the pieces. I wouldn't mind that so much if we were in the Glades, but I don't want to be set afoot so far from fresh water. See that big whip-ray! It's a beaut;—paddle up to it, Dick."

Dick paddled toward the fish, which was shaped like a butterfly, with a back six feet broad, covered with beautiful little white rings placed on a jet black background. The graceful creature fluttered along the surface of the bay with a bird-like motion, at a

66

speed that soon took it nearly out of sight of the boys. Dick followed it, as it zigzagged about the bay, sometimes skimming on the very surface and then disappearing in the depths for minutes at a time. Once it was out of sight for five minutes, and Dick had just stopped paddling, saying:

"Got to give it up. That big butterfly is the other side of the bay by this time," when Ned saw the broad back of the creature gliding beneath his harpoon, beside the canoe and a foot or two under the surface. His quick side-throw was doubly effective, for the harpoon was buried in the back of the quarry, while Ned and Dick were buried in the water of the bay. The center of gravity of the canoe's cargo of boys was at least two feet above the gunwales of the craft, and when Ned's side-thrust threw him out of balance, the canoe popped from under him, and as Dick sat on the stern of the canoe and quite outside of it, he was in the water as soon as his chum. The whip-ray had darted away at high speed as soon as the iron touched him, but before the line which was coiled in the harpoon tub had run out, Ned had seized the tub, which was floating near him when he came to the surface.

The end of the line was fast to the tub and when it was reached Ned was hauled through the water by the fish. If Ned had been built like a canoe, he would probably have caught the whip-ray, but the drag of the boy in the water was too much for the hold the iron had in the body of the creature, and the harpoon tore out. The boys managed to rock the water out of the canoe, but swamped it several times while trying to get in it without going ashore. After they had succeeded, Dick took the harpoon, while Ned sat in the bottom of the canoe with his paddle.

"Now go ahead and harpoon your fish and I'll show you how to keep a canoe trimmed. What you really need is a scow," said Ned.

"If I couldn't throw a harpoon over the side of a canoe without going over the other side myself, I'd give up fishing and try farming. Now just paddle softly in the wake of that big fin. Know what it is? I thought not. Well, it's the bayonet fin of the tarpon, my son, and if you'll paddle quietly and stay inside the boat, you shall have the fun of your life."

The tarpon was tame, and Ned paddled within twenty feet of it without frightening it, but Dick made a poor shot. The back of a tarpon is narrow and a small mark for a harpoon when thrown from behind the fish, and Dick's weapon grazed its side, while the pole fell across the back of the tarpon, causing it to give one wild leap and depart for regions unknown. Dick was now out for tarpon, and paid no attention to smaller fish, many of which came within

67

striking distance. Tarpon were scarce that day, and Dick's next chance was an hour in coming, and then the fish happened to be headed for the canoe. The boy had not learned the difficulty of throwing an iron through the coat of mail of a tarpon excepting from abaft the beam of the fish, and he drew in his harpoon with a beautiful four-inch scale fixed on its point.

"Take the harpoon, Ned. I couldn't hit a house."

"Yes, you could. You hit that tarpon. Only trouble was, you didn't know where to hit it. Keep on practicing. You said I'd have the fun of my life, and I'm having it."

Half an hour later Dick made a beautiful, long throw of nearly thirty feet, and the stricken tarpon leaped six feet in the air. For two hundred yards the frantic fish towed the canoe in a straight line, at a high rate of speed, and then began a series of leaps in the air. Some of these were long jumps which barely cleared the surface of the water, while others were from eight to ten feet vertically upward. The tarpon then darted away in a new direction, blistering Dick's hands as the line tore through them. For a quarter of an hour the drag of the canoe made little difference in the speed of the tarpon, but then it began to slacken and Dick was able to pull the canoe up beside the fish, which gave a leap and a sweep of its tail that drenched both of the boys and, if the tarpon had been a foot nearer, would have wrecked their craft. Again the creature dashed away, getting back most of the line that Dick had taken in. Once more the fish weakened, and the canoe was drawn up beside it, and once more it sprang in the air and dashed away. But with each fresh effort the tarpon became weaker, until Dick said to Ned:

"He's about played out. Better take the gaff next time I get near him and see if you can land him in the canoe."

"No," replied Ned, "he's your tarpon and you can gaff him yourself. He'll capsize the canoe when he comes aboard and I want to be ready to swim."

Dick drew the canoe beside the tarpon and, dropping the harpoon-line, held the handle of the big gaff-hook in both hands, ready to strike. But the fish saw the uplifted weapon and sheered away, swimming with renewed vigor, and Dick had to work for another half hour before his quarry was quiet enough for the blow. This delay was fortunate for the boys, since it left the tarpon too tired to struggle. When Dick sank the steel gaff deep in the throat of the Silver King and dragged it over the side of the frail canoe, Ned sat in the bottom of the craft with a hand on each gunwale, ready to balance the boat or swim, as events might indicate.

The boys took a lot of the big silver scales as souvenirs and then slid the body of the tarpon into the bay, where it was soon devoured by a couple of wandering sharks.

# CHAPTER XI

## GHOSTS AND ALLIGATORS

The boys spent a day exploring the bay to the east and south, finding but a single creek, which lost itself in the jungle after wandering a few miles.

"I don't believe we can get through this way," said Dick to his chum, as they were resting, after an hour of hard work, cutting away branches of trees and dragging the canoe. "Mr. Streeter told me that the Indians say there is no creek between the bays at the head of Broad River, where we are, and the rivers south of it. Suppose we work our way to the mouth of this river and then follow the coast down to Harney's, which is the next river south of us and the longest one in South Florida."

"All right, and we can explore that big creek running west from the foot of this bay, which we saw yesterday."

The boys found the creek to be deep with swift water, but so crooked that a snake would have had to slow up to get through it. After two miles of paddling, which advanced them about half a mile, they found themselves in a broad smooth-flowing river, the most beautiful stream they had ever seen. The big trees on the banks were clothed with airplants, draped with long, flowing gray moss and garlanded with flowering and sweet-scented vines. Sometimes an opening in the forest showed broad savannahs, or prairies, or disclosed groups of tall palmettos or magnificent royal palms, the grandest tree that grows. The water was mirror-like, and the great trees, capped by a mass of white clouds in the blue of the heavens, were repeated below in a reflection that was perfect. The boys paddled for a long time, silent as if in a dream, when Ned spoke in a voice so low that his companion could scarcely hear what he said:

"Does it make you think of Heaven, Dick?"

"Guess it does; only," added Dick, in a louder tone, "it will make you think of the other place, pretty soon."

"What do you mean?"

"It's a deserted river. Only ghosts stay here. The plantations are grown over, the houses rotting and little sticks in the ground tell where the old owners are. The climate is so bad that skull and bone notices grow on the trees. Then things happen. People eat something and die, or fall out of their boats and drown, or go out in the woods and stay till the buzzards find them. Oh, but it's the peaceful, lovely Rodgers River!"

"Why, where did you hear all that, Dick?"

"From Mr. Streeter. He talked a lot and I didn't forget much that he said. Then Johnny had heard the talk of convicts, and others who ought to have been, and told me about them almost in a whisper, for fear somebody would hear him."

"There's a rotting old shack, now, by that date palm. Are you afraid of ghosts?"

"No, rather like 'em. I wouldn't mind camping with them for a day or two, with you for company."

The house looked too spooky and snaky to live in, and the boys made their camp in the open, near a tamarind tree and, as they observed later, beside an overgrown grave. An old barrel under the eaves of the house was nearly full of rain water, which they were likely to need, since their only supply of fresh water was contained in a five-gallon can, which would hold about two days' requirements. The rain water was good and would have been better but for Ned's gruesome inquiry:

"You don't suppose it has been poisoned, do you, Dick?"

On their first afternoon the boys crossed the swampy jungle in the rear of the old plantation and found themselves on a typical South Florida prairie. On it were oases of fire-blackened palmettos, little ponds, palmetto scrub and bits of soggy meadow, in which they often sank to their knees, as they plodded across them. There were tracks of wild animals in the meadows and regular trails of alligators between the ponds. Billy stopped beside one of the ponds and grunted, as he had been taught by Johnny, until a little 'gator showed his head.

"See that alligator, Ned? Let's go in there and fetch him out."

"Not much do I go in that mud-hole, alligator or no alligator."

"Then, just you watch me," said Dick, as he took off his shoes and stockings.

"See here, Dicky boy, come out of there," said Ned.

But Dick kept on, wading all round the pond before he felt the wiggle he wanted. Perhaps his toes were less tough than Johnny's, or maybe he didn't manage them as well, for one of them got in a baby 'gator's mouth. Dick couldn't suppress a yell as two rows of

70

needle-like teeth sunk into his flesh, and he jerked his foot away so violently that he lost the chance of bagging his game. Then Ned came floundering through the mud and almost dragged him out of the pond.

"I mean to get that little alligator if it takes all day, only I won't try him barefoot again," said Dick, as he slowly drew his stocking over his aching toe.

Dick waded out into the pond again and for half an hour explored with his feet for the reptile he was after, but all in vain. Several times he thought he touched the creature with his shoe, but could not be sure. Then he waded ashore and began taking off his shoes.

"What are you going to do now, Dick?" said Ned.

"Johnny waded barefoot into just such a pond as that and brought out a 'gator. I told him then that what he could do, I could. I'm plumb scared to go in that pond barefoot, but that young Cracker, who's a year younger than I, waded right in without stopping to think whether it was safe or not. If Johnny was here he'd have that 'gator out of that pond, toes or no toes, and that's what I'm going to do," and Dick waded barefoot into the pond again and began feeling around in the mud with his toes.

"If you feel that way about it, I'm with you, Dick," said Ned, as he began to take off his shoes. But before he reached the water the reptile had been caught, and Dick waded ashore with the wriggling little alligator in his hand.

"There's a bigger one in there. He whacked me on the shin with his tail, just after I caught the little one. Let's get him."

The boys waded side by side, the length of the pond, several times without finding another 'gator, although the occasional roiling of the water showed that there were others in the pond. They were about to give up the hunt when something struck Ned's leg and, grabbing suddenly at the thing, he found that he had a five-foot alligator by the head. He held the jaws of the 'gator shut while Dick seized the hind legs of the reptile, and together they carried the creature ashore.

"I wonder where that fellow was hidden," said Dick, after the alligator had been safely tied. "My toes have felt in every inch of the mud in the bottom of that pond. Maybe there's another one. Let's get him," and Dick started into the pond.

"Wait till I get some clubs and I'll be with you. There may be a big 'gator in there who wouldn't be satisfied with a toe."

It was well they had clubs when they went back in the pond, for after a few minutes' searching, Dick struck something, and the

71

tail of a reptile came to the surface beside him. As he grabbed it with both hands, and hung on with all his strength, a long body curved upward from it, a big head was uplifted, and two rows of ivory teeth gleamed from wide-opened jaws before Dick's eyes. Before the boy could move or the beast strike, Ned's club came crashing down on the reptile's head. As the jaws closed and the head fell back, a second and yet more furious blow fell upon it. As they dragged the stunned or dead 'gator out of the pond, Ned said:

"I'm going to round-skin this alligator and save the skull, for mounting. I'll keep it in my den as a reminder of this trip and of you."

"If it hadn't been for your club, it would have been more of a reminder of me than it is now."

The alligator came to life a few times, while they were skinning it, and had to be killed over again, and the tail did some wiggling even after the spine had been severed. When the skinning operation was over the boys went back to camp, where they found an old kettle, in which they boiled the skull of the alligator and cleaned it of flesh and brains in preparation for mounting.

"How did you sleep last night, Dick?" asked Ned, the next morning.

"Didn't sleep at all. This place is sure bad medicine. First the hoots of the owls and the snarls of the wildcats kept me awake, then the booming of the big alligators worried me, and after I did get to sleep, the ghost of that alligator that we killed to-day shook his white teeth in my face, and I could feel the man in the grave under me trying to push me off of it. Let's get out of this river this morning, Ned."

As they paddled down Rodgers River, in the bright sunshine, Dick's spirits rose and when they were off the mouth of the river, headed down the coast and bound for Harney's River, two miles distant, he took in his paddle and, calling to Ned to hold steady, vaulted lightly from the canoe, without even jarring it, and landed on a sandbank in water that was but little above his waist. Stooping under the water he picked up clams of several pounds weight each, with which the bottom was paved, until clam-roasts for days had been provided for. Getting back into the canoe was a ticklish operation, but was accomplished without disaster, although a pailful or two of water was taken aboard.

# CHAPTER XII

## HUNTING IN HARNEY'S RIVER

The boys had chosen the last of the ebb tide for the trip down Rodgers River, which gave them low water for their work on the clam bar and a flood tide to help them up Harney's River. They made a false start at the mouth of the river by taking a channel that ran too far to the east and led them a mile or two out of their course, before they discovered their mistake and returned. After entering the channel, the course up the river, which averaged east-northeast, was plain, there being but a single branch to mislead them, in the first six miles. At the end of these the lower section of Harney's unites with a branch of Shark River to form Tussock Bay. This bay is a labyrinth of channels and keys and opens into creeks large and small, and water-courses shallow and deep, grass-choked and clear.

After exploring its mazes for miles, Dick and Ned found, near the northeast end of the bay, a tiny key marked by two tall palmettos, on which were the signs of an old Indian camp. Here they roasted a mess of clams and spent the night. An entire day was wasted in following creeks that led nowhere and blind trails. That night they slept again at the Indian camp and on the following day found a small channel which, through twisting creeks and crooked waterways, led to the broad waters of the upper section of Harney's River, which they followed until they were stopped by the Everglades. They made their camp by a lime tree which was burdened with fruit, and went out from it each day to hunt fish or explore and to study and chart the country about them. The waters of the streams were all flowing clear and fresh from the Everglades. The creeks were alive with fish of many kinds, and their surfaces dotted with the heads of edible turtles.

Alligators were abundant and otters could often be seen sliding down the banks, or in families, playing together in the water. Ned had seen a pet otter at Myers and wanted one for himself. He had brought with him an otter trap, with smooth jaws instead of the cruel teeth which are customary, and he set it near an otter slide. The next day as the canoe approached the point where the trap had been set the rattling of the chain that held it told of the victim it had made. The hind leg of the otter was held firmly by the trap, but he sprang fiercely at Ned as he came near, and the sharp teeth snapped together within a few inches of the boy's face as the short chain straightened out. The boys went back to their camp, where Ned made a cage out of the box in which they kept most of their stores, and then returned to their captive.

"How are you going to get him into the cage, Ned?"

"Hold his head down with a forked stick, take him round the neck with my hand so he can't bite, take the trap off of his leg and poke him in the cage."

"Ned! He'll eat you up. I'd rather tackle a wildcat."

"Just watch him eat me up. You stand by, when I've got a good hold, and take off that trap quick as you can. Then I'll drop him in the box and—there you are."

"No, we won't be there—not all of us. I wish I was the otter. He'll have all the fun."

Ned got his forked stick and, after a long struggle, in which Dick had to help with another stick, caught the otter's neck in the fork and held the creature firmly to the ground. Then putting his left hand around its neck he held the head down in the mud, and with his right hand clutched the skin of the animal's back.

"All right, Dick, take off the trap."

"Trouble's goin' to begin. Here goes," said Dick, and the trap was removed.

Like a flash of light, as Ned lifted the little beast, it thrust its head through the loose skin of the neck and turning backward bit Ned's hand to the bone four times in something less than a second. The otter would have been free, but that Dick, who was looking for trouble, had it by the neck with both hands and in spite of its biting, scratching and struggling, it was dumped in the box and the door of its cage closed.

"Been having fun! Haven't we?" said Dick, ruefully, as the boys, scratched, bitten and bleeding, stood looking at each other, after their victory. Ned's hand was disabled and so painful that Dick paddled the canoe, with its cargo of boys and pet otter, to their camp.

"Now, Ned," said Dick, "I'm the surgeon and you are to be respectful and call me Dr. Dick. Let me see your left hand first. I've got to decide whether to chop it off, or to try and save some of it."

"You look as if you needed some fixing up yourself, Dick."

"That will be all right. You shall have a chance at me—if you survive the operation."

Dick got a bottle of carbolated vaseline from their stores, tore up one of Ned's shirts and put the strips in boiling water. He then washed Ned's wounds with warm water and soap and dressed and bandaged them. His own injuries were less serious than Ned's, although more numerous, and although he spoke lightly of them,

74

his companion insisted on their having as careful treatment as his own. When the bandaging was over, Dick said:

"We ought to have a yellow flag to fly over this hospital. I wish we had a medical book to tell us what we've probably got. The only things I'm sure of are blood poisoning and hydrophobia. Then there's enlargement of the spleen. I've got all the symptoms of that."

"Your only danger is from melancholia, Dick. But what are we to do with the otter? That box is too small for his comfort."

"I'm not losing any sleep over his comfort. I thought I'd take him out of his cage every morning and lead him around the camp for exercise until you were ready to begin his education."

"It does not seem quite as easy to tame him as it looked before we caught him."

"Guess you mean before he caught us."

"Shouldn't wonder if I did. Couldn't we build a cage of poles, with some of these big vines woven in basket fashion?"

"That would be all right. We could watch him day times and you could put him back in the box every night for safe keeping. I don't think he's an otter at all. He just fits the definition of a white elephant."

On the day after his little difference of opinion with the otter, Ned's left hand and wrist were so sore and stiff that he could neither hold his paddle nor his gun. Dick, too, was partially disabled by the soreness of his arms, but he managed to get about in the canoe and shoot ducks enough for their meals. They could not induce the otter to eat anything, although it seemed much less fearful of them. The leg which had been in the trap was broken and appeared to trouble the animal, but they could do nothing to help it. Dick did propose to take the otter out of the cage and offered to set its leg if Ned would hold the creature. On the second day their wounds continued to be so troublesome that the boys stayed in their hospital camp. As they sat that afternoon in the shade of a lime tree, drinking limeade, Dick, the philosopher, began to question Ned.

"Don't you pity all these folks about here, Ned? Crackers, alligators, Indians, the whole ignorant lot of 'em. If they had got hurt as we did, they would have gone right on about their business. They'd never have found out that they were probably suffering from appendicitis and microbes and ought to go to a hospital and be carved up."

At this moment the bow of an Indian canoe glided silently into the tiny cove in front of the camp. The boys recognized one of the two bronzed, bare-legged Seminoles that stood so erect in the canoe, as from Osceola's camp. His response to Ned's greeting was a question.

"Whyome (whiskey), got him? Want him, ojus (very much)."

Ned told them he had no whyome, but brought out coffee and sugar and invited them to make a brew for themselves. He also produced grits and venison. The Indians sat down to a feast which lasted as long as any food remained in sight. One of the Indians looked curiously at Ned's bandages and smiled a little as he pointed to the box that held the pet otter. Ned nodded and asked the Indian, by signs, if he had ever been bitten by one of the creatures. The Indian held out his hand and showed the scar of a bite that must have nearly taken off his thumb. After the Indians had gone Dick looked ruefully over the diminished stores and exclaimed:

"There's going to be a famine in this camp if those Injuns hit us again."

The next day the boys were very much better and ready for work. Ned could not hold a paddle with his left hand, so they took a trip into the Everglades, where the water was so shoal that they used their paddles as poles and he could push with one hand. They left their stores in camp, for which afterwards they were glad, and pushed out several miles among the keys of the Glades, where Dick got a shot at a deer which was running from one key to another, but made a clean miss. They saw several alligators and in the afternoon chased one with the canoe. The boys could go faster than the 'gator, but the reptile could turn more quickly. At last the canoe was right behind the quarry and within a few feet of it.

"Give it to her!" yelled Ned, as he seized his paddle in both hands and threw his weight upon it.

"Here goes!" shouted Dick, as he threw his weight on his paddle, which, unfortunately, slipped from the point of coral rock on which it first struck. Dick landed on his back in the water, capsizing the canoe as he fell. When the young canoemen had picked themselves up, righted the canoe, and found the rifle, it was too late to look for the missing alligator, and they plodded slowly home to camp. They found their captive much tamer. He drank a little water, although he refused to eat. His leg was badly swollen and they were anxious about him, and with good reason, for when they awoke in the morning he was dead.

Ned's last, reckless thrust with his paddle had broken open his wounds and they became very painful. Dick dressed them again and warned him that he wasn't to use his hand until he had Dr. Dick's permission. They explored the creeks around their camp in the canoe, Dick doing most of the paddling, while Ned helped as well as he could, with his unhurt arm. The clear water of these little streams abounded with baby tarpon and other small fish, while often, in the deeper pools, turtles could be seen scurrying along the bottom. Dick had never told Ned of the turtle-catching that Johnny had taught him, so when he said, very casually, "Ned, I think I'll go overboard and pick up that turtle for supper," Ned replied:

"Don't be an idiot. You couldn't catch that thing in the water in a thousand years."

"Just hold the canoe steady and watch me." And Dick, resting his hands on the gunwales, threw himself overboard.

The splash frightened the turtle, which made off up the creek, but the boy was on his trail and, after a few futile grabs, had the reptile in his hand.

"Think that will do for supper, Ned, or shall I pick up a few more?" said Dick, as he put the turtle in the canoe.

"I'd like to know who taught you that, you rascal, playing roots on your poor old chum, who never had your chance to see the world."

While they were waiting for Ned's hand to get well, Dick got out the fly-rod and cast-net that came with his canoe and spent all his spare time trying to learn to throw the net. Johnny had given him a few lessons, until he thought he had learned to cast it. It was the kind of net which is used by the Florida Cracker, to the knowledge of which he is born, which he can cast when he leaves his cradle. The net was conical, six feet long with a ten-foot mouth, lined with leaden sinkers. The top of the net was closed, excepting for a small hole in which was fitted a small ring, through which puckering strings led from the mouth of the net to a 25-foot line, which was to be fastened to the fisherman's wrist.

For casting, about half of the net is thrown over each wrist and one of the sinkers held between the teeth. The net is then swung behind the fisherman, thrown forward with a whirling motion, the sinker in his mouth released at exactly the right instant and the net falls in an almost perfect circle wherever, within thirty feet, the fisherman wishes. That is the way the net behaved when Johnny threw it. And when Johnny arranged the net on Dick's arms, told him just what to do and watched him, Dick made some respectable throws, and thought he had learned the game; but now, away from his teacher, when he tried to cast it, net and leads went out in a solid mass that never could have caught anything, though it might have killed a fish by knocking it in the head. Dick, however, was bound to learn, and practiced by the hour, without seeming to make any progress, when suddenly the net began to go out in circles and his

77

casts became creditable. He was so fearful of losing his new-found facility that he practiced for the rest of that day, and lay down at night with what he called the toothache in every muscle.

But from that day fish was on the bill of fare of the young explorers.

When Ned's hand was well enough to be used a little, he began by fishing, sitting in the bow of the canoe, with the fly-rod, while Dick paddled. He caught several of the big-mouthed black bass, often called in the South fresh-water trout, and other small fish which they saved for the pan. Then the line was carried out with a rush by a fish that twice jumped one or two feet in the air.

"Got a tarpon, sure," said Ned, who had never taken one, and he became most anxious lest the fish escape.

For nearly half an hour he carefully played the fish, which never jumped again. When the tired fish was ready to be landed Ned found that his prize, instead of a tarpon, was a ten-pound fish which he did not recognize, but which he afterwards learned was a ravaille.

"Well, it was mighty good fun, almost as exciting as if it had been a tarpon," said Ned, who didn't know how foolishly he was talking.

They were down the river bright and early the following morning but, for the first hour, failed to hook any of the fish that struck. Then the hook was snatched and instantly a silver, twisting body shot ten feet up in the air. As it fell back in the water, the reel began to buzz and Ned's fingers were burned where the line touched them. Again and again the great fish leaped high in the air, while the line ran low on the reel.

"Paddle, Dick, paddle all you know," shouted Ned.

But Dick was already doing his very best. The tarpon changed his course, came back a little, leaped once more and again started off. But Ned had got a good many yards of line back on his reel, and was getting hopeful of landing his first tarpon. He was beginning to lose line again, when the tarpon turned around and, swimming straight for the canoe, leaped against Ned with such fury that the craft was nearly capsized, and when Ned had recovered from the shock his line was nearly out and the fish headed for a little creek that was almost overgrown with trees and vines. The first jump of the tarpon as he entered the stream carried him up among the bushes that hung over the water, but fortunately the line did not catch in the branches and, as the fish swam slowly up the little channel, the canoe was close behind him. Ned held the point of his rod low, that it might not catch in the bushes, but his heart was up in his mouth every time the tarpon sprang in the air.

78

"It's no use, Dick, we've got to lose him. He isn't a bit tired and the tangle is getting worse. Then if he turns back I won't have room for the rod and you can't turn the canoe."

"Never say die, Ned. If he gets away from you, I'll go overboard and pick him up."

"The creek's opening out into a big river, Dick. We may land him yet."

The tarpon stayed in the big river, swimming a mile or so and then turning back, while Ned put all the strain he dared on rod and line and, excepting when the tarpon made a rush, Dick held his paddle still and let the fish tow the canoe by the line.

"We've got all the scales we want," said Dick, "and I move we don't gaff another tarpon. When we have tired this one so it's through jumping, let's turn it loose. We don't need it to eat and I hate to feed sharks with such a beautiful creature."

"Sure!" said Ned. "And if it is as tired as I am it will give in pretty soon or die."

The tarpon grew weaker, his leaps lower and soon the canoe was held close to him, while Ned even laid his hands on the tired fish.

"Think we can take him aboard, Dick?"

"I think you can swamp the canoe and break the rod, all right."

"I don't mind swamping the canoe and we can take care of the rod. If you'll take the rod now, I'll hang on to his jaw and take out the hook, which I can see in the corner of his mouth. Then, if you will look out for the rod and balance the canoe, I'll slide that tarpon over the gunwale—"

"And we will all go overboard together," added Dick.

"No, we won't, but just as soon as we have fairly caught him and got him in the canoe, we'll slide him overboard again."

Dick took the rod, Ned removed the hook from the mouth of the tarpon and hoisted its head over the gunwale. The canoe canted over until water poured over its side, and the attempt would have failed but for the tarpon which, with a blow of its tail, threw itself up in the air and fell on top of Ned, who had tumbled into the bottom of the canoe. The sight of Ned hugging the big fish, which was spanking his legs with its tail, was too much for Dick, who sat down on the gunwale of the canoe in a spasm of mirth, and of course the craft was capsized. Ned clung to the fish for a few seconds until his captive had bumped him with its head and slapped him with its tail a few times, when he was glad to let it go. He then joined Dick, who was holding the rod with one hand and clinging to the canoe with the other, as he swam to the bank.

On the way back to camp Dick had several fits of laughter that made him stop paddling for a minute at a time and caused Ned to say:

"It's all right to laugh now, but that was my tarpon. I had him safe in the canoe and if you hadn't tipped us all into the river I'd have hung on to him."

"I'm awful sorry, Ned, but if only you could have seen yourself, you'd have had to laugh or bust. Besides, you had your fun. You caught your tarpon and you wouldn't have done any more if you had lain in the bottom of the canoe and let it spank you all night."

## CHAPTER XIII

### EDUCATING AN ALLIGATOR

The boys wished to explore the Whitewater Bay country, and spent several days following to their sources streams that led in that direction, until satisfied that no stream connected the two regions. Returning to Tussock Bay, they crossed it and entered a branch of Shark River, which led to Little Whitewater Bay. As they neared the bay a loggerhead turtle rose near them and Dick wanted to hunt it.

"We need the meat," said he. "We can smoke it and then it is as good as jerked venison."

"We haven't time to smoke it. We are in a salt-water country with only two or three days' supply of fresh water. We may not find any more for a week. We've just got to keep moving. I wish we had a keg of water. If we were to spill what we've got in that canoe we would have to hike in a hurry, back to the Glades or some other place where we knew there was fresh water."

On the eastern side of Little Whitewater Bay, the boys found a straight and narrow creek which led to Whitewater Bay. Paddling for six miles, east-southeast, across the bay, they were fortunate enough to strike the narrow mouth of what soon proved to be a broad river. They paddled long and late without Finding the fresh water they looked for, and camped on ground so wet that they had to cut branches to sleep on. As they kept on in the morning, the river they followed forked and they took the deeper branch. This in

80

turn split in two and again they followed the deeper branch. Near the close of a day of hard work the stream they were following opened out on a beautiful park-like prairie, while beside the canoe was an ideal camping site fitted by Nature to that end.

It was a circular bit of high ground, surrounded by big trees whose spreading branches, draped in moss, shaded it on all sides, while an immense growth of wild grape-vine canopied it overhead. The water that flowed past the camp was pure and sweet, fresh from the Everglades. There was heavy timber about the camp and more than once during the night the boys heard the tread of a wild animal. Once it seemed to be the step of a deer in shallow water near the camp, then it was the soft footfall of some catlike animal and when Ned raised himself on his elbow to listen to a heavier tread, the "wouf" of the startled beast told that Bruin had caught the offensive scent of the white man's camp. As the boys lay awake and talked while they watched the stars peeping through the canopy of vines above them, they heard the distant bellowing of a Bull alligator.

"Dick," said Ned, "do you s'pose we could find that 'gator? He must be fifteen feet long, from the noise he makes. I'd like mighty well to rope him. We could stake him out so he'd never, never get away and he would live for weeks if it took us that long to get him carried to Fort Myers. Dad would sure be delighted and pay all the bills like a major."

"Don't you think he'd throw in new rifles with silver plates and our names on 'em?"

"He sure would."

"Well, we haven't got the big alligator yet, but we'll hunt for him to-morrow."

Just as Dick spoke the distant report of a gun was heard.

"There goes your fifteen-foot alligator and both of our new rifles with silver plates and our names on them. Good-night."

The boys started out across the meadow in the morning on the hunt for the big 'gator. They carried a rope for the 'gator and Ned took his rifle to be ready for the bear that spoke to them in the night. There was no more danger of their losing their camp, for Ned had made a chart every night, of their course during the day, until his memory had learned to map every scene his eyes looked upon. As they crossed a bit of wooded swamp, they heard the step of some heavy animal in a jungle near them, but they could get no sight of the creature and the slushy mud through which it had waded left no prints that inexperienced eyes could read. They found little ponds from which small 'gators rose to their calls, but none of a size worth

81

thinking of. They saw one big alligator sunning itself on a dry bank, and spent an hour in creeping near it only to find that it was not over ten feet long. As it grew late and they turned homeward, Dick said:

"Ever since that otter of yours died I've wanted a pet in camp. We need one for a watchdog. 'Most any night we might be eaten up for want of one. Let's take home a young alligator and I'll train it. These ponds are full of 'em."

"I don't want you to go wading in any more ponds, Dick."

"That's all right. Don't have to. There are 'gator caves all round these ponds. You find one of 'em and I'll do the rest."

The boys hunted around several ponds till Ned found a hole in the bank of one, just under the surface of the water. Dick handed Ned a pole, which he had cut in the last bit of woods they had passed, and then made a noose on the end of the harpoon line which he carried. He arranged the noose around the hole in the bank and stood a little back of it holding the line in his hands.

"Now, Ned, just poke that pole down in the mud, all around, about fifteen feet back of this hole, and pretty soon you'll punch something. Then, you'll see fun."

Ned poked around in the soft ground for awhile, then:

"Look out, Dick! Something is wiggling."

"I'm all here. Let her come!"

Out came the reptile's head from the cave, straight through the noose which tightened around the alligator's neck, as Dick threw his weight back on the line. At first it tried to back into the cave, but the line held it. Then it plunged into the pond, but Dick soon yanked it out on the prairie. It scuttled over the prairie like a great lizard and when the boy jerked it back it ran toward him, but he side-stepped quickly out of reach of that open mouth. When the reptile became a little quiet, Dick dragged it to the pole which Ned had left sticking in the ground and walking twice around it had the alligator's head fast to the pole. Then stepping quickly up to the creature he seized it by the head, holding its jaws firmly together with both hands.

"Now, Ned, if you'll tie these jaws together, he'll be gentle as a lamb and we'll have a real pet that won't get away like a manatee or die like an otter."

"I'll tie it, and bully for you, Dick, boy! You did that in great shape. I shouldn't wonder if it made a pretty good pet, and I don't care how big its mouth is, it couldn't have a bigger bite than that otter of ours."

82

The 'gator was less than five feet long and quite babyish in its ways, but it gave Dick a lot of trouble as he was leading it toward their camp.

"Just boost him up on my back, Ned. He's only a baby and wants to be toted."

Ned found it a pretty vigorous baby when he tried to boost it and he got some spanks from its tail that made him think of his tarpon of a few days before. Finally Ned stood in front of his companion, and with his help the reptile was dragged up Dick's back with its forepaws on his shoulder. Dick hung onto the paws, in spite of the sloshing about of his pet's tail for about a quarter of a mile, when he dumped it on the ground and addressing it, said:

"There! You uneasy little cuss, you've got to walk. I don't mind your wiggling your tail, but you tickle my ribs with your hind claws and you pound my head with your hard old jaws. Now come along straight, or instead of being toted you'll get a lickin'."

When they reached camp Dick staked the pet out with a line long enough to let it get into the river when it chose. He took the rope from its jaws, leaving them free, and the 'gator never took advantage of it by trying to bite. At first the pet got very much excited when he was dragged out of the water and up on land, but after awhile he got used to it and seemed to almost enjoy it. Dick caught fish for his pet which always refused to eat them. Then Dick cut the fish in pieces and while Ned held the little 'gator, stuffed them in its mouth and then held its jaws together till it swallowed its food.

"See the baby 'gator sit up, Ned," said Dick one day, after he had been training it for some time. "I'll have him eating with a fork and drinking from a cup in a week."

## CHAPTER XIV

## ENCOUNTER WITH OUTLAWS

One day, just after the boys had returned from an unsuccessful hunt for deer and Dick was at his usual occupation of training his pet, they heard the sound of oars, and a skiff, rowed by a man who looked like a product of the swamp, landed beside the camp.

"Kin you fellers let me have a little salt to save my hides? 'Gators are pretty thick 'nd my salt's gi'n out."

"We have only about a bushel of salt, but you can have half; yes, we can spare you three-quarters of it. We only use it for specimens and there'll be enough left for us," said Ned.

"That's mighty kind o' you, 'nd I won't fergit it, tho' that won't be any use t' you, bein's ye ain't likely t' see me ag'in."

"Why not? You go to Myers, I suppose. We might meet you there and we'd be glad to see you."

"Thar's other folks 'd be glad t' see me thar, perticiler the sheriff. Ain't you fellers skeered, now yer know yer talkin' t' an outlaw?"

"Not much," laughed Ned. "If you are an outlaw you have probably had all the trouble you want."

"You bet I hev."

"Then you aren't looking for any more. So what is there to scare us?"

"Not a blame thing. But you boys is plucky. There's men 'd fight shy o' staying 'round here."

"Well, it doesn't worry us. We didn't suppose there was any one around here, though, and we wondered who it was we heard shooting last night and we are glad to find out. Did you get any big alligators?"

"'Twasn't me shootin'. I didn't shoot las' night. Say! You've gotter look out! I know them fellers. One on 'em's bad and you boys ain't safe. I'm goin' ter hang 'round, 'n if you smell trouble jest fire two shots 'nd trouble'll cum a-humpin' fur them fellers,"

"All right and much obliged, and if anything does come that we can't manage we'll remember you, sure."

Whenever the boys passed a pond on the prairie they stopped and grunted till the young 'gators came to the surface. One day Dick fired a shot near enough to splash one that had come up, but in ten minutes the reptile had forgotten his scare and again answered the call. Dick was disposed to wade in the pond and catch the little 'gator, but Ned coaxed him out of the notion and proposed that they find a cave and rope another 'gator to cheer up Dick's pet, which he said was getting lonesome. This pleased Dick and the boys spent half a day finding an inhabited cave, when they secured its occupant with no trouble excepting that, as the alligator came out of his hole, Dick slipped on the muddy turf and was dragged into the pond. The 'gator was soon brought out on the prairie and its jaws tied. It was larger than the one first captured, and Dick didn't try to carry it on his back, but led and dragged it the entire distance.

As the boys approached their camp they saw a skiff, with two rough-looking men in it, just being pushed from the bank. Ned called to the men, but received no reply, and the skiff was rowed rapidly away.

"That spells trouble," said Ned. "Those are the fellows that our outlaw warned us against."

The boys found their stores in some confusion and a lot of them had disappeared, and with them had gone Ned's rifle, which he had left in camp. Ned was quite too angry to speak and walked quickly to the canoe, followed by Dick.

"What are you going to do, Ned?"

"Going to get that rifle."

"All right. I'm with you."

"Dick, I'm going alone. It's a fool's errand and I don't want you mixed up in it."

"Maybe it is a fool's errand, I guess it is, and that's the very reason I'm going with you, Ned. You know I'm going, that I wouldn't miss going with you for the world and you haven't any right to ask me to be a sneak and crawl out of the trouble, for it is trouble and probably big trouble."

"Why, Dick, boy, I didn't mean to hurt your feelings, and I'm sure glad to have you with me, only you must let me manage when we find those fellows."

"Of course you'll run the thing and I won't interfere, unless it becomes mighty necessary, which is quite some likely."

As they got into the canoe Dick said:

"Don't you want the shotgun?"

"No. Got better weapons than that."

"Glad of it. You'll need 'em."

The boys paddled rapidly down the narrow river for several miles before they came up to the men they were seeking, who were then just getting out of the little skiff into a larger one which had a canvas cover and was evidently used as a camp.

Dick guided the canoe beside the larger boat and Ned spoke quietly to one of the men, who was scowling at him.

"You know what I have come for. I want my rifle."

"What rifle? I don't know anything about your rifle."

"I mean the rifle you stole from our camp this afternoon. I want it and I'm going to have it."

"See here," said the man, who was purple with rage, as he picked up a rifle, "I'll blow the top of your head off if you tell me I lie."

"You lie," said Ned calmly. "You are a liar, a thief and a

85

coward. Now give me that rifle. I am not going to ask you for it many more times."

"I won't give it to you and I don't know what keeps me from blowing your head off. I believe I will yet."

"I can tell you why you don't. Because you know there would be a hundred men on your trail who would never leave it while you were alive. Because you wouldn't dare show your face to man, woman or child, white, black or red, in Lee County or anywhere else. Because your own partner would be the first to give you up."

"He would, would he?"

"Yes, he would!" said the man referred to. "Don't be a fool, but give the kid his gun, or I will."

The rifle was handed to Ned and the boys paddled back to their camp. On the way Dick said:

"I was scared stiff, Ned, when that fellow took up his rifle and I saw how mad he was. Weren't you a little bit frightened yourself?"

"Not then. I'm a good deal scared now to think of it."

As the boys that night sat leaning against a log which they had made soft with masses of long gray moss, watching the dying out of the fire which had cooked their supper, another skiff touched at their bank, bringing the man to whom they had given the salt and also carrying the carcass of a fine buck.

"There, boys, better smoke what yer can't eat by termorrer. I'll show yer how."

"We know how and we're very much obliged. But we must pay for it, you know."

"I can't take a cent and it makes me feel bad t' have yer talk about it. Have yer seen them fellers yit?"

"Oh, yes. They called on us and we returned the call. We didn't happen to be at home when they called, though," said Dick.

"They come here t' your camp?"

"Yes. They certainly came."

"'nd you not here?"

"No."

"What did they take?"

"Stole a rifle," said Dick.

"I'll git it back. Don't yer worry, I'll git it back and I'll start now," and the outlaw rose from the log on which he was sitting.

"Don't go. We got the rifle back."

"How did yer do it?"

Dick told the story of the recovery of the rifle. The outlaw sat for a minute looking down at the ashes of the fire, and then,

86

speaking very slowly and with emphatic little nods between the words, said:

"And them's th' fellers I thought needed lookin' arter."

There was silence for some time and then Ned spoke in a voice that was low from suppressed feeling.

"My friend, I don't know your name. I don't know what you did. I don't ask it. But I believe you are too good a man to be living the life of an outlaw. Now, can't something be done to help you? If some men of influence worked for your pardon, couldn't it be got?"

"Reckon not. It's bin tried. I'll tell yer jist how 'twas. I killed a man. He worried me 'nd threatened me 'nd tried ter kill me with a knife, 'f I'd shot him then, nobody'd said nuthin', but I waited 'nd then I got scared, thot he'd kill me, 'nd one day I shot him. I was put in th' pen, then I was sent t' the chain gang 'nd set t' boxin' trees f'r turpentine. Saw a man flogged day I got thar. Sed I'd never git whipped if work would save me. I was the strongest man in the gang. Boxed more trees 'n anybody. More I did, more I had t'. I don't say I was whipped. If I was I didn't deserve it. If I was 'nd ever see th' man that did it I'll kill him. Know how turpentine gangs is guarded? Boy sits up on platform with rifle 'nd gives orders. S'pose yer sassy to him or he just wants fun with yer. When Cap—that's th' man that whips—comes 'long, boy sez feller's bin shirkin'. Then feller's tied t' tree 'nd Cap beats him till feller begs t' be killed. I don't want t' hurt anybody 'cept one feller, but I ain't goin' back t' no chain gang. If the sheriff holds me up, 'nd sez 'Come back or I'll shoot,' I'll say 'Shoot!'"

The boys were very silent after the outlaw's story and when he left them they shook hands warmly with him and asked what they could do for him; ammunition, food, clothing, money, anything they had was at his service.

"Don't want nuthin'. You've give me more'n you'll ever know," said the outlaw gruffly.

But the gruffness was a bit tremulous and there were tears in the man's voice.

The outlaw got in the way of spending his evenings with the young explorers and Ned pumped him dry of his knowledge of the Everglades, the Big Cypress and the lesser swamps of South Florida. He made charts from lines traced in the dirt to show rivers, bays, prairie land and swamps. Ned learned of hidden creeks that connected waters thought to be completely separated by land and of others that could be connected by a short carry.

# CHAPTER XV

## DICK AND THE BEAR

Dick wanted a bear and the outlaw showed him a near-by swamp where several of the creatures lived. Day after day Dick waded, wandered and watched in that swamp with the rifle, while Ned tramped in another direction carrying the shotgun, making maps of the country, and picking up occasionally a duck or Indian hen for dinner. Sometimes Dick got sight of a bear, but Bruin was shy and kept well out of range. One day, while sitting in some thick woods, hoping that a bear would wander near him, Dick heard a loud tearing sound that seemed to come from the top of a little group of young palmettos. He crept as slowly and silently as possible near the trees and saw a bear sitting in the top of a palmetto, tearing away the outer husk of the bud of the tree which is the cabbage of the Cracker and often serves as his bread. While Dick was creeping nearer to get a surer shot, Bruin tore out the bud and, with the cabbage in his mouth, dropped from the top of the tree to the ground, alighting on its fore shoulder. Dick didn't know that this was the way bears in that country usually came down a tree when in a hurry, and supposed the bear had met with an accident and was killed. He changed his mind the next instant when the creature came racing toward him. Dick and the bear were about ten feet apart when they saw one another. The bear had to turn quickly to keep from running over Dick, and Dick had trouble to keep from punching the bear in the ribs with his rifle when he fired at it.

No one was hurt on this first round and the bear thought it had escaped and so did the boy. Dick churned a cartridge from the magazine to the barrel of his rifle and watched closely the undergrowth through which the bear was running, hoping for another shot. Just as the splashing in the marsh grew indistinct and Dick realized that his last chance had gone, he got one glimpse of the bear as it sprang upon a log that lay across its path. Dick threw his rifle to his shoulder with the quick motion of the sportsman who takes a woodcock on the wing, and fired. The bear, which was distant more than a hundred yards, disappeared and it seemed to the boy scarcely worth while to follow it. It was only the notion to look for the mark of his bullet on some tree near the log that induced him to wallow through the swamp to where he had last seen the bear. To his amazement he found a piece of bone and some fresh blood on the log. He had no thought now of abandoning the trail. He followed it through swamp and jungle, sometimes losing it

88

where the ground was hard or where it crossed the path of an alligator. Often when he became fearful that he had lost the trail a smear of blood on root or leaf told him that he was on the track. From former hunts and the study of Ned's maps, he knew the general lay of the land, but he stopped often and noted his course, for he meant to follow that trail and camp on it if necessary until he lost it finally or found the bear. The animal seemed to know all the bad stretches of marsh and thorny bits of jungle and, as the hours passed and night drew near, without his getting a sight of his quarry, he consoled himself with the thought of what Mr. Streeter had told him:

"A man is never lost in the swamp so long as he knows where he is himself."

Dick knew he wouldn't starve. There were always birds to be shot, alligators which he could kill with a club, and palmetto cabbage which he could dig out with his knife. He had his matches in a watertight box, a little bag of salt in his pocket, the swamp water was fresh, and what more could a hunter-boy ask for? He felt so cheerful that he began to whistle, which brought him bad luck, for he stumbled over a root which caught both feet and threw him head-down into a deep pool of mud. He was half strangled before he got out and was looking down shudderingly into the morass out of which he had crawled, when he missed his rifle and knew he had got to get back into the mudhole. It was so deep that he laid a branch across it to cling to, before venturing in. A big moccasin crawled from under a root beside the pool of mud as Dick stepped in it and the boy shut his teeth tight as he forced himself to wallow through the slimy, snaky mass from which his flesh recoiled.

He was waist-deep in that broth of mud when his feet found the rifle and he stooped down into it and groped around among roots that felt like living, squirming reptiles before he recovered the weapon. When he had scraped the most of the mud off of himself and out of the rifle it was too dark to follow the trail and Dick walked to a near-by thicket where he hoped to find better ground for a camp. He was peering into a dark recess in the thicket when a fierce growl within a few feet startled him terribly, but told him that he had found his bear—or another one. Dick was about to run, when a picture of Ned facing the outlaw formed itself in his mind and after that the bear couldn't have kicked him out of its path. As the boy's eyes became accustomed to the gloom he saw the bear lying within six feet, with jaws half open, and eyes fixed upon him. Dick believed the bear was dying, since he failed to spring upon him, but

89

he thought a bullet would make things safer and he raised his rifle. He pointed the weapon at the animal's head, but it was too dark to see the sight of the rifle, the brain of the creature was small, and Dick, remembering that a bear with a sore head is likely to be cross, dropped the muzzle of his weapon to the fore shoulder of the beast, and fired. The bear scarcely moved, but its eyes closed and Dick was prudently waiting before touching it, when he heard the distant report of a gun and knew that Ned was worried about him. He fired an answering shot and then, finding a bit of dry ground beside the body of the bear, decided to eat his supper the next morning and lay down to sleep with his head on his new bear robe.

At daylight he heard the report of Ned's gun and fired his rifle in reply. The bear was so heavy that Dick had trouble in handling it and before he had finished skinning it the report of a gun within two hundred yards showed that Ned was out hunting for him and had taken the right course.

"Hope you didn't worry about me," was Dick's greeting as the boys met.

"Nope, didn't worry after you answered my shot, but I was mighty envious of you, for I knew you had got hold of something. I didn't believe it was a bear. Were you scared, Dick?"

"Yes, I was, a heap, but I pulled through," and Dick told his chum of the thought that braced him up.

Ned tried to speak roughly, but his voice trembled and he looked affectionately at his companion as he said:

"See here, Dick, boy, you can cut out all that outlaw talk. The gun business was all bluff and you know it as well as I."

"You looked pretty white, Neddy, for a fellow who didn't think he was taking any risk. But if you'll tell me now, honest Injun, that you didn't think there was any danger when you faced that convict and called him a liar, a thief and a coward, why I'll never speak of it again. I noticed that your pet outlaw, who said the fellow was a murderer, three deep, didn't seem to think that you had done anything so very amusing in giving that fellow the lie and all the rest of it."

"I see you are round-skinning your bear for mounting. I'm glad of that. Some day I'll see it in your house and we'll be talking about last night."

"That skin is for you. I want you to have it stuffed and put where it can watch your alligator."

"I'm not going to take all the trophies of this trip. You can bet your life on that."

"Don't get slangy, Neddy. You aren't used to it and it isn't becoming. Besides, we may never get these little souvenirs out of the wilderness."

By which remark Dick proved himself to be a prophet.

The trail of the bear had been roundabout and had brought Dick within less than a mile of the camp. The buzzards were gathering and Dick remained to guard the meat while he finished removing the skin and cleaning the skull. Ned made two trips with good loads and then, taking all they could carry, the boys returned to camp, leaving a big feast for the bird scavengers.

## CHAPTER XVI

### IN THE CROCODILE COUNTRY

One evening while Dick had one of his alligator pets sitting up on his tail, teaching him to sing, as he told his chum, Ned said:

"Crocodiles are a lot more interesting than alligators and the Florida crocodile is nearly extinct. All that are left are in a little strip of land near Madeira Hammock, which is only a mile or two wide and eight or ten long. Let's go down to Madeira Hammock and catch some to look at. We can turn them loose after we are through with them."

"Mr. Streeter says there is no way to get through to Florida Bay, where Madeira Hammock is, by water from Whitewater Bay."

"Your outlaw says there is, only you have to tote your canoe some."

"He isn't my outlaw. I don't sit up nights making maps with him, and anyhow we can't tote the canoe through a mangrove swamp, and that's what we're up against if we go that way."

"But our outlaw—the outlaw, if you like—says we can find little creeks up toward the Glades that will take us almost through."

"All right. We'll start in the morning. I wish we'd cured about a ton or two less of that meat. We'll have to make a lot of trips across the carries. You don't see any way to take my alligators along, do you?"

Two days were spent in following creeks that led to nothing and then one was found with a deeper channel which led them for miles, after which it broke up into several little waterways, which were almost without current and so shallow that the boys had to wade and drag their canoe. Their progress was slow, and they slept on a bed of brush which had lumps and knots to bruise every soft spot on their bodies. Their next trouble was a strip of mangrove swamp which a cat couldn't have crawled through. After following along the mangroves for an hour they found a creek which entered it. As they followed this creek it grew wider and deepened. There was a slight current that flowed with them; the water was brackish, and they knew it led to the Bay of Florida and that the Madeira Hammock was near.

The mangrove gave place to a better growth, the soil became richer and vegetation more luxuriant. Soon they had to cut away vines and branches to clear the way for the canoe, but they counted their troubles over. They were paddling gaily ahead when they saw in front of them a branch that stretched across the creek about a foot above the water. They had met plenty of similar obstructions, but this was different. There was a big wasps' nest on the branch and the air was filled with flying little pests. It was impossible to get around the nest and it was doubtful if there was another creek that would take them through.

"Let's get some dry palmetto fans and make torches. Then we can burn and smoke the wasps out," said Ned.

"Dunno as I want to wade up to that nest and set it afire. Ouch!" said Dick, who had sat down on what he thought was a stump, but had turned out to be an ants' nest. "Holy smoke! Don't these things bite? I don't believe wasps are in it with them. Anyhow, I'm going to find out."

Dick took the oar that was used to pole the canoe and wading straight toward the nest struck it a blow that most fortunately knocked it to the water, while a second blow sent it under the surface. A few of the outlying insects stung the boy and he had a dozen little lumps to show for a day or two, but he had captured the fort and drowned the garrison and the canoe passed in peace.

The creek emptied into a wide bay on the high bank of which the boys camped. It was part of the Madeira Hammock, the most beautiful native forest they had seen. At daylight a large crocodile was floating on the bay near the camp, but sank out of sight as the campers showed themselves. From the bay the canoeists entered a deep river with high banks on which were growing madeira, wild sapadillo, palms of several kinds and other varieties of trees. In the sides of the high banks at the water line the boys saw holes which they believed to be the caves of crocodiles. In the mouth of one the water was muddied and Dick cut a long pole which he poked into

92

the hole. At first he felt something seize the pole, but could not afterward find the creature. He then took the pole on the bank and thrust it into the ground where he thought the reptile was most likely to be. When he had worked thirty feet back from the bank he felt something move and the next instant Ned, who had stayed in the canoe at the mouth of the cave, was nearly capsized by the rush of a great beast nearly the size of the canoe.

"Why didn't you grab it, Ned? What is the use of my driving game to you, if you let it slip through your fingers?"

"Perhaps you think that was one of the alligator babies you've been nursing. You didn't see the big head with the tusks running out of the top of it."

"No, but I mean to see the next one. It'll be your turn to do the punching while I rope the critter."

"If you had got your rope on that one and held on, you'd be in his cave now, inside the owner's tummy."

The next crocodile was not far away and the hunters saw it crawl into its cave. Dick stood on the bank over the cave and arranged the noose on the end of the harpoon line around the mouth of the cave, while Ned paddled the canoe a few rods down the stream. Dick had the line fast to his wrist, but Ned wouldn't punch it until it had been made fast to a chunk of wood instead.

"What difference does it make?" grumbled Dick. "If the chunk goes overboard I follow it. See?"

Ned hit the crocodile on his first poke and Dick had his hands full from the start. He would have been dragged into the river within a dozen seconds, but for Ned's coming to his aid. The crocodile was as quick as the alligators had been slow.

"If he digs round as fast on land as he does in the water there's goin' to be a circus when we get him out on the bank," said the panting Dick.

"And you wanted to be tied to his mammy by the wrist. This is only an infant. It isn't nine feet long."

But it was, and a foot over that, yet when they got the reptile on the bank and drew its head close to a sapling, they tied a piece of the line around its knobby head without any trouble. From that moment the crocodile was tame, and soon Dick was handling him fearlessly, although Ned warned him that if he didn't keep out of the way of that tail he'd be knocked endways. But Dick sat on his back, pulled his tail and tried to lift him on his own back without the crocodile showing displeasure in any way.

"Ned, this thing is a peach. Why not send him to your father? He could be taken to New York in a baby carriage or led like a puppy dog. There would be no such trouble as there would be with a manatee. He's a curiosity, too."

"If it was the big one I believe it would be worth trying. That fellow must be as big as they come. I wish we had fixed for him."

"It isn't too late. Let's lay for him to-morrow."

The crocodile hunters camped beside their captive and Dick spent the afternoon trying to educate it. He talked of taking the string off of its jaws, but Ned stopped that.

"I'm afraid he might eat the wrong thing, by mistake, and then I'd have to go home alone. I suppose I could take the crocodile along in your place. Your mother might like him as a kind of souvenir."

"But see how gentle he is and how mild his eye. He doesn't whack around with his tail like an alligator and I think he likes to have me sit on his back."

"That's only his slyness. Look at him now." For the crocodile, thinking itself unobserved, was crawling slowly toward the bank of the river. When it reached the end of its tether and could go no farther, it lay down and, lifting its head, looked all around as innocently as if it never dreamed of escaping, but had just moved a little way to get a better view of the scenery.

Every hour or two of the next day the boys called at the cave of the big crocodile, but never found him in.

"Well, we'll go at it again to-morrow," said Dick.

"We will be doing something else to-morrow. We've got to hike out of here, and keep moving, too. Last drop of water has just gone into the coffee pot," and Ned turned the empty water can upside down.

"Hope you can find the creek that leads to the fresh-water country. I don't believe I could. We came through too many twisty, narrow places. We sure don't want to be three or four days finding it. I'm awful thirsty now."

"You must stop thinking about it. I believe I won't try for that creek. It's a regular Chinese puzzle up among the mangroves, and I'm not a bit sure I could follow our trail back to fresh water. I'd rather take chances of that river that leads more to the east. I know it can't go through to our bay, but it must lead up to the Everglade country where the mangroves won't be so bad. We may have to do some toting, but we will be sure to find water by to-morrow night or the next day at the worst. But I won't go that way unless you think best. It's too serious a thing for me to decide alone."

"Oh, I'm with you Ned. I might live till day after to-morrow without water, but I wouldn't have a ghost of a chance beyond that,

94

and we might be three days in your Chinese puzzle country. Wow! but I'm thirsty."

"Say that again, Dick, and I'll confiscate your coffee. I'm going to save half of it for breakfast, anyhow. So go slow. You're on allowance now. We will have breakfast before daylight. I want to start as soon as we can see. It's a lot cooler before sun-up."

"I'll wake easy. I'll be so thirsty—Oh! excuse me, I forgot. But Ned, would you mind if I took my crocodile along in the canoe? He wouldn't take up much room and I could sit on his back. I could lead him across any carry and I've grown quite fond of him."

"You had better stop talking nonsense and get some sleep. You may need it."

"Yes, I know. 'Most anything may happen. You'd feel bad to think you had refused a poor boy's dying request—and he your chum, too. Can't I have my little pet crocodile?"

When the sun rose the young explorers had already paddled several miles and were in a labyrinth of little bays from which they followed channel after channel until each one shoaled down to a few inches in depth. Finally they found one that deepened as they advanced, although its banks came nearer together and the branches of big trees closed over it.

"This is all right. Fresh water soon," said Dick joyfully.

But he was soon to be disappointed. For the little creek ended in a round shallow pond, a hundred yards across and entirely shut in by thick bushes. Dick became very blue and even Ned was discouraged.

"I hate to go back for miles and begin all over again, just when we are so far along in the right direction. We can get through these bushes and walk a mile or two, and perhaps climb a tree and see what the country looks like," said Ned.

"I'd rather do anything than go back," replied Dick. "Let's paddle round the edge of this pond and see where the bushes are thinnest."

They paddled along the shore of the little lake, finding the water so shallow that it barely floated the canoe, until just where the bushes seemed thickest it deepened to several feet, and parting the bushes disclosed a deep but very narrow creek through which the water slowly flowed. There was no room to paddle and for more than a mile the boys dragged the canoe by taking hold of overhanging branches. Sometimes they could lift branches that crossed the creek over the canoe as they passed. Sometimes they had to lie down in the canoe to get under the obstructions and often they had to stop to cut away limbs of small trees. They were finally stopped by the trunk of a large tree which had fallen across and completely blocked up the creek. Just beyond it two palmettos had fallen in the stream, one of which lay lengthwise in the channel. It would have taken days to remove the obstructions and the young explorers explored the swamp near them to find a possible carry. They found that a hundred feet behind them the woods were thinner and they could cut a path through which they could carry the canoe and stores.

"This is going to take all the rest of the day," said Ned, "and it will be a dry camp after a heap of hot work. What do you say to leaving this till to-morrow, and putting in this afternoon hunting for the best route and looking for fresh water?"

"That's me," replied Dick. "Let's hike in a hurry. Only don't you lose your way. We have got to get back to the canoe and you're the guide."

"Don't you worry about that. You may have to go slow, but I won't lose myself and I will bring you back to the canoe," said Ned.

Instead of following the creek, Ned bore off to the north where the woods seemed more open and soon reached a stretch of dry, open prairie. On the border of it stood a tall mastic tree with a lightning-blasted top and many branches which made it easy to climb. Ned was soon in the top of the tree making a mental map of the country round about.

"It is all right now," said he as he climbed down. "I can see the open Everglades within four or five miles, and there is something that looks like a slough that is only half as far away. We'll leave the creek in the morning and cut our path this way, instead of around those trees. It won't be as much work, either. We can do some of that work to-night and camp right here. Then in the morning, at daylight, we will start out with the canoe on our shoulders and tramp till we find water to float it."

"But how about water to drink? I need it worse than the canoe."

"Where there's water for the canoe, there will be water for you. It's Everglade water from now on."

"I wish it would begin this minute. There's a little mud-hole that looks pretty wet. Do you think that might be fresh?"

"Only way to find out is to try it." A minute later Dick called out.

"Come here, Ned, it's muddy, but it's fresh. Oh, isn't it good!"

As Ned approached the pool Dick, who was lying on the prairie beside it, lifted his face from the water of which he had been drinking, and was turning to speak to his companion when the head

96

of a great alligator, with wide open jaws, was thrust violently out of the pool, just touching the boy's face. Dick fell back on the prairie and scrambled away from the pool. It was a minute before he spoke and then he said to Ned:

"Let's get back to work. I don't want another drink for a month. It makes me sick to think of it."

The slough was farther away than Ned thought and the road to it lay through a marsh. Often they sank to the waist and wallowed for rods, carrying the canoe which seemed to weigh a ton, or dragging it beside them. Moccasins were plentiful, but the boys were too tired to be worried by them. They had to make two more trips to carry their cargo, and on the last one, as Dick was staggering under a load of smoked meat and a heavy, salted skin, he was heard to say:

"I wonder why I killed that bear. I will never kill another one."

There was dry ground beside the slough, under some willow trees, and the explorers were glad to rest there for the night. A duck flew down by the willows as if seeking to camp with them and he succeeded, for they had him for supper.

## CHAPTER XVII

### AMONG THE SEMINOLES

The young explorers had found an uncharted route from the Bay of Florida to the Everglades and the work before them was now easy.

The water was deeper than was needed to float their canoe, and the grass too light to trouble them. They sheered off and avoided all bands of saw-grass unless they found trails across them. The Glades were dotted with little keys of bay, myrtle and cocoa plum. These were small and usually submerged. A few larger keys were covered with heavier timber, pine, oak, mastic, palmetto and other woods. In these, deer were plentiful and bear and panther sometimes found.

The boys went to several keys before they found one with dry land enough for a camp. It had been used for camping by the Seminoles for many years and was the only bit of land above the surface of the water for miles. On it were piles of turtle shells, while

97

scattered about were bones of deer and alligator and skulls of bear and smaller animals. A cultivated papaw which some Indian had planted within a few years, stood twelve feet high and was filled with great melon-like papaws, each one of which weighed from five to ten pounds.

"Better than cantaloupe," said Dick as he finished half of a big one as a preliminary to his supper, "but what's this you are giving us for coffee?"

"Coffee's out," replied Ned. "The fellows that took the rifle cleaned out most of the coffee."

"Why didn't you make 'em give it back when you had 'em on the run?"

"Reckon I was glad to get out of it as easy as I did. Then I had said enough unkind things to them for one time."

"Sorry you think you were unkind. Your feelings must be a good deal torn up. But you haven't told me what I'm drinking. Tastes something like the sassafras tea I used to get dosed with when I was a kid. It's pretty good, though."

"It's something like it. It's made from the leaves of the sweet bay tree, which grows on all these islands and all over this country. Sweet-bay tea is all you're going to get to drink, excepting water, from now on."

"What is that fruit that looks like a big stubby pear on that curious-looking tree there?" inquired Dick.

"Custard apple."

"Does it taste like custard?"

"Yes, if the custard has been mixed with turpentine."

The explorers made little progress the following day. Bunches of thick saw-grass turned them back. They found shallow water where for long distances they had to paddle slowly to avoid little pillars of coral rock that came close to the surface and endangered their fragile canoe. Most of the afternoon was vainly spent in searching for a camping site. They found a key where the water was shoal and made a bed of poles and branches. Both of them chose to sleep on the bed they had made. Whether this was simply politeness or because both were afraid of rolling out of the canoe nobody else knows. The poles and branches sagged under their weight until both were wet. Then such a deluge of rain as is seldom seen outside of the tropics fell on them. They got out in the dark and tied their canvas sheet over the canoe. They didn't need it for themselves. They were already as wet as they could be.

In the morning they dried themselves—so Dick said—by rolling into the water and sloshing around. They made a cold lunch

98

of smoked bear, cold hominy, or grits as it is called in Florida, and water, choosing to wait for breakfast until they should find land enough for a fire. During the day they saw high trees to the eastward and made for them. Here they found a Seminole camp of several families.

As they landed from their canoe they saw several pickaninnies, for Seminole children are not called papooses like children in other tribes of Indians, watching them from behind trees and boats. The squaws whom they met were equally shy and kept their faces hidden. Ned spoke to several of them, but they gave no sign that they even heard him.

"They don't like your looks," said Dick. "Let me speak to the next one."

The next one was a young girl and Dick was very confident, as he addressed her, with his very best smile. But he was turned down as badly as his chum, for the girl didn't see him at all. At the camp they found one old Indian and several squaws. The Indian welcomed them with a grunt and the question,

"Whyome (whiskey), you got um?"

"Whyome holowaugus (bad), no got um," replied Ned. The Indian grunted again and conversation ceased. Dick was sitting on the edge of the table which serves also as floor in a Seminole camp, when he heard a low growl just over his head. He looked up and saw, crouched on a shelf within four feet of him, a full-grown wild-cat, or bay lynx, which seemed disposed to spring at him. Dick tried to keep from showing how much he was scared, but he asked Ned to find out if the wild-cat would bite. To Ned's question, the Indian nodded emphatically and replied,

"Um, um, unca, ojus (yes, heap)." Dick moved away, but the creature fascinated him and he came back. Dick never could resist the temptation to play with wild animals and he put out his hand to the wild-cat, saying:

"If that Injun can tame that beast, I can."

"That Injun understands you, just as well as I do. He only pretends he doesn't so as to make us try to talk his confounded lingo."

A half smile stole over the stolid face of the Indian, either on account of what Ned was saying or because Dick's hand was slowly approaching the wild-cat. The paw of the lynx flashed out and back so quickly that it could scarcely be seen, but the blood began to flow from several deep, parallel cuts on the back of the boy's hand. Dick still held out his hand, scarcely moving a muscle, while Ned called out:

99

"Come away, Dick, that beast'll scratch out your eyes."

"Wonder what it would do if I cuffed it?"

The Indian appeared to understand this, for he spoke sharply to the lynx, and going up to it patted its head and stroked its body lightly. He then motioned to Dick to do the same. To Dick's great delight the wild-cat not only allowed him to stroke it, but even purred as well as a wild-cat can.

"Ned, I've got to have that cat. I've given up all my other pets because you didn't want them in the canoe, or there wasn't room. Now Tom will take care of himself and won't need any toting. Shouldn't wonder if he'd feed himself, too."

"That's what I'm most afraid of.

"Don't worry. I won't let him eat you. Ask old Stick-in-the-mud there what he wants for his beastie."

Ned talked with the Indian and reported to Dick.

"He says he will sell for one otter skin like that one in the canoe."

"How could he see that skin from here? Tell him it's a whack. Only he must make Tom go with me if there is any trouble about it."

"He says wild-cat go with you, you brave boy, not afraid of him. Says somebody get scared, he eat 'em up."

"Ned, you old hypocrite, you made that up."

"Honest Injun, I didn't. I told it straight, just as I got it. That Indian likes you."

"Why don't he talk white man lingo to me, then, instead of his old gibberish that he can't possibly understand himself? Ask the old snoozer what's cooking in that pot. It smells bully and I'm hungry."

Ned turned to the Indian and pointing to the steaming pot, said:

"Nar-kee? (What is it?)"

"Lock-a-wa. (Turtle.)"

"Esoka bonus che. (I want some.)"

"Humbuggus cha. (Come eat.)"

The boys took turns with the big, wooden, family spoon and found the mess very good. There was another kettle of which the Indians ate freely into which Dick dipped his spoon. He made a wry face as he swallowed the portion he had scooped up and said to Ned:

"Tell your copper-faced friend that he had better give that swill back to the pigs he stole it from."

"Be careful, Dick, he understands."

"Then let him say so in a decent language and I'll apologize for

100

hurting his feelings, but I won't say that stuff is fit to eat, not if I am tied to the stake."

Dick spent one afternoon getting acquainted with the Indian children, in which he succeeded so well that when he came back to the camp streaming with water, the whole bunch, although they were quite as well soaked as he, followed him screaming with laughter, quite like white children.

"What is the trouble?" inquired Ned as soon as the youngsters gave him a chance to be heard.

"Only the usual thing. These Indians don't know how to manage their roly-poly canoes and I'm afraid I'll be drowned before I get 'em taught."

Dick had found a big family canoe that looked as if it couldn't capsize and had made signs to an Indian boy to go out in it with him. Before they were fairly afloat all the pickaninnies belonging to the camp had piled into the craft. From the smallest squab to the biggest boy, the Indian children danced about in the canoe without disturbing its equilibrium. The boy in the stern, standing on the extreme point of the craft, set his pole on the coral bottom and threw his weight back upon it until his whole body stood out almost parallel with the water behind the canoe. Dick stood on the tiny deck on the bow of the boat, but with every thrust of his pole the canoe wabbled till the pickaninnies balanced it. But Dick improved with practice and as he grew confident, threw his weight on the pole in true Seminole fashion. He would have pulled through with credit, but for the slipping of his pole on a point of coral rock, when he fell heavily in the water, capsizing the craft as he went overboard. At first the boy was alarmed for the safety of his cargo of children, but soon saw that they were as much at home in the water as on land and were quite capable of caring for themselves. After Ned had heard what had happened he called the attention of the squaws to the ducking of their babies without causing the faintest gleam of interest to cross their stolid faces.

After another day of eating with the Seminoles and sleeping on their tables, Dick announced that Tom and he were tired of Injuns and wanted to light out. The whole Indian family saw them off, even the squaws coming half way to the canoe from their camp. Dick carried Tom on his shoulder and the lynx stepped into the canoe as if it had always owned it and curled up on the canvas of the tent.

"Where do you want to go, Dick?"

"What's the use of asking me? You have been talking

Everglades and Big Cypress in a steady streak, for two days to that old Injun. You must have a map of his brain by this time."

"We can go through the Everglades to Lake Okeechobee, out through the canal and down the Caloosahatchee, but the Everglades will be much the same as we have seen, only more and worse saw-grass and so harder work. If we go to the east we will pretty soon come out at the coast which we want to avoid. I think we had better strike across to the prairies and the border land between the Everglades and the Big Cypress Swamp. Bear, deer, panther and wild turkey are to be found in that country, and we won't have to hurry so much to get through in the time we talked of for the trip. What do you say?"

"The woods for me, every time. Then I think it would be better for Tom's health. I am afraid he would get melancholy if we kept him on the water too much. Let's put in a big day's work and get somewhere. I can stand sleeping in the water once in a while, but don't like it as a regular thing."

They put in their big day's work without getting very far. They struck shoal water in the morning where little pillars of coral, rising almost to the surface, threatened to tear a hole in their canoe. When they got overboard and waded, the same sharp points of coral hurt their feet and bruised their shins. During the afternoon they held their course, as best they could, for a tall palmetto, which, lifting its head above a waste of water and grass, gave promise of land enough for a camp beneath it. They dragged the canoe through a narrow strand of saw-grass, but were turned westward by a heavier band of the same obstacle, and finally made their camp for the night on a bushy little submerged key, where Ned lay on top of the canoe and was kept from sleeping by the fear of rolling over into the water, and Dick lay on a bed of brush that soon settled into the water with him. At first Tom climbed a little tree, but didn't seem pleased with his quarters. He looked at Dick's bed for a moment and turned in for the night with Ned in the canoe. Good progress was made on the following day, for the boys were tired of trying to sleep on the water and meant to find land enough for a camp before another night. They found much open water, most of the grass was light and the few strands of saw-grass they encountered were easily avoided. They saw few keys and all of those were submerged. So again when night came there was no dry land for a camp and the bed of branches was built up in the shallow water. About midnight Ned, noticing that his companion was restless, said to him:

"Dick, can you sleep any more?"

102

"Sleep any more?" said the indignant Dick. "I haven't slept any, yet."

"Then let's get out of this and paddle the rest of the night. It's full moon, paddling isn't half as hard as trying to sleep on that bed and we may get somewhere."

"Good thing, and I move that we keep paddling till we get to those woods you talked about, if it takes a week. Tom votes with me. Motion carried."

About the middle of the forenoon they saw a clump of palmettos on a key, for which they headed at once, where they found ground which had been often camped upon. Dick climbed a tree and could make out a forest near the horizon, in the west. A few more hours' work would see them out of the Glades, but they chose to rest for the remainder of the day.

"There goes your pet. That's the last of him," said Ned, pointing to the lynx in the top of the tree, which Dick had climbed.

"He'll come back all right. If he doesn't I'll go up and fetch him by the scruff of his neck."

Dick was right, for when the wild-cat saw the stores broken into for dinner he came down for his portion of meat and then curled up for a nap on his canvas in the canoe. Tom tolerated Ned, but never permitted any familiarities from him, while Dick could handle him as he chose and the lynx only smiled, in his own fashion.

To reach the woods they were aiming for the boys left the Indian trail they were on and, after forcing their way through a strand of saw-grass, found themselves on a prairie, bounded on the west by a heavy growth of cypress, oak and other heavy timber, while the prairie itself was made beautiful by picturesque little groups of palmettos which were scattered through it.

## CHAPTER XVIII

### DICK'S WILDCAT AND OTHER WILD THINGS

The Everglades had been crossed and that great region of romance was no longer a mystery to our explorers, who found a dry, shaded site for their camp on the border of the swamp which they planned to explore and there fitted up for a long stay. They stretched their canvas, tent fashion, and gathered grass and moss for their beds. A round, deep pool of clear fresh water was just beside the camp, and after one rattlesnake and a few moccasins that claimed squatter's title had been killed they felt that nothing was lacking. In the evening the distant gobbling of a turkey told the hunters what would be the first duty of the next day. When they started out on the hunt prepared to be gone for one or more days Dick was troubled for fear Tom might not understand his long absence and skip out. He had a long talk with the lynx and told Ned that he thought Tom would be good. Then he got out two days' rations for the animal, which it ate up at once. There was more dry land in this swamp than in those farther south to which they had become accustomed, and traveling was better, or rather, less bad. Yet to persons with less experience than the young explorers it would have seemed to be as bad as it was possible for it to be. For half a day the boys tramped and waded in the swamp without finding the game they were looking for. They had found other birds, some of which they would have shot for their dinner had they not been afraid of frightening the wary turkeys, which they believed were not far from them. Alligators were plentiful, large and small, but the boys were not hunting for hides and Dick said that Tom was all the pet he cared to have charge of for the present. Early in the afternoon they sat down to rest under a big tree and were eating their lunch of smoked meat and cold hoe-cake when a turkey gobbler lit on a branch of the tree under which they were sitting. The turkey was in plain sight and less than twenty feet from them, but Dick's shot-gun was resting against a tree fifteen feet from its owner, while Ned's rifle lay on the ground five feet from his hand. Both kept as quiet as graven images, for they knew that at the motion of a hand the big bird would take flight. If Dick's gun had been within five feet he would have jumped for it, trusting to be ready with it to cut down the turkey before it could get out of sight among the trees. But a run of fifteen feet made his chances too small and he waited to see what Ned would do. Ned's rifle lay just out of his reach, and before he could lay his hand on it the bird would be on the wing and quite safe from anything he could do with a rifle. At last Ned began to push himself inch by inch toward the rifle, while Dick sat silent and breathless with excitement. Very slowly Ned progressed until his hand touched the rifle. Before he could move it the fraction of an inch, the turkey saw the trouble in store for him and was off. Ned grabbed the rifle and took a harmless snapshot at the bird, while Dick rushed for his gun and sent after the turkey, which was then a hundred yards distant, a shower of shot which could never have overtaken it.

"Next time I eat I'm going to feed myself with one hand and hold my gun in the other," said Dick. "I think I'll stay home to-morrow and keep camp. Tom will go hunting with you. He's got sense and he always keeps his weapons handy."

"Keeps 'em too handy for me. I don't like the way he looks at me sometimes. He acts as if he wanted to feel of my ribs to see if I am fat enough for his purposes. I reckon I'm the one to keep camp. My rifle was right at my elbow, but I didn't seem to know enough to use it. Dick! Look at that hole in that tree and all those insects around it. It's a bee-tree. There's a barrel of honey there that belongs to us!"

"Do you s'pose the bees know that it belongs to us, or will they make trouble for us?"

"Of course they'll make trouble. You can't rob a hive without being stung."

"I'm going to keep camp to-morrow, just as I told you, and let Tom go with you. Wonder how he'd like to climb that tree."

"We will chop down that tree to-morrow and likely get stung a lot, but you know, Dick, you wouldn't stay away for a farm."

"Better not try me. I wish I had a sheet-iron jacket and stove-pipe pants. Let's go home. I want to see Tom and tell him about it. I'm afraid he's lonesome."

But Dick didn't tell Tom anything, for when they got back to camp Tom had gone. Dick scarcely tasted his supper and his sleep was restless and troubled. He woke with a scream, from a terrible nightmare in which a wild beast had him by the throat and was crushing him to death under his tremendous weight. He was happy when he woke to find that his dream was true. For Tom had come home and showed his joy at the sight of Dick by leaping on the boy's chest and licking his face and neck. Even Ned rejoiced that Tom had returned and stroked his back, which for once the lynx graciously permitted.

"You are glad that Tom has come back, aren't you, Ned?" said Dick as he laid his face against the soft fur of the wild-cat whose purring sounded so like a low growl.

"Oh, yes. I'm glad. 'Course I am. Only wish all of 'em would come back, the two alligators, the crocodile and the dead otter. Then we'd start a menagerie and I'd tell fearful stories of man-eaters while you went into their cages with a big whip in one hand and a small cannon in the other."

When the boys started for the bee-tree they carried a bundle of dry palmetto fans, an axe, and a bucket for the honey.

"Shall we tote the guns?" asked Ned.

105

"What's the use? Don't either of us know how to use 'em. Better leave 'em with Tom."

But the guns did not stay with Tom, or rather Tom did not stay with the guns, but quietly followed the boys as a pet dog might have done. He stepped daintily from root to root and walked along fallen logs and the branches of trees which he climbed, easily keeping up with the bee hunters, without muddying his paws, while they wallowed in mud which was usually knee-deep and occasionally a foot more. Before tackling the tree they built a fire some fifty yards away, which they made smoke by putting on rotten wood and wet moss. They intended to hide in this smoke if the bees attacked them while they were chopping down the tree. The palmetto leaves were to be kept until the tree had fallen and were then to be made into smoky torches, under cover of which the boys hoped to secure the honey. They took turns in slinging the axe and resting, yet the exercise and the bees together kept them pretty well warmed up. For, after a while the bees began to take notice of the knocking at their door and occasionally a few of them dropped down and stung the chopper and the looker on, quite impartially. The art of wood-chopping has to be learned before one is born. The children of back-woodsmen can sling an axe as soon as they can stand. Boys born as near New York City as Dick and Ned were, never can learn. They think when they go up in the Adirondacks and chew down some trees with an axe, that they are chopping wood, but their guides who lie around smoking their pipes while the sportsmen sweat over the task, know better and slyly wink at each other while they praise aloud the skill of their employers.

When the boys stopped work and went back to their smudge to give the bees a chance to rest, and to find out if mud really drew the poison out of the little lumps that covered them, the tree had been cut nearly half through. Any Nature-lover would have known that a beaver had been at work, while everyday folks would have suspected a saw-mill.

Dick missed Tom and at first was troubled, but finally discovered him sitting on a branch behind a tree around which he could look without making himself conspicuous.

"Shall we wait till to-morrow to finish the job?" asked Ned.

"Not much. By to-morrow my face will be so swollen that I can't see and the rest of me so sore that I can't move. Let's make a big smudge at the foot of the tree. I'd rather be smothered by smoke than stung and poisoned to death by those little beasts."

The smudge worked and the bee hunters had no more trouble until the tree fell, when they got into the thickest of the smoke they had made. This did not save them altogether, for the bees were very numerous and very mad and a few dozen of them got far enough in the smoke to leave their marks on their enemies. When the insects had quieted down and were gathered in bunches on logs and stumps, looking stupidly at the wreck of their home, the boys made another smudge near the hole in the fallen tree which led to the home of the bees. They sounded the hollow tree and found it only a shell where the honey was stored and a little work with the hatchet laid open the storehouse of the insects. A few of the homeless bees lit on the comb they had made, other bees gathered on the cypress knees which abounded in the swamp and through which the great cypress trees breathed, but their spirit was gone and they made no attack on the destroyers of their home. Of the comb and honey which the boys found in the tree they were able to carry away less than half and they wondered if the bees would have the sense to save what was left or if some wandering bear would scoop it in for his supper.

As the young bee hunters started for camp laden with their spoils, Tom stepped softly out of a nearby thicket, licking his chops and apparently thinking of the delicate lunch of fat tree-rat he had just eaten.

"Dick," said Ned, as they were lazily resting against a log, after a supper that was mostly dessert, having consisted of a little smoked bear and a lot of honey, "something has got to be done for the larder. We go for honey when we need meat. We let Indian hens which we can get, escape on the chance of turkeys which we can never bag. We are looking for deer that are miles away and overlooking ducks that are trying to fly into the pot."

"I'm not overlooking much, Neddy, since that turkey biz. I've got my gun in my hand this minute and here's a chance to use it."

As Dick spoke he raised the gun to his shoulder and fired. A little black creature, thirty yards away in the grass, sprang into the air and fell to the ground. Both of the boys started for it, but Tom was ahead and looked back upon them, growling fiercely, with his fangs fixed in the throat of the dying creature. Dick tried to coax the lynx to give up the creature he had seized, but the animal was filled with the fierceness of his race and even Dick dared not touch him. The creature which the cat held in its claws was clearly a rabbit, little and jet black, unlike anything which either of the boys had ever seen before.

"I've heard of these little Everglade rabbits," said Ned. "Tommy told me of a key in the Everglades where there were plenty of them. If we had time we might look it up."

"How much time have you got, Neddy?"

"Another month will use up the time I said I would be gone. I left that word for Dad in Myers. Guess he's there now and maybe my sister with him. He won't worry a minute till the time I set is up, after that there'll be trouble."

"What kind of trouble?"

"'Most anything," laughed Ned. "Might be a lot of nurses out looking for a lost baby."

"He won't be frightened about you if you're not quite up to time, will he?"

"Not exactly frightened, but he will want to see me, and I'll be glad enough to see him, and sis, too."

"I knew you had a sister, but you never talked about her much."

"She's a nice child, alle samee. I think you're going to like her. She's a little your style of foolishness."

"What's that?"

"Oh, it isn't very bad. But you haven't had much to say about your own self, lately. You never told me exactly what took you around by Key West. Why didn't you come straight to Fort Myers instead of taking the tiny little chance of finding me in the big Everglades?"

"Well, I'll tell you. You see, mother knew how much I wanted to go with you on this hunt and she begged me to let her foot the bills. Of course I couldn't stand for that, you know, and—"

"Oh, Of course not, you stuck-up little donkey," interrupted Ned.

"So I started as a stowaway on the Key West steamer—"

"You cheeky little imp! Did they put you in command of the ship when they found you?"

"No, only put me in the fireroom, shoveling coal in the furnace."

"But that's not boy's work. What business—"

"Hold on, Ned, wait till I get through. The captain was bully. So was everybody else. I went to him soon as we were outside Sandy Hook and asked for a job. I was independent about it. I believe I offered to swim ashore if he didn't happen to have a job for me. He gave me an easy one, for a boy, but I struck and asked for a man's work, and got it—in the fireroom. But I pulled through, Neddy, and made good, though once or twice I did have to call myself hard names and think how you'd have hung on, if you'd been in my place. Yes, everybody was good to me. One passenger wanted to pay for a

108

first-class passage for me and I had hard work to beg off, and—but that's all."

"Dick, you mustn't talk that way about me. You make me ashamed. I wouldn't have stuck it out in that fireroom for one day. Now how about your time for the trip? Will a month suit you?"

"Yes, that's all right. I wrote mother from Key West and told her the hunt would be a long one without any chance to mail a letter and that she was not to worry because there wasn't a show of danger in the whole business. Of course mothers do worry a little when there isn't any reason."

"Yes, mothers do worry, foolishly. Pity yours couldn't know how faithfully Tom looks after you. She'd be so relieved."

On the day after cutting down the bee tree the boys were glad to stay quietly in camp. Ned's neck and arms were badly swollen and Dick's eyes could scarcely be seen. Both of them lay awake nearly all night, but it was uncertain whether this was due to the pain of the stings or the quantity of honey they had eaten.

Tom shed his fierceness soon after he had disposed of the rabbit and again became friendly to Dick, who, even while he petted him, explained that he could never quite trust him again.

Every evening turkeys could be heard in the swamp near the camp. Every morning they had departed. One morning Ned said to Dick:

"I'm turkey hungry and I'm tired of shilly-shallying. The way to get anything is to get it. Let us get a turkey. We'll start out for it now and come back after we have got it, and not before."

"All right, Neddy, we goes for it, we gits it and we comes back when we gits it and not afore."

The boys started out with their usual equipment of weapons, salt, matches and axe. They crossed the swamp without finding the bird they sought and then, as they were hungry and tired, Dick shot a fat young ibis and broiled it for their dinner. After dinner they crossed the meadow to a narrow strip of woods, beyond which, on a wide stretch of prairie, they saw three bunches of turkeys. The bunch nearest them appeared to be a hen turkey with her family, each member of which was about as large as its mother. They were a long rifle-shot away, and a shot, if it missed, would send every turkey to cover for the day. The same thing would happen if either of them set foot on the prairie.

"Our best chance," said Ned, "is to wait for them at the edge of the prairie. It's getting late and pretty soon they'll be looking for places to roost among these trees. They may come right here. Anyhow, by spreading out we will cover quite a stretch of woods. It may be too late for the rifle but the shotgun ought to do something."

"That means that you're tired of my society, Neddy. So I'll go and hide myself on the edge of the prairie, a little further off than you can hit anything, in case of you mistaking me for a turkey."

Soon after Dick had reached his station, the turkeys began to feed toward the woods. Two of the bunches went to the opposite side of the prairie. The hen turkey with her grown-up family fed slowly toward Dick's hiding place, but, when just out of range, appeared to become suspicious and turned toward Ned. Slowly she walked, darting her quick-moving head in every direction as she searched trees and bushes for hidden enemies. The younger turkeys put much faith in the wariness of the old lady and stalked fearlessly behind her. Ned waited for a chance which he thought couldn't be missed and, avoiding the mother turkey, shot down one of her brood. Instantly the flock was in the air, following its leader down along the edge of the forest. This brought them directly over Dick, who neatly cut down another member of the family. While Ned was dressing the turkeys and building the fire for the broiling of one of them, Dick was climbing a young cabbage palm and cutting the bud from its top.

"Couldn't tell this palmetto cabbage from big fresh chestnuts, by the taste," said Dick. "I'm going to roast that other turkey at the camp to-morrow with his whole inside crammed full of chestnut stuffing."

While the turkey hunters were eating their breakfast of cold turkey a doe, followed by a fawn which was still in the spotted coat, walked out on the open prairie within fifty yards of them and gazed at them without a sign of fear.

"They know we wouldn't shoot a doe or a fawn," said Ned. "That's what makes them feel so safe."

"Wonder if they would have felt as safe last night, before we got those turkeys?"

On their return Tom, met the turkey hunters a quarter of a mile from their camp and they wondered whether he had heard them coming, or happened to be strolling that way. He looked so earnestly at the turkey which Dick was carrying that the boy said to him:

"See here, Tom, that's my turkey and I won't stand for your laying a paw on him. So you had better be good unless you are looking for a mix-up with me." Tom looked cowed, but showed his friendly feelings by walking beside Dick, rubbing against his legs and purring in his half-growling fashion.

# CHAPTER XIX

## A PRAIRIE ON FIRE

"Dick," said Ned as they rested against a log, having their regular after-dinner, heart-to heart talk, "we had better hiepus (light out), if we mean to get to the coast and bring up at Myers on time, besides taking in all we want to on the way. We know the Harney's River route like a book and we've been over the Indian trail to Lawson's River, so we've got to find some new way out. There is a chain of salt-water lakes between the Everglades and the rivers of the west coast and we must get into them. I have made a pretty fair chart of the country and can tell how far across the swamps and prairies it is to almost any point, but how much of that distance is easy water and how much tough swamp or boggy prairie is what I don't know, but what we have got to find out. We have explored the country right around here pretty well and now let's put in a day working the canoe through the grass to the south, then leg it westward till we strike salt water."

"That sounds well," replied Dick, "and then, you know, if your charts don't pan out straight, you can always ask Tom or me. Wonder if you half appreciate your privileges, having us along to take care of you."

The young explorers "lit out" as proposed and, after a day of hard work and easy work, of open water and thick saw-grass and of clear channels and half dry meadows, camped beside a little slough on the border of a swamp, in the jungle of which it soon lost itself.

The first excitement of the new camp came in the night when Tom, who was sleeping, as usual, beside Dick, sprang up with a fierce cry, which they had never before heard from him, and dashed into the woods near the camp. There came from the woods the battle cries of warring animals, but soon all became quiet and the cat came back, but he growled at intervals throughout the night.

"What got into you, Tom?" said Dick to the lynx the next morning, after he had looked him over in vain for marks of a fight. "Was it jimjams, or only a bad nightmare?"

Tom listened gravely and looked as if he could have explained a good deal if only Dick had understood his language.

Tom followed the boys through the swamp on the morning of their first tramp, but when they struck a marshy meadow where the water was knee deep and the mud as much more, with no trees to make it pleasant for a poor cat, he looked reproachfully at Dick and turned back toward the camp. At the end of the meadow was a

111

dense thicket which Ned entered first. He had only advanced a few steps when he turned back and held up his hand in warning to Dick. The thicket in which they stood was on the border of a big prairie of rich grass in which more than a dozen deer, nearly all bucks, could be seen feeding, with only their backs and antlers showing above the tall grass, excepting when some buck of a suspicious mind lifted his head high and gazed warily about him.

"Isn't it us for the big luck, Neddy?" whispered Dick. "When I ate that very last bit of turk this morning I wondered when I'd get another meal and Tom asked me in confidence if we meant to let him starve. And now, just look. There's venison enough for the rest of the trip."

"It don't belong to us yet. You want to be mighty cautious. You can sneak up to that tree with the rifle and wait till that nearest buck shows up in good shape and then drop a bullet somewhere around his fore-shoulder. Don't fire at his head unless you have to. The brain is a mighty small mark, and you're not playing to the gallery down here."

"Ned Barstow, what are you talking about? Take your own rifle and shoot your own buck. If you don't I'll let out a yell that will scare the whole bunch to Kingdom Come. I don't run to you with my gun, whenever I find game, and ask you to shoot it. You mean well, Neddy boy, but sometimes you get mistaken. I'm afraid I didn't begin this trip right. I ought to have given you a lickin' every day, just to keep you in your place."

Ned crawled out to the tree with his rifle and watched for his chance. The nearest buck was within easy range, but the grass hid his body and when the creature, scenting his enemy, threw his head high in the air Ned sent a bullet through his brain. As the boys were dragging the carcass to the woods where they proposed to skin and cut it in two for carrying to camp, Dick said to Ned:

"Do you know what hypocrite means?"

"I s'pose so, but what are you trying to get at?"

"Hypocrite means a fellow who tells his friend that the only way to shoot a buck is through the body, coz the head is too small to be hit, and then goes out himself and sends a bullet plumb through the center of the brain of the beast."

"But Dick, I couldn't see the shoulder."

"Neither could I. You can't sneak out that way."

A strong wind from the northwest sprang up while the boys were finishing their supper of broiled buck's liver and they built a wind-break to protect them while they slept. The wind became a gale, but they slept soundly, soothed by its roaring. They were

112

rudely wakened by the crashing of some wild animal through the brush of their wind-break and, sitting up, saw that the whole western sky was lit up and all beyond the dark meadow was a lurid mass of flame. The roar of the fire mingled with that of the gale, while, as the swirling columns of flame bent to the earth and swept the meadow, the crackling of the grass was like the rattling of musketry or the spitting fire of a hundred Catlings. Soon the air became filled with sparks and cinders, and thick with smoke.

"We've got to mosey, Ned. Reckon there isn't any time to waste, either. Shall we take the meat?"

"Got enough to do to take care of our own."

There was plenty of light, but the flickering shadows of the trees caused by the wavering flames made the steps of the boys uncertain as they fled from the flames that were following so fast. Ned fell headforemost into a thicket of the terrible Spanish bayonet and it was only the excitement of the hour that made the pain bearable. They floundered across the narrow swamp and into the marshy meadow often waist deep in the mud and more than once both of them fell flat in the water of the marsh. The narrow belt of timber which they first crossed checked the fire and although tongues of flame crossed it and a few trees took fire, while live coals were scattered broadcast over the marshy meadow, the fire died out without crossing the belt of woods that first stopped it. The boys crossed the marshy meadow to the swamp which they first entered when they left their camp the previous morning. As Ned's Spanish bayonet wounds kept him from sleeping, the boys sat up and talked till daylight.

In the morning the wind had gone down and a few burning trees and little columns of smoke were all that was left of the great fire of the night.

"If you will go on to camp, Ned, I'll go back and get that venison. It must be well smoked. Hope it didn't burn up. Give my regards to Tom. If he isn't good tie him up."

"Guess I'll go with you, Dick. These stickers hurt worse when I keep still. Then you will need help to carry the venison. I hope the buzzards haven't got at it. We can leave our guns here."

"No, thank you. My gun goes with me. I have had trouble enough from not having it handy."

They found the hide of their buck had been destroyed by the fire, but the venison had only been roasted and partly smoked and they made their breakfast on it. The outsides of the palmettos, on the prairie where Ned shot the buck, were still burning and the trees looked like big sticks of charcoal, but palmetto trees get used to that

113

and are seldom harmed by it, though it does spoil their beauty. The boys walked out in the ashes of the grass of the meadow and were sorry they did, for it made them look like the burnt ends of matches. When they got back to camp Tom came out and sniffed at Dick and then, instead of rubbing against his legs, went back and lay down. Dick spent the rest of the day working over Ned's face and body with tweezers, pulling out bits of thorns. When he got through the boys were about equally tired.

Ned's wounds were so painful that for several days the explorers stayed around the camp and Dick amused himself and his chum by worrying a family of young alligators that lived in a pond near the camp. He grunted the little ones to the surface until they were tired of being fooled and refused to respond and he drove the largest one out of its cave in the bank until the reptile refused to play any more and would not come beyond the mouth of his cave. Then Dick cut a pole leaving a bit of a branch sticking out like a barb at the end and poked that in the hole till the alligator grabbed the end of it. Dick now pulled good and hard, the barb caught in the reptile's lower jaw and the boy soon had him out of his cave and up on the prairie. The 'gator was lively and Dick had to chase around the prairie a lot after him and finally get Ned to help before he could tie it. Tom didn't approve of the new member of the family, but he made no trouble while the camp was awake. The alligator became very restless at night and got in the habit of thrashing around almost constantly. In the morning his tail was seen to be raw and bleeding and day by day it grew worse. Tom was suspected, but always denied having had anything to do with it, with an expression of such injured innocence when accused that Dick had to believe him. One night, however, a heavy blow was heard, accompanied by a yowl from Tom and followed by some sort of scrimmage. In the morning Tom had a mussed-up look and the reptile had a number of fresh wounds. As the camp was moved that day and Ned continued to object to taking an alligator in the canoe the reptile was turned loose. He walked with dignity out on the prairie until he was near the slough, when he scuttled hastily to the water and plunged in.

The new camp was in a little glade on a creek which the explorers had followed for about three miles west from the Everglades. They paddled through the creek till it melted in the meadows; they poled their canoe along the channel which the grass concealed; they dragged it by hand under bushes which covered it, until the little glade opened to them and showed enough dry ground for a camp and several shallow streams winding around clumps of bushes, but always stretching out toward the west. At daylight the young explorers were again on the move, dragging the canoe along twisting streams not deep enough to float it, until they struck a larger stream in a heavier growth. The little streams disappeared, the water grew deeper, but the jungle became worse, and every yard of their path had to be carved out with their knives.

"This doesn't look very hopeful," said Dick as they stopped the heavy work for a few minutes' rest. "Hadn't we better go back a ways and hunt up a more open trail?"

"Not on your life," replied Ned. "We are on the right track and we've got to fight it through. The only thing I'll stop for is a mangrove swamp, and I'll try mighty hard to get around that. But we won't find any mangrove swamp to trouble us."

"You seem to know just what we're going to find on this trail, if you call it a trail."

"I know what we ought to find, and that's better."

"Why is it better?"

"Because then we'll know if we're on the right track."

"All right, Neddy, I quite agree with you. I only wanted to know that you were sure of your ground."

The trees became heavier in a narrow belt along the stream, but open sky could be seen beyond them.

"Don't you want to walk across to that open place, Ned, to find out what kind of country it is?"

"I know now. It's open prairie or swamp and the next big water we strike will be the salt-water lakes. We will probably come to a fresh-water river first and that pretty soon."

"Conceit's good for the consumption, Neddy. What do you want to bet on finding that river in an hour?"

"I'll eat my hat if we don't find it in a quarter of a mile. I won't bet on the time, because at the rate you're working it may take three weeks to get there."

"Ned, you're a wizard, for there is the river."

The river flowed gently between high banks, densely wooded. The waters were alive with fish, and long-legged wading birds of the heron family stalked over the shallows in the stream. An hour's paddling brought the canoe to the mouth of the river, where camp was made. The water beside the camp was fresh, but the salt-water bays spread out for miles before them.

"Everything is easy now," said Ned. "These bays are in the Ten Thousand Islands and lead to the head waters of the rivers of the coast. We may get tangled up in these keys, aground on the flats or cornered up in some of the bays and perhaps lose a few

115

days, but we're safe to get out without hard work or trouble of any kind."


## CHAPTER XX

### DICK'S FIGHT WITH A PANTHER

"I've always noticed, Ned, that when everything looks simple and easy, it is a good time to expect trouble."

"Not this time, Dick."

But it was this time, and that night Ned had his last care-free sleep for weeks.

"How long shall we camp here?" asked Dick.

"Better stay here for a week or two. We can hunt in the woods back of us and explore all these bays. This may be the last fresh water we will find on the trip, so we don't want to leave it till we are ready to pull straight through to Myers."

In the morning the boys started across the woods on the bank of the stream, hoping to find a buck on the prairie beyond them. When they reached the prairie they saw three deer near its farther end, about half a mile away. They went back in the woods and started to work their way around the prairie to its farther end where the deer were. It took them some hours to get where the deer had been, only to find that they had gone. They saw them again on a smaller prairie and once more tried to get near the creatures by creeping through the woods. When the hunters were as near the game as they could go without getting out of cover the animals were yet a hundred and fifty yards distant. One of them was a fine buck and Ned watched it, rifle in hand, for many minutes, hoping it would come nearer. As the deer fed they sometimes came nearer and his hopes rose, only to sink into his boots when they turned away. At last he gave up waiting for a better chance and fired. The buck threw up his head, looked around for a moment and trotted quietly away, entirely unharmed, followed by the other deer.

"It isn't our day, Dick," said Ned, ruefully, as he watched the disappearing animals.

"Here goes for something to eat, anyhow," replied Dick, as he dropped a curlew that was flying over them. After broiling and eating the bird, together with some hoe-cake which they had in their

116

pockets, the boys resumed their hunt for deer. They saw several more during the afternoon, but ill luck followed them and they finally set out for camp empty-handed.

As the boys were passing through a thick clump of trees on the bank of the river, about two hundred yards from their camp, Ned was suddenly held back by a clutch on his shoulder, and turning his head, saw Dick's face upturned and his eyes fixed on the large branch of a big tree just before them. As Ned looked upward he saw the form of a huge panther, or mountain lion, crouching upon the limb and apparently about to spring upon him. The animal was within ten feet, every muscle was tense, his long tail was waving slowly and Ned stood motionless, charmed by the living beauty of the beast, until he heard Dick's whisper in his ear:

"Shoot, Ned!"

The hypnotic spell was broken and Ned slowly raised his rifle to his shoulder, while the panther crouched lower and waved his tail more quickly. In another second it might be too late, and once more Dick whispered:

"Shoot, Ned! Quick!"

The bullet struck the beast and the next instant Ned was knocked down by the body of the brute. He was unharmed, however, for Dick had jumped between them and it was in Dick's arm that the panther's teeth were set and Dick's shoulder and side that were being raked by its cruel claws. In an instant Ned's clasp knife was being driven into the body of the beast whose throat Dick's hand was clutching in a feeble effort to keep from his face those long, sharp fangs.

Bullet and knife had done their work and the panther was dead. But Dick was unconscious and covered with blood which was flowing from deep gashes in his arm and a side that was torn from shoulder to waist. Ned half carried and half dragged the unconscious Dick a few yards to a level piece of dry ground and examined his wounds. Bad as they looked, there was no spouting of blood from an artery, or heavy flow from a large vein. With simple bandaging and care the boy would get well, and Ned's relief was so great that he was almost happy. He removed what the panther had left of Dick's shirt, which was sodden with blood, and tearing off his own, bandaged the wounds from which blood was still flowing. He then filled his cap with water from the river and sprinkled Dick's face, but failed to bring him to consciousness. He was wondering what next to try when Dick opened his eyes and smiled weakly.

"Did he hurt you, Neddy?"

"No, he didn't hurt me, thanks to you, Dicky boy. Now I'm

117

going to bring the camp here, in the canoe. Can you get along without me for half an hour?"

"Sure. Don't forget Tom."

Ned didn't forget Tom. He thought so much of him that he took his rifle with him when he went to move the camp. For he was without a shirt and was stained with Dick's blood and therefore very doubtful how the lynx would behave. But Tom merely sniffed at him and when the canoe was loaded stepped aboard as coolly as if his passage had been paid for. When the canoe landed at the new camping ground Tom took a few steps toward Dick and then suddenly sprang into the woods and away, as if witches were after him. Ned was surprised at first, but remembered that Tommy, the Seminole, had once said to him:

"Wildcat eat 'coon, panther eat wildcat," and he ceased to wonder why Tom had run away.

Ned stretched the canvas over Dick, built a camp fire, got out a clean shirt for himself and tore up another for bandages. He washed Dick's wounds, which had ceased to bleed, with warm water and soap and put fresh bandages on them. After he had gathered a lot of moss and made a soft bed for the invalid, he picked up Dick's gun and walking a few steps down the river bank, shot a curlew that sat on a branch by the stream and was young enough to make a broil or stew for the invalid.

"Been breaking the law, have you, Neddy?"

"I'd break anything, to get you some nice chicken broth such as I am going to make now."

At daylight Ned saw that Dick was sleeping quietly and taking the shotgun started out in search of a breakfast suited to a sick boy. When he returned, an hour later, he had a brace of ducks, a little brown Florida rabbit and a 'possum. Dick was awake when he returned and when offered his choice of the game for his breakfast chose all of them. Ned stewed the rabbit and broiled a duck, giving Dick a little of each, but the 'possum looked fat and greasy and he kept it for himself.

"Dick," said Ned after breakfast, "shall I roll that beast into the river, or do you want his skin?"

"Want it, of course. I've got no hard feelings against him."

"Want him skinned for mounting or a rug?"

"Rug, I guess. Think I'll enjoy walking on him."

The big cat was nearly eight feet long, including his tail, and was so heavy that Ned found skinning him a hard job. After he had finished he had to cut a stout stick for a lever, before he could get the carcass into the river. The bad luck of the hunters seemed to

118

have run out, and game began to come to them. Ducks flew over the river beside the camp and plovers often lit on a bank near them. Ned went out for deer and came back in an hour with half a buck on his shoulders. When he approached the camp he saw Dick sitting up and tossing bits of hoe-cake to a 'coon that was watching him with some suspicion from a distance of three or four yards.

"You ought to have seen him, Ned. I had him half tamed. He took little bits of wet hoe-cake that I threw him and rolled them up into balls with his funny little hands before he ate them. In an hour more I'd have had him eating out of my hand."

"He'll come back to-morrow, Dick. You've got a way with you that wild things understand."

"It's only that I really love them and they know it."

The 'coon did come back the next day while Ned was out exploring the bay in the canoe and, although he did not eat out of Dick's hand, he came within a few feet of him and showed very little fear. When Ned returned, the 'coon scrambled to the top of a little tree and looked down on the boys in a friendly way. Day by day the 'coon became more intimate with Dick, even to eating out of his hand, but always scampered away when Ned came back. On the third day, as Ned came in from an exploring trip, instead of the 'coon he found his old friend Tom, the lynx, sitting beside Dick with the air of a trained nurse.

"Bully for you, Tom; I'm glad to see you back," said Ned.

"I'm not glad he's come back, the murderer. He has killed my 'coon."

"You remember what my Indian said. 'Panther eat wildcat, wildcat eat 'coon.' Shall I shoot him, Dick?"

"Shoot Tom? Well I guess not. He didn't know any better. I'm awful sorry the 'coon has gone, but I'd hate worse to lose Tom."

"How did it happen?"

"I was feeding the 'coon, and had just put out my hand to rub his head when he jumped in the air and started for that tree like a streak of lightning. He never got there, though. Something was after him like two streaks of lightning. I didn't know it was Tom till it was all over. That wasn't very long, either. If there had been any time I'd have had Tom by the ears or tail and taught him a thing or two."

"Glad you didn't have time, Dick. I'm afraid Tom might have taught you a few things. Don't you think you had better get over what one cat has done to you before you tackle another?"

"But Tom isn't that kind of a cat, Ned. I'm not afraid of his hurting me much. He might scratch me a little at first, but he'd be

119

sorry for it, soon as he had time to think it over. Wouldn't you, Tom?"

"Cats are cats, Dick, and I don't think it's safe to leave you alone with that wildcat. You are too weak to help yourself if he really tackled you."

"But he won't attack me. So what's the use of talking about things that aren't going to happen? You are a good boy, Neddy, but you've got your limitations and you can't appreciate Tom."

Ned spent much of his time coddling the invalid. He paddled out in the lakes and among its keys. He explored the waters and the woods and brought Dick wild grapes with much character and cocoa plums with little; sea-grapes with juice that had the taste of claret and the color of blood; figs, of which Dick said: "De breed am small, but de flavor am delicious"; wild sapadillos that were sweet as honey, but chewed up into a solid ball of soft india rubber; and mastic berries that were delicious to the taste, but stuck like a porous plaster to the roof of the mouth. He got out the rod and caught mangrove snappers from under the banks and sheephead from their hiding places among sunken logs and snags. He dove for turtle that he never got and hacked at young palmettos for buds that he did get.

Days followed days and though Dick grew better he didn't grow strong. Ned got anxious and told his chum that he was going to take him to a doctor. Dick laughed and said:

"You are my doctor. I've great confidence in you and don't care to make a change."

"Glad to hear it. Your doctor, in whom you have such confidence, desires to consult with his brother physicians in Fort Myers regarding your case, and you will light out with him to-morrow."

The next morning a little canoe with a cat couchant in the bow, a young invalid comfortably reclining amidships and a husky youth in the stern started down the river and into the salt-water lakes. The first day's run was a short one and the camp was made on a bit of high ground covered with thin grass and shaded by a group of palmettos. It was bordered about with cocoa plums and sweet-smelling myrtle, on one of which flourished an orchid, the vanilla bean, which made heavy with its fragrance the whole camping site.

"But there lurked a taint in the clime so blest,
Like a serpent coiled in a ring-dove's nest"—

and as Ned stood dazed by the enchantment of his environment, he was brought to earth with a jar by the whirring of rattles almost under his feet. Every muscle of the boy was tense with

120

excitement as he stood motionless, knowing that death, in a horrible form, was within striking distance of him. The strange, paralyzing music of the dreaded "King Snake" of the Indians seems to come from all sides and until the threatened victim can see the reptile the motion of a hand may be fatal. The seconds seemed minutes to Ned as he waited and watched, waited and watched, before he saw the fascinating, dreadful, gently swaying head and the lightning play of the forked tongue within easy striking distance.

He felt that if he jumped, the snake, so much quicker than he, would sink the glistening white fangs of that wide-open mouth deep in his flesh before he could get out of reach. He compelled his quivering nerves to hold steady while he slowly, inch by inch, moved away from the coils of the angry reptile. When Ned was six feet from the rattlesnake he sprang back and stood, almost fainting, quite out of reach of the reptile, which continued to wave its head and jar its rattles, but with less passion. The boy had often been told never to leave a rattlesnake alive and he looked around until he found a stick about five feet long, with which he returned to the field of his fright. The rattler had uncoiled and was creeping away when Ned rushed up and struck at him. The snake coiled like a flash and striking back, sunk his fangs in the stick within a foot of the hand of the boy. Again Ned struck, and the snake returned the blow, both of them missing their marks. Then the stick fell on the coils of the reptile and the back of the rattlesnake was broken. After a few finishing blows Ned dragged the six-foot creature by the tail to the bank and was thrusting it into the water when Dick called out:

"Don't you want to save the skin?"

"Don't want to save anything to remind me of it. I never expect to get the frightful sight of the open jaws and white fangs of that beast out of my dreams."

Dick rested in camp the next day with the lynx, while Ned explored with the canoe, looking for the head of some river of the west coast that led to the Gulf, or for enough dry land to serve for a camp. Every water course that he followed, sooner or later closed up on him. He paddled four miles to the west through a long bay, only to find that there was no outlet on the western end, excepting a narrow creek which he followed until he could drag his canoe no farther. He followed floating wisps of manatee grass, freshly torn up by the roots, hoping to find the manatee which had spilled them, that he might follow him to a channel which would lead out of the wilderness. He discovered the manatee and was nearly swamped by the first dash of the frightened creature. Then he lost track of the animal after a long chase among the innumerable keys of the so-

121

called Ten Thousand Islands, and found that he was himself lost. He paddled until it was dark and for an hour after that, when he gave up hope of finding his camp that night.

He had a map of the country in his brain, but that was for daylight use only. He was hungry, and that was nothing; but he was parched with thirst from his long labor, and that was everything. He had seen no dry land during the day, and it was hopeless to look for it at night. It was never easy to keep the canoe balanced; if he dozed for an instant he would certainly roll it over. He had made up his mind to sentry duty for the night when through the darkness there came to him a gleam of light from a far-distant fire. As he approached, it brightened and sent up a crackling flame, in the blaze of which Ned saw the tall palmettos of his camp.

"Were you worried, Dick?" he asked after the first warm greetings were over.

"I sure was. I thought you couldn't get lost and wondered what had happened to you. Tom was uneasy, too, and I reckon he is out looking for you now. He went away in a good deal of a hurry. I made a lighthouse out of those palmetto fans that you cut for my bed, just on the chance of your having lost your way."

Tom came home about daylight and lay down beside Dick, where he grumbled and growled as if he were a man with a next-morning headache.

When daylight came and Ned began to bestir himself, he missed the cheery "Good-morning" of his companion, who was not able to lift his head from his pillow of palmetto. His wan smile went to Ned's heart, and the boy had to busy himself with the fire to hide his emotion. Every hour of that day he watched over the invalid, and from time to time tempted him with bits of broiled bird, heron soup and sips of hot tea made from leaves of the sweet bay. Ned's acquaintance with sickness was slight and his apprehension great, so that the night was a sleepless one and the day that followed brought no relief to his mind. Another day brought new anxieties. Dick was no better, and Ned couldn't bear to leave him, for the invalid's thirst was continuous, but now the supply of fresh water was running low, and a trip back to the river was imperative. He put the bucket, with what water was left, beside Dick's bed and said:

"Dick, boy, I've got to go for some water. I'll have to be away a few hours, but I'll get back the first minute it is possible."

Dick put out his hand, and his smile was cheery, though his voice was weak as he said:

"Don't you worry, Neddy. I'm all right for all day. I don't need anything but amusement, and Tom will 'tend to that."

"I'm afraid to leave a big wildcat with you when you are so weak. I am going to take Tom with me."

"Don't do it, Neddy. He'd only be in your way, and I do want him for company. You don't understand Tom; he likes me and I like him. Please don't take him away."

"Of course I won't take him away, Dick, boy, but you will have to be very good and keep cheerful and get strong and well to pay me for leaving him."

Ned's apprehensions made the day a hard one for him. He was afraid of capsizing the canoe and being unable to get back in it. He imagined a tarpon jumping into it, a shark swimming against it, or a porpoise smashing it. When he reached the river of fresh water he carried the canoe up on the bank and tied it to a tree while he walked along the river bank and shot a few tender young birds for the nourishment of the invalid. His nerves were so unstrung that he feared to go far lest he lose his way, and was even apprehensive of failing to find on his return the camp where his companion was awaiting him, although the path to it was plain as a pikestaff. Ned's meeting with Dick was a joyful one, for the boy was clearly better and his voice stronger, although his first words were:

"Don't go away again, Neddy. You've been gone a year, and I thought you were never coming back."

By careful economy the five gallons of water which their can contained was made to last as many days for the three of them, for Dick insisted that Tom must share the rations of food and drink of the other members of the family. Each day Ned made a little trip around the keys nearest the camp by way of doing the marketing for his family, and returned when he had shot enough birds for its daily needs. He was happy in the thought of the invalid's increasing strength, but dreaded the necessary trip for fresh water. Dick surprised him by bearing the separation with cheerfulness, and his voice was so much firmer and his strength so obviously on the mend that Ned began again to plan for his return to civilization.

On one of his marketing excursions Ned saw a skiff containing two men about a quarter of a mile distant. He waved his hat to the men and paddled toward them, but they rowed away. He followed, but was unable to find them, and concluded that they were outlaws, who did not care to extend their acquaintance. After this he paddled about on the lookout for some one who might help him to carry Dick to the outside world, for he had given up the idea of attempting it by himself.

# CHAPTER XXI

## CONVALESCENCE AND CATASTROPHE

Ned's hopes and plans were suddenly changed, and he no longer hoped for help, but planned to take Dick to the coast himself. For Dick was getting well. There was no doubt about it. His appetite came back, until, instead of urging him to eat, Ned waited for him to ask twice for food before giving it to him. He was still thin and weak, but his spirits bubbled over, and his laughter was on tap, ready to be turned on any minute. He began to clamor for a move toward the coast, but Ned was obdurate and refused to stir for a week. Then one day Ned started out and paddled some miles toward the coast, examining the shores of the keys and the mangrove-lined banks of the salt-water rivers for a camping-ground. He could have made his own camp on the overflowed meadows almost anywhere, but Dick was still an invalid and Ned was always anxious about him. Six miles from the camp, where he had left Dick with Tom, Ned found a good camping site, marked by a freak palmetto with a trunk that branched into two stems about midway up. The ground was covered with palmetto scrub, which Ned examined carefully for rattlesnakes, after which he got out his fly-rod and caught a mess of fish for supper. On his return to camp the lynx sprang into the canoe, seized one of the fish and growled so fiercely that Ned thought best to let him keep it.

"Fresh water is all out, Dick," said Ned that night, "so I'll start at daylight and go back to the river and fill up. I'll take it slowly and be here about noon. Then we can start out and make easy work of being in the new camp long before sun-down."

"Ned, I can paddle all right, and I'm going to help. I am sick of being a baby."

"Go 'way, chile, you make me tired. Don't forget that I'm your doctor," replied Ned.

"Do you see any chance of getting to the coast?"

"Yes; pretty sure thing. I found a deep channel near the camp with some porpoises playing in it, and I think it's near the head of one of the big coast rivers. I am almost certain it's Rodgers River."

Ned was a tired boy when the day's work was done and the young explorers were settled in the new camp, but a night's sleep braced him up so that he agreed to his chum's plan to make a dash for the coast, for Dick had said:

"What is the use of losing a lot of time in prospecting for a soft spot for me to sleep? We can be on the coast to-night within sight of

124

houses and help if we need it, which we don't, for I'm going to do my share of the paddling. I know that coast and you don't, so I'll naturally be boss."

When the little canoe had been loaded with all their stores and trophies, and the boys were ready for their final trip, Tom stepped gravely aboard, and seating himself in the bow, turned to Ned with an expression which Dick translated as:

"I am here, you may start the engine."

Ned dipped his paddle deeply in the water, that with his every stroke flowed more swiftly. The banks became well defined, and although the stream was so crooked that it flowed by turns to every point of the compass, its general trend was to the west. The river broadened and the channel deepened, the forest on the banks became more heavily timbered, and the boys recognized the beautiful Rodgers River. Curlews and water-turkeys watched them from the trees; herons flew lazily up from the shoals as the canoe approached; porpoises, going out with the tide, rolled their backs out of water and gave sniffs of affright as they saw the canoe beside them. The fin of a great shark, longer than their canoe, cut the water as its owner swiftly pursued a six-foot tarpon, which escaped by leaping in the air within thirty feet of the canoe, toward which it was headed. Another clash of the shark brought its huge body within its length of the boys, while the great mouth, with its rows of serrated teeth, razor-sharp, opened wide to take in the tarpon, which leaped wildly ten feet in the air, and turning, plunged head-down straight for Ned as he sat in the canoe, paddle in hand. Dick started up from his seat, while Ned tried to fend off with the paddle, but the hard, pointed head of the big tarpon tore through the bottom of the fragile canoe as if it had been paper. A minute later the shattered canoe was floating down the river, while everything sinkable had gone to the bottom.

Tom, who had been asleep in the bottom of the canoe, was swimming for shore, and Ned, who had not for a second lost his presence of mind, was treading water and supporting the unconscious Dick, who had been struck by the tail of the tarpon as the big fish crushed the canoe. Even as the tarpon struck the canoe Ned was reaching out for Dick, and the boys went down together.

Then to Ned came the struggle for life—for two lives. His only thought was of Dick. Dick mustn't drown; Dick's face must be kept out of the water; he must get Dick ashore. He swam high, wasting his efforts to keep Dick's head above the surface. Strength goes fast when one struggles in the water, and Ned was soon gasping for breath. As he struck out more and more feebly for the bank, while

125

the current swept him down the stream, he sank lower and lower, until only his eyes were above the surface and his lungs seemed bursting for want of air. A great shark swept past him, and the wave from the big fish rolled over him. He felt his senses going, his muscles refused to respond to the call of his brain. His grasp on Dick was loosening, and the thought of this roused him to renew the struggle. To save Dick he must save himself; he must breathe; he must not exhaust himself, and above all his mind must not wander. He was so tired; for himself he would have given up the struggle and dropped into rest, but for Dick—never! A great calmness came to him. He rolled over with his head thrown back until all but his face was under water. This floated clear of the surface as he lay back and drew air into his smothered lungs in great gulps. He began to kick out with his feet and was soon swimming on his back toward the bank, making fair progress with little effort. Some of his strength came back, and he found that he was easily dragging Dick along, happily with his face upward. Hope took the place of despair, and Ned felt that now he could swim for hours. He saw the overhanging branches of trees above him and knew he was nearing the bank. Then suddenly he found himself aground on a shoal with water less than knee-deep. He dragged the unconscious form of his companion into the jungle on the bank, and a great wave of thankfulness rolled over him as he felt the weak beating of Dick's heart, which was followed by the familiar smile as the boy opened his eyes.

"Well, Neddy, what have you been doing now, and what are you going to do? Last time I saw you a thousand-pound fish was dropping on your head. Seems as if he hit me, too."

"Going to make a camp for the two of us, feed us, and get us out of the wilderness. That's what I am going to do," replied Ned.

"You'll do it, all right; but what have you got to work with?"

"Pocket-knife and some matches. First thing I'll make a fire to dry you. Then I'll forage. You see, Dick, we've got to stay right here until you get strong enough to travel. I can make a palmetto shack big enough to keep the rain off in half a day. The worst trouble will be fresh water, but I think I can fix that. I know how to get things to eat. I have picked up a couple of old cocoanuts, and I'll bring them to you in an hour full of water. Then to-morrow I will start early and find that old shack where we camped in the graveyard. You remember that old kettle there? Well, I'll bring it here full of fresh water. Then if you don't get well pretty quick I'll leave you plenty to eat and drink and find my way to the coast. I can do it in a day, and have your old friend, who don't believe we know a manatee from a tarpon, up here with his boat the next day sure."

126

"Don't do it, Neddy. I'd be thinking of a hundred things happening to you, and the night would be pretty lonesome without even Tom."

Ned started away from the river through a wooded swamp, and before he had gone a quarter of a mile struck a prairie on which several deer were feeding. The animals seemed to know that he had no weapon, for they showed no alarm until he had walked some distance toward them. There were a number of small ponds near him, and as Ned approached the nearest one a small alligator slipped from the bank into the water. The boy had provided himself with a short, heavy pole, and he waded fearlessly in after the 'gator; but although the pond was not thirty feet across and he explored every foot of it, he could not find the reptile. He finally came across an opening in the bank, in which he thrust his pole, when it was promptly seized by the alligator. Ned tried to pull the reptile within reach, but when the head came out of the cave it was larger than he had looked for, and before he had made up his mind to tackle it the creature had let go of the pole and gone back in his cave. Then the boy got earnest and determined to have that alligator if he had to crawl into the cave after him. He sharpened a bit of branch that stuck out beside the big end of his pole like the barb of a harpoon, and again thrust it in the cave. Soon he had the reptile fighting mad with his head out of the cave, when he pushed the pole into his open mouth, and catching the barb in the soft skin under the alligator's jaw, just as Dick had done weeks before, hauled him out of the cave and dragged him out on the bank. When a few yards from the pond the reptile broke loose from the barb and started back for the pond. Ned was after him like a tiger and struck two or three smashing blows on the creature's head with his pole, and then, as the reptile neared the water, threw himself on its back and seizing its jaws held them together while he turned the brute on its back. At first the alligator lashed out with its tail, but soon became quiet; and then Ned got out his knife and severed the spine of the reptile.

The water of the pond was so nearly fresh that its taste was only slightly sweetish, and after Ned had drank all he could hold he filled his two cocoanuts for Dick. On his way to camp he hunted up a young palmetto for the bud or cabbage which grew in the top of the tree. The sharp edges of the great, tough leaves tore his flesh as he climbed through them, and it was only after more than an hour of hard work with his knife that he secured the cabbage he was working for. By this time the water he had drunk had oozed out through his pores. He was so parched with thirst that he took a long walk back to the pond and filled up again.

127

That night Dick and Ned had broiled alligator steak and palmetto cabbage for supper. Both suffered so much for want of water that Ned started out at daylight to find the old abandoned plantation. Dick was pale and his smile so wan that Ned's heart was sore at leaving him. He was too earnest to think of trivial things, and he sloshed through the swamp without thought of the swaying heads of little speckle-bellies in his path, or the great, ugly cotton-mouth moccasins that moved slowly aside as he wallowed through their lairs. He stopped long enough on the border of the prairie to find a club, with which he fiercely pounded to death a rattlesnake, upon whose coils he had nearly stepped when the locust-like warning found its way to his consciousness.

After about three miles of tramping, during which he waded waist-deep across two sloughs, the prairie opened upon familiar ground, and Ned knew that he was opposite the plantation he sought. In the decaying building he found an old bucket that would hold three or four gallons, and a couple of quart cans in which water could be boiled. From a tamarind tree he gathered the half-dried fruit with its sweet acidity, and in the old garden he discovered a few stalks of sugar-cane. He picked up a rusty fish-hook and from an old net got a quantity of string. Then filling his bucket with rain water, he started back to Dick and the camp. The journey was a hard one, and though he refused to drink a drop of the water, half of it was lost on the way. The weight of it pressed him down in the mire of the sloughs until he sank to the armpits as he held the heavy bucket on his head. Dick laughed aloud with joy, even if it was a bit hysterical, when Ned got home to camp.

"Been lonesome?" asked Ned after Dick had drank a quart of water and looked as if he wanted a gallon more.

"Not very. Tom has amused me," replied Dick, as he pointed to a branch over his head. Ned looked up, and there was Tom gazing benignly down upon him.

"Wonder if Tom is hungry?" said Ned.

"Guess not. I tried him with a piece of alligator steak, and he turned his nose up at that."

"What do you think he would say to a mess of fish?" and Ned produced his fish-hook and line. Dick's eyes glistened.

"Oh! I am so hungry for some broiled fish."

Most Florida streams are alive with fish that are not fussy about the tackle with which they are taken. Ned baited his hook with a piece of alligator, which was promptly seized by a salt-water cat. The cat-fish was given to the wildcat, which grabbed it fiercely. Two mangrove snappers were the result of a few minutes' fishing.

128

Ned put some tamarinds in one of the quart tins, which he filled with water and then stirred with a stick of sugar-cane which had been peeled and split.

Dick perked up a good deal during his supper of broiled fish, palmetto cabbage and tamarind water, after which Ned made him a tin of tea from the leaves of the sweet bay. In the days that followed Ned gathered oysters, which he found some distance down the river, caught fish and killed several heron and a young curlew with sticks. The broils, roasts and stews which he made would have done credit to a professional cook. He wanted to set snares for rabbits and birds, but had to give it up owing to the difficulty of making a snare which would distinguish between Tom, whom he didn't wish to catch, and the rabbits which he wanted.

Dick was improving, but so very slowly that Ned determined to find his way to the coast and get help. He put it off, at Dick's request, for several days, until they had been in camp a week, when one afternoon it was agreed that Ned should start early the next morning. Dick, who was feeling very blue at the prospect of Ned's leaving him, was lying on his bed of moss when suddenly he sat up.

## CHAPTER XXII

### THE RESCUE

"Listen, Ned, listen! There is a motor-boat in the river. Don't you hear it?"

"I don't hear it, Dick."

"But you must hear it. It's growing plainer every minute. It's a four-cycle engine, and a fast boat, too. I can tell you that. Who can it be? Do you suppose it is your father looking for you?"

"I hear it now. No, it isn't Dad. My time isn't up for several days yet. After that anything might happen, but until then Dad won't lift a finger toward looking me up."

"Oh, Ned! It's coming nearer, nearer, nearer! There! It's 'round the bend. Of course, you see it now. How it is coming!"

"You bet it's coming. You ought to see the water pile up against the bow. It's a glass-cabin launch. There's a man standing on top of the cabin. I think he sees us, for he is pointing this way, and—

the boat's headed straight for us—hear that whistle, and—Dick, Dick, boy!—there's a tall man and a girl standing in front of the pilot-house, and—oh, Dick! it's too good to be true, but it's Dad and Molly!"

"Molly?" said Dick.

"Yes, my sister, you know. Sometimes we call her Mary."

"I didn't know your sister's name was Molly. What does she look like?"

"Just watch that girl who is waving her hat as if she was crazy. That's Molly."

Ned was in the launch before it touched the bank, and Mr. Barstow was holding his son by the hand, although neither spoke, while Molly had her arms around Ned's neck and was laughing, crying and talking by turns.

"You blessed, blessed Neddy! What did happen to you? We were frightened, oh! so frightened."

"Ned," said Mr. Barstow, "your friend, young Williams, was with you. I never saw him, but I hope no harm came to him."

"No, daddy; Dick will be all right, now you are here, but he has been very, very sick, and I was dreadfully afraid he wouldn't get well, and all his trouble came because he saved my life without thinking of his own. Come right ashore and see him."

"Shall I come, too?" asked Molly.

"Sure," replied Ned. "He wants to see you especially."

A moment later Mr. Barstow had one of Dick's hands in both of his own.

"My boy, my boy, what made you run away? The hue and cry is out for you in Key West. Why did you never tell me that you were Ned's nearest friend? Why didn't you tell Molly who you were? Ned has talked to her for years about you. Come here, Molly, and tell your friend Dick Williams what you think of him for hiding his name from you."

But Molly didn't tell him just then. For Dick's strength had been overtaxed, and when his eyes met Molly's he promptly fainted.

When Dick had recovered, Ned invited his father and sister to dine before going aboard the motor-boat, and as he was busy preparing the meal and his father had much to hear from him, the care of the invalid fell upon Molly, a duty which she performed to the apparent satisfaction of her patient.

"Those oysters are lovely," said the girl as she speared with a chop-stick a small one which had been roasted in the shell.

"Yes. Ned waded through half a mile of mud to get them."

"I wondered how Neddy got so muddy. I was so glad to see

130

him that I just hugged him, and now I ought to be in a wash-tub. Just look at me."

Dick obeyed her so literally that she added a moment later:

"I mean look at the mud on my dress."

The broiled snappers were pronounced the finest fish ever served, the palmetto cabbage better than cauliflower, and then the girl asked:

"This white meat is pretty good. What is it?"

"Alligator."

"Really?"

"Really and truly. You said you liked it."

"I didn't know it was a reptile. Why didn't you tell me? I wouldn't have eaten it if I had known."

"Ned wouldn't have liked it if I had told. He is my doctor, you know, and I have to mind him."

"You don't need a doctor any more. What you want is a nurse."

"That's so. I could mind her easy," said Dick.

"Oh, I meant a man nurse," said the girl.

Ned produced some joints of sugar-cane for dessert, and made a can of after-dinner sweet-bay tea, and then began to ask questions.

"Daddy, I want to find out whether you and Molly are crazy or whether I am. You never saw Dick before. You said so half an hour ago. Dick never saw you or Molly. He said so half an hour ago—"

"But Ned—" interrupted Dick.

"You keep still. I've got the floor. Now, Dad, you and Molly rush up to this chap, whom you never saw before, and fall into his arms—"

"Neddy Barstow, I didn't do anything of the kind. But I had seen him and I did know him," said the girl.

"Now, there you go. How ever did you know this chum of mine, who never saw you?"

"How did Dick save your life, Ned?" asked Mr. Barstow in a voice that wasn't quite as steady as usual.

"I can tell you," broke in Dick. "He didn't do it at all. That's how."

"Dad, when our canoe was wrecked, we lost the beautifullest skin of the biggest kind of a panther—eight feet from tip to tip. Dick saw the panther first, when he was ten feet from us, ready to jump. I fired at the beast, and he sprang for me, but Dick jumped at the same time and got between us, so the panther landed on him and I was saved. That's why he is sick now. I s'pose that is what

131

knocked his memory endwise, so he don't remember anything about it."

"Mr. Barstow," said Dick, "I wish you would ask Ned who it was that swam ashore with me when the big tarpon smashed the canoe and knocked me out. Yes, and he almost lost his own life in saving mine. Please ask him. I want to see if he has lost his memory."

Ned tried to speak, but Molly had her arms around his neck, saying nice things to him.

"See here, sis, doesn't part of this belong to Dick?" said Ned, and got his ears boxed very promptly.

"Did not Dick tell you, Ned, that he came from New York to Key West on the steamer with us, and that Molly and I got acquainted with him, and that he then slipped away at Key West so that we could not find him?" asked Mr. Barstow.

"Never told me a word. Dick, you gay deceiver, you pretended to tell me everything, and you left out the most interesting part. You probably thought I wasn't interested in Dad or Molly."

"But, Ned, I never knew they were your father and sister until just now. I told you everything that seemed worth speaking of."

"Hear that, Molly? This young man says you didn't seem worth speaking of. Can't you get even with him for that? Now, tell me how you happen to be here, you and Dad. I told Dick that he wouldn't move a finger for us till the time of my vacation was up."

"You were all right about that, Neddy. He wouldn't budge an inch, for I tried to make him start out and hunt you up, and he refused until—Well, one day the boat that carries the mail between Key West and Chokoloskee picked up, out in the Gulf of Mexico, a broken canoe that everybody seemed to know was the one you and Mr. Williams were out in. Then Mr. Streeter made a night run to Myers, got Dad out of bed, and things began to happen. Of course, I was coming, so I got into a few clothes, skipped my breakfast and was aboard this boat barely in time not to be left, for Dad was just plain crazy. But before he came away he chartered everything in sight and told the men not to leave an unexplored channel in the whole Ten Thousand Islands."

Ned held out his hand to his father without speaking, but Dick looked at the girl with more gratitude in his eyes than she could possibly have deserved, although she seemed willing to accept a good deal of it.

"Well, boys," said Mr. Barstow, "if you are ready we will go aboard. I don't see much that you will care to take with you."

"Nothing but Tom," said Dick. "Can't he go? He'll be good."

132

"Of course he can. But who is Tom?"

"Oh, he's nothing but a savage old wildcat," replied Ned. "He'll probably eat us all up but Dick. He has eaten some of him already."

"Oh, what a beauty!" cried Molly, when Tom, who had been sitting in a tree over their heads, was pointed out to her. Dick soon coaxed the lynx, which sat there looking suspiciously at the strangers, down to his shoulder.

"Can't I pet him?" asked Molly.

"No!" said Ned.

"Yes," said Dick, and Molly stepped forward and laid her hand fearlessly on the soft fur of the beautiful creature. Tom began a low growl, but Dick talked soothingly to him, and in a few minutes he became quite friendly with the girl.

"There!" said Molly. "Now we're friends, and I can play with him all I want to."

"Oh, no, not yet. You must promise that you won't touch him unless I am with you," said Dick.

"Of course, I won't promise. I'll pet him when I please."

"Then poor Tom will have to stay here."

"Do you mean to say that if I don't make that ridiculous promise I can't have Tom?"

"Tom belongs to you the minute you make that promise, but not before."

"Well, Mr. Williams, I make the promise rather than lose Tom, but as for you—" And the blank which Molly left was filled with feminine possibilities.

A bunk was fixed up in the cabin of the launch for Dick, and the throb of the heavy engines became a steady hum as the boat turned down the stream, with water and spray curling up from its bow and heavy waves from its propeller breaking with a sullen roar on the banks of the river. Dick's bunk must have been uncomfortable, for very soon he crawled up on deck and, going forward to where he could lean back against the cabin, sat down, looking pale, but not unhappy. Molly, who happened to be on the bow of the boat, was so indignant with him that she told him he ought to have a guardian, and then went below and brought back an armful of pillows and cushions, with which she proceeded to make life a burden to Dick. Then, as she seemed about to go away, Dick began to talk to her about the old plantations on the river and tell her the ghost stories that belonged to them, until she sat down near him. "I hope you don't think I was rude about Tom? I was only—" But Molly interrupted him.

"You need to be good and strong before I tell you what I think

133

of that." And the girl walked away from him so indignant that she didn't return for nearly two minutes.

As the launch neared the mouth of the river a yawl-rigged craft with an auxiliary engine had just entered it. Her captain was sitting on deck with his right hand grasping the wheel, his body leaning forward, rigid as bronze, while his roving eye scanned water and sky, reefs, banks and keys. A roll of the wheel, and the launch darted toward him. When within a hundred yards the whir of the big engine and the chugging of the two-cycle motor of the yawl stopped, and as the boats were passing each other, Mr. Barstow hailed the skipper of the yawl.

"Oh, Captain Hull! All's well. The boys have been found. Spread the news. Hunt up the other boats and all hands report to me at Myers."

"Aye, aye, sir!" came from the bronze statue, and the chugging and the whirring began again as the yawl resumed its course, while the launch wove in and out among the oyster reefs, that guard the mouth of the river, at a speed that would have torn the propeller out of her had she struck one of them.

Dick's eyes sparkled as the Gulf opened out, and the launch turned down the coast to clear the bar before making her course. Before him were the waters where the waterspout destroyed the Etta; the Shark River bight was near, and in the distance the cocoa-palms of the Northwest Cape could be made out. He turned eagerly to the girl beside him, and was telling her the story of the waterspout when Mr. Barstow came to them and said:

"Run away, little girl, I want to talk to Dick."

"So do I," said Molly as she made a little face at her father, who laughed at her.

"You mustn't think you own Dick. Go play with Tom, there. He looks pretty amiable just now."

"But he won't let me play with Tom. He's mean about that."

Dick began to explain, but the girl had gone.

"What are your plans for your future, Dick?" asked Mr. Barstow.

"I am going home and going to work at anything I can find to do."

"How would you like to work for me?"

"I don't know of anything else in the world I would like so well." And Dick fairly beamed.

"Then, if the work suits you, your engagement will date from to-day."

"What will be my duties, sir?"

134

"First a vacation to get well in and visit your mother. Then you and Ned will go to my timber property in Canada, familiarize yourselves with the present methods of working it, and suggest any improvements that occur to you, and make the best estimate you can of the amount and kind of lumber I have. I don't care for present returns, but I wish the property administered in accordance with the most advanced knowledge of the science of forestry."

"Mr. Barstow, you are good to me, too good, and I am as grateful as I can be, but I can't take money for amusing myself. You would be paying me for taking the most delightful excursion in the world, and there wouldn't be any other side to it. I couldn't make good to you in any way. I don't know anything about lumbering, forestry or practical surveying."

"Don't begin by criticizing your employer, Dick. Just make believe that he knows what he is about. I am not paying you for what you know now, but for what you will know in a few months. I am expecting great things of you. The science of forestry and economic methods of lumbering are fairly well understood in Canada. You will find yourselves with young men of education and enterprise, enthusiasts who think nothing of starting out alone on snowshoes for a week or a month in the woods, where the mercury in the thermometer often freezes. You will find your work cut out for you if you only keep up with them, and I am hoping that you will get near the head of your class. I want you to learn the business from the beginning to the end from the planting to the cutting of the tree, and from forest to freight car. So don't fear that you will not have a chance to earn your salary. Your pay and Ned's will be the same. It will take good care of you, but you will not find much over to waste. Here, Molly, come back and hear the rest of that romance that I interrupted. And don't look so cross at me next time I speak to Dick."

"Isn't he the nice old daddy?" said the girl to Dick, as she sat down near him. Dick looked as if he thought so too, but was troubled to find words to express all he felt. The launch, which was now flying up the coast, was just opposite the shack of the fisherman whom the boys had hired to help with the manatee which couldn't be found. Dick was telling the girl the story of the manatee when Ned put in an appearance.

"Run away, Molly. I want to talk to Dick."

"Neddy Barstow, when daddy says 'Run away, Molly,' I have to go, but when you say it, I stay right where I am. See?"

"But this is important, Molly. It's business."

135

"So am I important, even if I'm not business. If business is in a hurry, it can go ahead; if it isn't it can wait."

"Dick," said Ned, "Dad thinks we need a little vacation before going to work, and he offers to take us on a cruise in the Gypsey to the Bahamas and to Cuba, or to charter a light-draft boat that could go through the Bay of Florida and let us finish our cruise in the crocodile country, beginning where we turned back when the fresh water gave out. Maybe he will let Molly go."

"Let Molly go!" repeated the girl mockingly. "Only question is whether she will let you go. But I thought you said it was business. That isn't business; it's fun. We choose the small boat and the crocodiles. That will be new. I know all about the Gypsey now."

"Shall we let it go at that, Dick?"

"Sure. Wonder if we can find my crocodile again."

## CHAPTER XXIII

### MOLLY AND THE MANATEE

A week later the party of five (for both Molly and Dick insisted that Tom belonged) was sailing down the coast in the Irene, a half houseboat with auxiliary engine, which was sailed by Captain Hull. An engineer and a darky cook had been engaged, but the three young folks held a meeting and then announced that Dick had been elected engineer and Molly chief cook, with Ned as assistant. They added that the man engineer and the darky could "go bounce." When they notified Mr. Barstow of the result of the meeting he told them to see Captain Hull and that if they could stand their own cooking and engineering he thought the captain and himself might manage to live through it.

The captain grimly assented; said that he had been wondering where he could sleep his cook when it rained; that Dick couldn't be a worse engineer than the one he had engaged, and that he hoped he would keep sober more of the time than the other one was in the habit of doing.

The Irene was of less than three feet draft, and towed or carried on her davits a small launch and a skiff. Excepting when the wind was especially favorable, the sails were kept furled, and an awning stretched above the cabin-top made of it a pleasant lounging

136

place. When the Irene was opposite the mouth of Broad and Rodgers rivers, the whole party, including Tom, who kept beside Dick, were sitting on the cabin roof, and Mr. Barstow said to his son, as he pointed to Broad River:

"Is that the river where you caught your phantom manatee, that wasn't there when you brought a fisherman to get it? You know the story is all over Myers that you saw a porpoise and imagined the rest. How was it, Ned?"

"Yon've made a lot of fun of me, Dad, and Molly has bothered the life out of Dick about that manatee ghost. Now, if you will let Dick and me boss this boat for three days, no questions to be asked, we'll show you a sure-enough manatee and give some folks a chance to think up real handsome apologies."

"But supposing you don't make good?"

"Then Dick and I will do a whole lot of kow-towing ourselves."

"What do you say to that, Molly?"

"See here, sis," interrupted Ned, "it's up to you to put up or shut up. If you don't give us this chance to make good you are not to say 'manatee' again on this trip."

"Give 'em what they want, Daddy. They can't do much harm in three days, and just think of the fun I'll have with them afterwards."

"Well, hoys, you shall have your chance. It may prove a good lesson to you."

"You heard that, Captain? Dick and I are boss for three days, and we want this boat to start up Broad River immejit!"

"Tide's jist a-bilin' out of the river. It'll take all day to get anywhere. Hadn't you better anchor at the mouth of the river till it turns? We can run up the river in the night, so you won't lose any time."

The Irene's anchor was dropped behind the bar that lies opposite the mouth of the river, and Molly and the boys went out in the skiff to call on a family of pelicans which were keeping house on a little coral key, surrounded by oyster reefs, between Rodgers and Broad rivers. As the skiff neared the key the old birds flew lazily away and lit on a mud-flat a hundred yards distant, but the pelican children waddled around on the oyster reef without showing much alarm until Dick caught one, when the indignant bird struck him with its big bill and punched holes in his hat. As the tide fell the oyster bars were uncovered, the water shoaled on the mud-flats, and the boys gathered oysters from one, and clams weighing from half a pound to four pounds each from the other.

A fire was built on the reef, bread and coffee brought from the Irene, and Mr. Barstow and Captain Hull invited to a picnic supper which they were polite enough to say they enjoyed greatly. After supper Molly and the boys took a walk on the beach on the north side of Rodgers River and amused themselves by chasing the crabs that were skurrying along close to the shore to keep out of the way of their enemies. They had a lot of fun, but caught no crabs, until Dick went back to the Irene for a scoop-net and a bucket, which he soon filled with the crustaceans. Molly had never before seen shell-fish growing on trees, so Dick cut a few oyster-bearing branches from a mangrove tree and roasted bunches of the bivalves on the beach. When the sputtering of the oysters on the branch told Dick they were cooked, he hauled the limb from the coals, sat down with his companion on the beach, and with sharpened sticks the young people picked the roasted oysters from their shells, while Dick told the girl of that other picnic on the coast near-by after the waterspout had wrecked the Etta. They talked after the oysters were eaten and the fire had gone out, until Ned's voice came to them:

"Do you kids expect to settle here and grow up with the country? Don't you know it's 'most night, the tide's been right for the river for an hour, and everybody is waiting for you?"

When they reached the Irene, Mr. Barstow proposed putting off their start until morning to give Molly and him a chance to see the river as they sailed up it. Mr. Barstow replied to a quizzical look from his son:

"Of course, this doesn't come out of your time, Ned. You are to have your full three days."

"Maybe you'd like to see some fire-hunting," said the captain. "There are 'gators in these rivers, and there's time before the moon rises to find one or two. If you don't want one killed I'll fire a blank cartridge at him, unless you'd like to shine the eyes of one yourself."

"I don't think I'll try any fire-hunting, but I should like to see it done," said Mr. Barstow.

Dick was proud of his sculling, and at his request it was arranged that he should scull the skiff for the captain, while Ned was to pole the little motor-boat, in which his father and sister would go with him. Before they had gone far Dick found that he had overestimated his strength, and that handling the heavy sculling oar was too much for him. Mr. Barstow offered to pole the motor-boat, and Ned took Dick's place at the oar in the skiff, where Dick remained as a passenger. They entered Broad River and Ned sculled slowly along the bank, while the beam of light from the lantern, which was bound to the captain's forehead, played along the surface of the water under the mangroves that overhung the banks and sometimes swept the banks above the water. In the shallow places

138

mullet leaped wildly as the rays of the bull's-eye lantern fell on them, while porpoises sniffed and tarpon splashed in their light. Sculling was hard work for Ned, who had none of the easy and graceful swing with which Dick threw his weight on a sculling oar, a skill which he had acquired during his life on the sponger. Several times the oar jumped out of the scull hole in the skiff, and once Ned nearly went overboard. But a little extra noise didn't much disturb wild creatures that were fascinated by the light; and on the land 'coons sat motionless, two dots of greenish light told of a hypnotized wildcat, and when all on the skiff saw the light reflected from two big, round eyes, while the captain held the beam from the lantern steadily upon them, Dick whispered:

"What is it?"

"A big buck. Wish I didn't have a blank cartridge in the rifle," replied the captain.

They cruised for half a mile up Broad River, then back to its mouth against a tide that made the captain take the oars of the skiff, to which the painter of the motor-boat was then fastened. Then Ned sculled to the mouth of Rodgers River, where, upon a little beach, the captain first saw the gleam for which he had been looking. Then for a few minutes Dick took the oar and slowly and more slowly sculled toward those little round stars. Soon the light from the bull's-eye on the captain's forehead showed the head and body of the reptile, which remained as motionless as if cast in bronze, while Dick held the skiff in place that the launch might come near. With the roar of the blank cartridge came the scream of a girl and the quick scrambling of the alligator into the water. Every one wanted to continue the hunt, but the rising of the moon put a stop to the sport.

In the morning the tide was rushing up the river, and with it came rolling porpoises and schools of leaping tarpon.

"Couldn't you catch one of those tarpon?" asked Molly.

Dick said nothing, but Ned shook his head slowly, and Molly understood that he couldn't so quickly forget that desperate struggle in the water, during which two lives hung by a thread after a tarpon had wrecked their canoe.

As the Irene sailed up the river birds flew from the trees on her approach, alligators slid from their beds on the banks, and otters lifted their round heads above the surface of the stream. Six miles from its mouth the river spreads out into a bay, and as the boat was entering it Mr. Barstow called out:

"There is your manatee, sure enough, boys!"

A big, ugly head appeared beside the Irene for an instant,

followed by a column of water thrown in the air by the huge porpoise-like tail of the frightened animal. The anchor was quickly dropped and the little motor-boat, with Dick at the wheel and Mr. Barstow and Molly as passengers, started in pursuit of the sea-cow. Captain Hull and Ned were in the skiff, which was towed by the motor-boat. Every few minutes the long eel-grass of the shallow bay choked the propeller of the motor-boat. Then the motor was stopped, the skiff pulled under the stern of the power-boat, and Ned, with half his head and shoulders under water, tore the grass from the wheel. For two miles all eyes scanned the surface of the water without sight of the quarry; then came a shout from Molly:

"There it is!"

"Take the wheel, Molly; it's your manatee," replied Dick.

And the girl, without a hat and with her loosened hair streaming down her back, headed the power-boat straight for the creature, which was distant about the eighth of a mile. Twice the grass choked the wheel and twice with desperate haste it was cleared by Ned. The boat had gone many yards beyond the place where Molly had seen the animal when there was a great swirl in the water beside the craft, followed by other swirls, which grew less and less as they led in a straight line up a broad tideway that opened into the upper end of the bay. A moment later another series of swirls was seen and followed, after which, for a time, nothing was seen, although four pairs of eyes were scanning every inch of the stream ahead of the boat. Then came a cry from the captain, who had been cannily watching the water behind the craft. The sea-cow had turned around, and, swimming silently beneath the boat, would have escaped but for the glimpse the captain got of him as he rose to breathe just before reaching a bend in the stream, which would have hidden him from his pursuers. Soon the motor-boat was again on his trail, never to leave it till the creature was a captive. For the manatee was tired and had to come to the surface for breath at shorter and shorter intervals, until the power-boat almost ran over him at every turn.

"Turn us loose!" shouted Ned, and in a moment the skiff was free and being sculled by the captain toward the quarry, while Ned stood in the bow with a noosed rope in his hand. Soon the manatee rose beside the skiff, so near that Ned laid the noose over the creature's nose. But it didn't stay there, for a column of water rose in the air, and when it subsided Ned was swimming two yards from the skiff.

There was a cry from Molly in the motor-boat which no one noticed, for in half a minute Ned was back in the skiff and the

140

pursuit was on keener than ever. Every ten seconds the manatee came up to breathe, every time he rose he was driven back under water by the blow of the rope across his nose. Finally the half-strangled creature lifted his whole head out of the water and held it there long enough for Ned to slip the noose over it. The next instant the blow of the manatee's tail deluged the boy with water and jarred the skiff from bow to stern, which was then dragged through the water at a rate which for minutes left the motor-boat behind. The sea-cow carried the skiff around keys, through deep channels, over shallow banks and under bushes that projected from the shore, until the animal was fairly tired out. As the speed of the creature slackened, Ned drew the skiff close beside him, and plunging overboard, threw his left arm over the neck and with his right hand grasped the right flipper of the manatee. Then Captain Hull took a hand, and pulling the skiff up to the manatee was soon swimming beside him and clinging to his left flipper.

Dick slowed down the motor, while Molly kept the boat circling around the swimmers until the manatee surrendered and became quiet as a cow. The motor was stopped, and the sea-cow was brought beside the boat, where Molly patted the head and laid her hand on the soft lips of the gentle creature.

"Now, Daddy," said Ned, "Dick and I want a certificate that this isn't a phantom manatee or a porpoise."

"I'll certify to that, Ned. You boys have made good, although nobody ever doubted it, anyway, for the fisherman was only having a little fun with you."

The manatee was so tractable that Captain Hull swam back for the skiff, while Ned loosened his hold on the flipper of the creature. Suddenly a cascade of water half-filled the power-boat, drenched every one in it, and the manatee disappeared. Ned was chagrined, but Mr. Barstow cheered him:

"It is all for the best, Ned. He had done all he could do for us. We hadn't time to arrange for his shipment, and so had to set him free. The only thing I am sorry for is that I didn't go overboard, too, and have some of the fun. I am just as wet as you are, without having anything-to show for it."

"Me, too," said Molly, whose red cheeks and sparkling eyes shone from among streaming mermaid tresses, and whose pretty frock had been deluged.

"Dad," said Ned, after they were back on the Irene, "you know Dick and I are in command for two days more."

"I thought you were to have charge for three days, or until you found a manatee."

141

"No, sir; three days—seventy-two hours, and not a minute less."

"What are you going to do with all that time?"

"I have elected myself senior boss and Dick junior boss, and we are going to show you and Molly the Everglades. The Irene will start down Broad River at once. But Molly is to take the power-boat through the cut-off to Rodgers River, and down that river to its mouth, where she will find us. Oh, by the way, Dick will go with her as engineer, but subject to her orders."

When the Irene was opposite the cut-off, the power-boat, with Molly and Dick on board, was set adrift and was soon twisting and turning at half speed as it followed the channel of the crooked creek. Swimming through the creek would have made a snake dizzy, and the girl at the wheel had to keep it spinning. There were logs to be dodged and sharp-ended stumps to be avoided. Trees lay nearly across the stream, leaving barely the width of the boat to spare, and others under which the boat had to be driven between flexible branches, while the steerswoman crouched low down in the craft. There were birds and beasts on the bank, fish and reptiles in the water, but the girl could spare them scarcely a glance. Great spiders hung in midair on nets that stretched from bank to bank, and Molly's face was matted with webs that she could not avoid, while her teeth were tightly clenched lest she scream when the hairy legs of a spider with a spread of five inches traveled across her face. Dick saw her trouble and came forward to where he could lean ahead of her and take the brunt of the spider's work. Molly spared him a grateful glance, but got in trouble for it the next instant. For just then a quick turn of the craft happened to be necessary, and although Dick helped to roll the wheel, it was too late, and because of the inattention of a moment the motor-boat crashed into the bank. The pilot and engineer were thrown violently against the wheel, but nothing was injured excepting the temper of the girl, who said to her companion:

"That was all your fault, Dick Williams, and I wish you would go back to your engine. I will try to manage the wheel by myself."

After two miles of squirmy navigation the boat came out into the broad, beautiful Rodgers River, down which they turned; and when Dick pointed out where the tarpon had wrecked their canoe and stunned him, and told of Ned's struggles to save his life, the girl's voice trembled and there were tears in her eyes as she listened and asked questions. The tide was low when they arrived at the mouth of the river, and Molly ran the boat on one of the oyster bars that form a network across the entrance to Broad and Rodgers rivers. Almost the instant the boat touched, Dick was overboard heaving on the bow, and soon had the craft afloat. Then turning to Molly, he said, while mischief sparkled in his eyes:

"I am sorry I ran you on that bar, Miss Barstow."

"You shouldn't bear malice, Dick," replied the girl.

## CHAPTER XXIV

### TO THE GLADES IN THE "IRENE"

They found the Irene waiting for them near the mouth of the river, with Ned impatient to be off to catch the inflowing-tide from the mouth of Harney's River, which was about two miles down the coast.

It was still daylight when they crossed the bar and passed the little key inside the mouth of the river, but they sailed up the stream by the light of the stars, which gave mystic beauty to the smooth water and the shadowy outlines of the tropical forest that bordered the banks of the river. Captain Hull anchored the Irene for the night in Tussock Bay, at the head of the lower division of Harney's River, because, as he said, he needed all the daylight he could get when he tackled the crooked courses between Tussock Bay and the Everglades.

When the anchor was hoisted in the morning, Dick was at the wheel, which he held on to when the captain came up to relieve him. The captain stood by as the boy steered across the bay, and wondered at the chance that kept him for miles on exactly the right course. As the boat was passing Tussock Key, Dick headed up to the northeast.

"Too far north," said the captain. "Course is east-southeast."

"No talking to the man at the wheel," said Dick, and Captain Hull laughed and waited for the trouble that was coming. But no trouble came, and the Irene twisted in and out, always in plenty of water, for a mile and a half of crooked creek, until it floated in a wider stream, the banks of which were covered with long prairie grass, when Dick handed over the wheel to the captain, saying:

"Guess you know the rest of the way, don't you, Captain? If you get in any trouble call on me."

"That was one on me," said Captain Hull as he took the wheel.

143

"I never came that way before. Wonder who taught you piloting? Mighty few pilots can find their way up this river."

"I came that way," said Dick nonchalantly, "because the water is deeper and there is less grass. The other river is pretty shallow and gets badly choked up at this season."

"That's so," replied the captain, "but I'd like to know who told you."

It took the rest of the day to reach the Everglades. There were narrow streams so crooked that the Irene had to be poled around the sharp corners, broad, shallow rivers, so choked with eel and manatee-grass that every five minutes one of the boys went overboard to clear the clogged propeller, and twisting creeks, through which the water of the Everglades poured so swiftly, that to make headway and avoid snags kept the captain busy at the wheel and the boys fending off from the banks with oars. Sometimes for miles the channel was clear; and while the captain stood at the wheel the rest of the exploring family sat upon the cabin roof and chattered like children about the turtle and terrapin heads that dotted the surface, the leaping young tarpon, grave old alligators, shy otters, and birds that flew from the trees or soared overhead.

The sensitive Tom resented Dick's neglect, and was seen sitting on the after end of the cabin, in front of the wheel, making friends with the captain. Every few minutes Tom put out a paw and rested it on the captain's hand as it rolled the wheel. Then Tom would look up in his face, and finally rubbed his cheek on the captain's hand, and after that became his shadow. That night Tom abandoned his sleeping place beside Dick's bunk and turned in with the captain. Dick was a little annoyed at first, but his conscience told him that he had neglected Tom, and had himself to blame.

When the anchor was dropped, the Irene rested in a solid mass of lily pads, with her bowsprit extending over the border of the Everglades, which stretched out eastward, a great, grassy, overflowed meadow, dotted with keys, to the horizon. A slough of clear water, deep enough to float the little power-boat, zigzagged out into the Glades, and the captain, with Mr. Barstow, Molly and Dick in the craft, followed it for more than a mile. There was water enough over the light grass of the Glades to float the skiff, which Ned poled through a carpet of white pond-lilies, that here and there covered the surface. Many little grassy mounds showed where an alligator had his cave. From one of them an alligator slid out and started across the Glades at full speed. Ned was soon on his trail, poling like mad. He was nearly up to the reptile when it swung around and darted away at right angles to its former course, gaining many yards on its pursuer, for the grass prevented the quick turning of the skiff. Time after time the reptile repeated this dodge, time after time the boy was near enough to have touched the alligator with a pole, but always he dodged, until Ned was too exhausted to follow the creature any farther.

"Oh, I wish you could have caught it," said Molly when Ned returned.

"We'll get one to-morrow sure," said Dick, while Ned's only comment was:

"Don't you get Dick to try fool things, sis."

"Captain," said Dick that evening, "I want an alligator, and if you will help Ned pole in the skiff in the morning until we are near enough to one, I'll either put a rope over his head or go overboard and grab him."

"Don't try that on these 'gators; but I'll rig up a harpoon for you, and if you can hit one with that there won't be any trouble in getting him."

"I don't want to kill the thing with a harpoon."

"I'll fix that. I'll stop down the harpoon so you can't drive it more than an inch beyond the hide, and the 'gator will never know he's hurt. He'll think a fly lit on him."

In the morning, as they were about to start on the 'gator chase, Ned said to his father:

"This is our third day and our last chance, so we have got to keep busy."

"Not quite," replied Mr. Barstow. "You and Dick have done so well that you can stay in command until I have to call you down."

"Where do I come in?" said Molly. "Haven't I got something to say about things?"

"Looks as if you were having too much to say now. You mustn't try to influence the officers of this ship or lure them away from their duties."

The little face that Molly made at her father wasn't quite respectful, but Mr. Barstow only laughed at it.

On this day of the 'gator hunt, Molly took the wheel and her father ran the engine of the motor-boat, while Ned and the captain poled the skiff and Dick stood in the bow with the harpoon pole. They soon started a nine-foot alligator out of his cave, and after a chase of ten minutes and a few sudden turns were so near the reptile that Dick fixed his harpoon to the end of the pole and stood ready. Twice he threw and missed, and each time many yards were lost while the pole was being recovered. Dick was so mortified at

145

missing that he offered the harpoon to the captain, who refused it, saying:

"You threw all right and almost got him last throw. You'll fetch him next time."

The captain's prophecy was fulfilled and at the next throw the harpoon pierced the soft hide of the hind leg of the reptile. From the beginning of the chase the alligator had been making for the river and was within a hundred yards of it when struck. They headed it off from the river and Dick dragged on the line while the others poled until the skiff was beside the 'gator. A heavy blow on the bow of the boat from the tail of the reptile and the big open jaws with their rows of great gleaming teeth that swung before Dick's face made him drop the line and fall backward into the skiff, while the alligator started off in a new direction. On the next approach the creature turned on the skiff again and though the captain fended it off with an oar the reptile had the best of the battle. Several times Dick brought the skiff near the alligator and tried to lasso it with the painter of the boat, but the reptile was too wary for him. The captain suggested running the reptile into the river, saying it would be easier to take it aboard from the deeper water. As soon as they gave the brute a chance it plunged into the river and towed the skiff two hundred yards down the stream, then turning and rising to the surface the alligator came with open mouth at Dick, who sprang from his place in the bow and, seizing the painter, the boy soon had a rope around the head of the brute and its jaws tied. They tried towing the alligator up the river to the Irene, but it is easier to drag an anchor than an alligator. Then as Dick was winded the captain and Ned finally hauled it aboard the skiff, where for a time it amused itself by trying to smash the skiff or knock somebody overboard with its tail. It became perfectly quiet before the Irene was reached, when the captain dragged on the rope which bound its jaws while Ned boosted with his arms around the tail of the brute. But the alligator was playing 'possum and had Ned just where it wanted him and, with a swing of its powerful tail, lifted the boy in the air and neatly tossed him overboard. It was fortunate for Ned that he was holding the alligator so tightly that it was more of a push than a blow that he received. As it was, the breath was so completely knocked out of him that for an instant he could not swim and was drifting with the current, feebly paddling with his hands, just enough to keep afloat, when he felt Dick's supporting hand and heard a voice in his ear:

"Don't say you're hurt, Neddy."

146

"No—no—not a—bit. Nothing but—the talk—knocked out of me. Gee! Wouldn't he make a fine spanking machine?"

Both of the boys were glad when the captain came for them with the skiff and they were saved a hard swim against the current.

"Where is our alligator?" said Ned to the captain. "Hope you didn't turn him loose."

"Nope. He's all right. He slipped back into the water when you went in swimming, and of course I knew you wanted him looked after first, so I gave his line a turn round the big cleat. When I left he was trying to pull it out."

When the boys were back on the Irene, Molly clung to her brother's hand, hardly able to speak, while Mr. Barstow said to his son:

"Is that the sort of thing you boys have been doing in your odd hours when you were not squabbling with panthers or mixing up with tarpon? I am afraid you need a traveling guardian to look after you."

A hundred feet was added to the rope that held the alligator and he was left to pasture in the water until the Irene was ready to sail, when he was hauled aboard the skiff and lashed there. While he was being tied he was perfectly tame and peaceful, but, though he looked as if butter wouldn't melt in his mouth, no one trusted him and even the captain fought shy of his tail.

For two miles from the Glades the river was broad and the navigation, excepting for many bunches of moss and manatee grass, was easy. Then came half a mile of a twisting narrow creek, in places not twice the width of the Irene, through which poured swiftly the whole volume of the big river. At the head of this creek the captain came to anchor.

"We won't get through this creek without a lot of trouble. The current will throw us against the bank a dozen times and we haven't speed to prevent it and couldn't turn the corners if we had. The launch must go ahead and keep the bow of the big boat out of the bushes if it can. Then we can't be bothered with the skiff or the 'gator. We'd likely lose both. Somebody must take the launch and tow the skiff through and then come back, if he can get back, and help the big boat through. I hate to do it, but we can't tow the skiff and, of course, it would be torn off of the davits in two minutes. We are going to scrape the sides and perhaps tear out half the rigging of the Irene, anyhow. Now who volunteers to tow the skiff through the creek? I can't go because the launch may not be able to buck the current and get back and I must stand by the big boat."

147

"I volunteer," said Molly, "if you can get anybody to go as engineer."

Every one laughed at this, excepting Molly, who blushed a little, and Dick pulled the power boat up beside the Irene as if he were afraid that somebody would change her mind if there was any delay.

"Can she do it and is it quite safe?" asked Mr. Barstow.

"Do it as well as anybody. They may swamp the skiff or get caught in a corner, but they can get out on the bank without anything worse than a ducking."

As the power boat started, with Molly at the wheel, Dick standing by the motor and the skiff hauled close under the stern, the captain called out to Dick:

"Full speed. It's your only chance to get through. Don't bother with the skiff, but keep an oar handy to fend off from the bank." The speed of the boat was doubled by the current and Dick's heart was in his mouth as the banks flew past and some log-guarded point threatened to smash the bow of the boat. But Molly was quick to see the coming peril and the wheel rolled swiftly to starboard or port, always in time to avert it. There were double turns which the boat could never have made but for the rush of the current which often swept them aside from a stump or log that it seemed impossible to avoid. It was a thrilling experience to both pilot and engineer, and when the broad, placid river opened before them and the perilous trip was past, the girl turned a flushed and beaming face toward her companion and said:

"Wasn't it just lovely?"

And the boy replied with enthusiasm:

"It was glorious!"

Dick fastened the skiff to a tree on the bank, gave a look at the lashing of the alligator and the return through the creek began. There was nothing exciting about this trip. As the craft was working against the current, the flow of the water balanced the power of the engine, and log stumps and points on the bank were passed slowly, inch by inch. Often there was no progress and then the boat was steered close beside the bank and Dick pushed with his oar against the trees until less swift water was found. The run down the creek was made in three minutes. The return 'took half as many hours. On the Irene all were anxious but the captain and Tom. At the end of an hour Ned was for starting down the creek with the big boat, but Captain Hull said:

"No. It may take them three hours. Give them two at least. If we start now we'll make sure of a smash-up."

In another minute the motor of the launch could be heard, although it was half an hour more before the wanderers were welcomed aboard the Irene and their story told.

"It's our turn for trouble now," said the captain, "and we're likely to get it, good and plenty."

"Want me to tow?" said Dick.

"Sure," replied the captain.

"Me, too?" inquired Molly.

"No," replied the captain, rather sharply. "It isn't piloting this time. You can't steer the launch much while it's fast to the big boat. Best you can do is to fend off and then you're likely to get caught, and when you do get caught and fifteen tons comes down on you at ten miles an hour, somebody has got to be spry."

"Is there much danger to whoever goes in the little boat?" asked Mr. Barstow.

"Some, not much. It's the big boat that is likely to get caught and if the launch did get stuck and we couldn't sheer off it would only mean a quick jump and a little swim and—a busted launch."

The Irene started down the creek with her engine at half speed, the captain at the wheel and Dick standing in the bow of the motor boat with an oar at hand. Molly stood in the companionway at the captain's request because he feared her being swept overboard by overhanging branches. Mr. Barstow and Ned were stationed near the bow with long poles for fending off from the banks when necessary. The first trouble came from a wooded point on the starboard side, but Dick swung the power boat to port while Ned nearly went overboard as he threw his weight on the pole with which he was fending. The bow cleared the point, though the bowsprit swept the bushes and a low-growing branch tore out the screens on the starboard side. Before the point was passed Dick had the launch on the starboard side, working to turn the Irene before she should strike the opposite bank. The efforts of all hands failed to make the turn in time and a stump by the bank caught in the jib-stay of the boat and held her fast. As the stern of the Irene swung on the point she had nearly passed, she lay broad-side to the current, subject to all its power.

"We're in for it now, if that jib-stay don't part pretty sudden," said the captain.

And before the words were out of his mouth the eye-bolt that held the stay broke short off and the Irene's bow swung down the stream. The boat was not caught badly again, although her fore rigging on the port side was carried away and her sides somewhat scarred. The only accident that threatened was prevented by a

149

precaution which Dick had taken. He had fastened his tow line to the stern of the launch with a knot that could be slipped and led the end of the line forward to where he stood by the wheel. It happened that when nearly through the creek it became needful to drag the bow of the Irene far to port. Dick did this, but found himself in a pocket from which he could not escape and in position to be dragged stern first under the bow of the big boat. A quick jerk on the towing line, and the launch was safe behind the Irene. There was no more trouble for the big boat, which a minute later was headed down the broad but shallow river, at half speed, while Dick picked up the skiff with its alligator passenger who slowly opened one eye when spoken to. In a few minutes the Irene was traveling at full speed toward Tussock Bay while her joyful passengers sat on the cabin roof and talked of perils which had passed.

From Tussock Bay to the coast, the Irene sailed by way of a branch of Shark River. The deep water of this river near the Gulf of Mexico was roughened by a high wind and the rising and falling of the skiff seemed to excite the alligator which for hours had been as quiet as if he were asleep or dead. Slowly lifting his huge head over the side of the skiff he gave a lurch which strained the rope that held him and enough of the weight of the reptile was on the side of the skiff to capsize it. The captain, who first heard the struggle and saw the upset of the skiff, shouted to Ned, who was below oiling the engine, to shut off the power. Before the Irene lost her headway Ned was in the river with the alligator, resting on the bottom of the skiff which he rolled from over the reptile to save it from drowning. Instantly the freed jaws of the alligator opened wide in his face and the boy threw himself backward in the water and swam swiftly away from his dangerous companion. The rope had slipped from the head of the reptile, which now seized the gunwale of the boat and thrashed about until he had freed himself from the rope which bound him, after which he quickly disappeared. Half an hour later Ned was pouring his grievances into the ear of his chum, who was resting in his bunk from the fatigue of the morning.

"Don't you think, Dick, it was bad enough to be scared to death by a whopping old alligator that I thought was going to bite me in two, without being scolded by everybody on board for recklessness? First there was Dad, and he uses pretty powerful language when he gets real earnest, then Captain Hull gave it to me like a Dutch uncle, and even Molly lectured me and squeezed out a few tears. I told Dad it wasn't half as bad as your jumping in the way of that panther, but he said that was altogether a different thing and had some sense in it."

150

# CHAPTER XXV

## IN FLORIDA BAY

After the Irene had sailed twenty miles down the coast and was about opposite East Cape (Sable) Captain Hull asked for his orders.

"Isn't Madeira Hammock on the coast, about thirty miles from here?" inquired Ned.

"Yes, but you will have to go seventy to get there. You've got to go way round by the keys."

"Isn't there water enough for the Irene along the coast?"

"Isn't enough to float the skiff. You can go about ten miles. After that there's an inch of water and I reckon a mile of blue, soft, sticky mud. I've been a few feet down in it and the farther I went the softer and stickier it got."

"Suppose we go the ten miles you talk about what will we find?"

"Tarpon, sharks, porpoises, lots of fish, birds and enough sawfish to make a picket fence of their saws all around the coast."

"That's us, Captain," said Ned.

And the Irene's mud hook went to the bottom that night in eight feet of water off Joe Kemp's Key.

In the shoal water over the broad banks which lay to the south and east of the Irene the bayonet fins of many tarpon rose high above the surface as the fish beneath them pursued their prey. Often the two fins shown by a wandering shark swept swiftly across a bank, or three big reddish fins moving in a straight line slowly behind a great, swaying, four-foot weapon marked the course of a fifteen-foot sawfish. There was water to float the power boat in the channels between the banks, and families of porpoises or dolphins were always ready to serve as pilots and point the path through these labyrinthine waterways. A school of porpoises, rolling in the water and leaping in the air, passed the motor boat as if they had been telephoned for in the greatest haste. Two minutes later, a quarter of a mile away, a great splashing could be seen and huge bodies hurled in the air, which seemed to be filled with flying fragments.

The power boat, with Molly at the wheel, started for the fray at its best speed and when it reached the battlefield its occupants saw a little band of porpoises in the midst of a great school of silver mullet. Each blow of a porpoise tail sent several mullet flying in the air, each blow that was struck was followed by a quick turn or leap

151

of the agile animal for the victim which it caught before it fell. Ned and Dick were in the skiff which had been towed by the power boat, hoping to harpoon a sawfish or a shark. They had not before thought of the swift and wary porpoise. They called to the captain to cast them loose, and soon Ned was poling the skiff toward the busy porpoises while Dick stood in the bow of the skiff with his harpoon handy. Quick as a flash the porpoises separated and scattered in every direction and the boys followed several in vain. Then Molly took a hand in the game and sent the power boat at one after another of them until the captain called to her:

"If you'll stick to one you'll run him down."

Then Molly kept steadily after a single porpoise, until the animal came to understand that it was the chosen victim, and quickly put half a mile between it and its pursuer. In a few minutes the half mile between them had vanished and the creature made another frantic dash. After that it swam back and forth as if confused, and traveled in narrowing circles, wasting its strength, while the wheel of the pursuing boat rolled back and forth without ceasing as it followed the course of the animal or took short cuts to head it off. The boys came near with the skiff, but the worried quarry paid so little heed to them that soon Dick sunk his harpoon in the tail of the porpoise. All the life and strength of the creature seemed to come back and it threw a column of water in the air which nearly swamped the skiff, while Dick's hands were torn and blistered by the outgoing harpoon line, before way could be had on the skiff. The frantic creature tore back and forth, sometimes striking the skiff a powerful blow with its tremendous tail as it passed, sometimes towing it at high speed until Dick, who was not yet strong, was more tired than the porpoise. He changed places with Ned and the two were nearly worn out when the porpoise surrendered.

They took the harpoon from the animal's tail and tried to drag the creature over the gunwale of the skiff, but found it too heavy for them. At length they lifted and dragged the porpoise up on the gunwale of the skiff which they pressed down until the water was beginning to flow over it. Half of the animal was now over the side of the skiff and the boys threw their weight backward expecting to roll the porpoise into the bottom of the craft. This would have happened if the porpoise had kept still, which it neglected to do. With a blow of its tail on the water the animal threw its own body forward and Ned and Dick found assistance instead of resistance as they pulled, and promptly went over backward into the water with the porpoise and the capsized skiff on top of them. When they got to the surface their captive had escaped, but the power boat was beside them with three highly edified occupants. After the skiff had been righted and bailed out and the floating poles, oar, hats, and line tub gathered in, Ned saw the fin and swaying tail of a shark cutting the surface of the water near them, and calling on Dick to take the harpoon, began to pole the skiff toward the tiger of the sea.

"Look out," shouted the captain. "That's a shark. You'll lose your iron if you strike him."

Th captain spoke too late, for the shark was struck and the skiff was towed at speed for a hundred feet by the angry fish, which then turned and rolled up on the taut line till it caught the rope in its mouth and bit it in two as easily as scissors snip thread.

"Told you so," said the captain. "A shark always bites the line and often rolls up in it. An alligator always rolls up in it, but can't bite it. I've had an alligator roll up against a skiff and pretty near come aboard after I'd harpooned it. There's another harpoon on the Irene, and I'll fix it to-night with a few feet of wire for the next shark to bite on. I reckon it'll give him a surprise."

Molly was in full command of the power boat for the day, and as harpooning was over, she ran it at her own sweet will. Sometimes the captain helped her with a hint when he saw her heading for water that was too shoal. The course she took was southerly and brought her near Man-o'-war Bush, from which rose hundreds of man-o'-war hawks, or frigate pelicans, the most graceful bird on the continent, excepting the fork-tailed kite. These birds soared high overhead, circling, rising and falling with scarcely a perceptible motion of their wings. From another key a flock of roseate spoon-bill, or pink curlew, flew at the approach of the boat, while young herons sat fearlessly on branches of trees or spread wings and stretched long legs as they fled in affright.

That night Mr. Barstow called a council on the cabin top.

"Boys, I would like to have you make Miami in four days from now, if you can manage it."

"That's easy," said Ned. "We can make the trip in a day. That leaves us one day here and two at Madeira Hammock to find Dick's pet crocodile."

"If you're going to Miami by way of Madeira Hammock," said the captain, "you'd better allow two days for the trip. You're likely to get some tangled up in that country."

"Then we'll cut out our day here. We have had our share of fun out of this place. What is there in that bay to the east of us, Captain?"

"There's a creek that leads to the Cuthbert Rookery, but it isn't

153

the season for that. It's a hard trip anyway, through small salt-water lakes and little overgrown creeks where you have to drag your skiff most of the way. And you've got to carry all the water you drink and you won't find that a joke."

"We have had all we want of that kind of country, Captain, so we'll hike out of here at daylight and get to Madeira Hammock quick as you can find the way."

"I can find the way now, anyhow as far as Lignum Vitae Key, and if the tide doesn't bother me too much in the cut, maybe to Hammer Point. Beyond that I want daylight and then I ain't sure. Do you want to make a night run?"

"Sure," said both the boys together.

"If you will excuse me from any share in this night navigation," said Mr. Barstow, "I think I will turn in. How is it with you, Molly?"

"Oh, I'll stay up a while and help Captain Hull navigate the ship."

The moon rose soon after the anchor was broken out, and its light reflected from the white canvas of the bellying sails and the tops of the white-capped waves, gave a dream-like beauty to the night. Captain Molly called to Engineer Dick:

"Stop that noise in the engine room!" and Dick promptly shut off the gasoline from the motor. Captain Hull made no complaint of this mutinous interference with his authority, but said:

"That's right, we don't need the engine now and I reckon we ain't going to need it to-night."

The wind was fair and strong from the north, and every minute its sweep grew wider and the waves bigger as the Irene drew from under the shelter of the cape. The captain and Ned stood by the wheel, while the girl and Dick sat on the front of the cabin in the moonlight, watching the white water that rose from under the bow of the clumsy craft, with each heavy blow that it struck upon the waves.

As they sailed the wind grew stronger and at Horse-neck Shoals the crest of breaking waves covered the deck of the Irene with foam. Following the swish of each heaving wave as it lifted and swept past the boat came a heavy jar as the craft struck in the soft mud beneath her and her headway was checked.

"It's all right," said the captain, in answer to Ned's look of anxiety. "I expected her to touch, but she'll pull through."

No one else was alarmed, for Mr. Barstow was asleep in his bunk below, while Molly and Dick were too busy watching the effect of the moonlight on the breaking waves and the distant keys to

154

notice that anything unusual was happening. Soon the water became deeper, the waves ceased breaking and subsided, and the Irene sailed smoothly on till she was hauled up in the wind to enter the cut in the bank near Lignum Vitae Key, through which an adverse tide was pouring. Dick was called from his post near the bow to start the motor, which was kept running until the boat had made her way through the channel between the white banks that showed clear under the moon as daylight could have made them. Then the motor was shut off and Dick returned to his post and resumed his study of moonlight effects as its rays fell on the palms of Lignum Vitae, the line of outer keys, the Matecumbies, and the jewel of an Indian Key, of which he told Molly the legend. At this Molly jumped up and said:

"It's all too lovely for anything and Daddy has got to come on deck and see it."

She went below and when she returned had Mr. Barstow in tow, to whom she pointed out the beauties of sea and sky, of clouds and light just as Dick had been doing to her. Then she went for Captain Hull, who turned the wheel over to Ned and came forward, where he answered the rapid fire of the girl's questions, about Shell, McGinty and other keys as they passed them and about the channel and cuts through which their course lay, until he assured her he had told all he knew and if she remembered it she was as good a pilot as he. But questions continued until, having passed Tavernier Creek and neared Hammer Point, the Irene was anchored for the night.

All hands were on deck when the rays of the next morning's sun first fell on the mirror-like water about them, but Ned spoke sadly as he said:

"I've shipped as cook and I s'pose I've got to get breakfast, but I wish my assistant didn't waste so much of her time."

"If you'd let me keep the cook I hired we'd have crawfish for breakfast," said Captain Hull.

"Where would we get them?" inquired Ned.

"Every one of these coral keys is built on crawfish and Snake Creek here is full of 'em."

"Then after you've shown us a lot of crawfish and we've caught them we'll have breakfast."

Captain Hull lashed two tarpon hooks to broomsticks, and getting in the skiff with Molly and the two boys, poled to the nearest key. Beneath the water the steep coral banks of the key were filled with deep holes from out of many of which long feelers projected. Pushing a hook into one of these holes the captain gave it a quick turn and brought out a squirming, squeaking imitation of a young

155

lobster. Then he handed the hooks to the boys. Ned got overboard and began to haul out crawfish at the rate of two a minute. Dick was less successful, for Molly had promptly commandeered his hook and left him nothing to do but watch her when she tried to hook the shell-fish. They didn't get many fish and when Ned came along with a bunch of crawfish which he dropped in the skiff, he said:

"Here, you kids, you aren't earning your salt. Just take my hook, Dick, and catch some crawfish. I'll help Molly do whatever she's doing."

On the way to the Irene Molly called out:

"Oh, the beautiful, beautiful, bubble!"

"Don't touch it," shouted Dick.

But he was too late, for Molly had picked up a Portuguese man-o'-war and sat wringing her hands with the pain of its poison. For, while nothing in nature is more exquisite, few things are more virulent than this animated, opalescent, iridescent bubble with its long, delicate, purplish tentacles.

Molly's hand pained her all that day and the next, while Dick's commiseration was boundless, but was kept in restraint by Ned, who frequently assured both of them that, although a surgical case, it was probably not quite hopeless. A run of two hours in directions that varied, but averaged northwest, brought the Irene to Madeira Hammock, where the anchor was dropped.

## CHAPTER XXVI

### MADEIRA HAMMOCK AND—THE END

Mr. Barstow wanted to explore Deer Key which was nearby and Ned took him there in the power boat. The captain took Molly and Dick out in the skiff to show them a crocodile and Dick stood in the bow with the harpoon while Molly sat amidship and the captain poled. Almost as they left the Irene they saw a crocodile swimming under water near them, but failed to get another sight of him. They cruised vainly in open water, beside banks and in narrow channels. Finally while going through a narrow creek a wave rolling high ahead of the skiff showed that some big creature was fleeing before them. The next moment a four-foot weapon of a hand's breadth, armed with a double row of teeth, was lifted for a second above the

156

surface and was followed by the three fins, tandem, that proved the presence of a sawfish. Dick fairly quivered with excitement as he held his harpoon at ready.

"Captain," said he sharply, "will there be the least bit of danger to Miss Barstow if I strike that fish now?"

"There'll be some, of course. If he turns round and comes back at us in this narrow creek the only safe place will be in the bottom of the boat."

"Dick Williams, don't you stop for me. I'm not a bit afraid. If you don't harpoon that sawfish and give me his saw, I won't speak to you for a week," said the excited girl.

"No use, Molly, I wouldn't do it if it meant that you'd never speak to me."

"If Miss Barstow will wait on the bank for half an hour you can bring her the saw, all right," said the captain, who seemed anxious to oblige both of the passengers.

"Put me ashore quick, then."

The girl was soon standing on the bank and the chase was renewed. A hundred yards farther up the narrow stream the great sawfish was found swimming slowly across a bank where the water was shoal, with his two fins and tail showing in line above the water. As the harpoon pole was lifted and Dick's every muscle strained for the throw, the captain shouted:

"Throw three feet ahead of that forward fin. That's where his back is."

The harpoon struck the fish in the middle of his wide back and as the freed pole splashed in the water the sawfish made a mighty swirl and was off at express speed. The line was strong, the barb of the harpoon was under the tough leather of the creature's back, and the skiff seemed to fly through the water as Dick gave the line a turn around his hand and the captain fended the skiff from the banks when sharp turns were made by the flying fish as it followed the channels of the crooked creeks. Sometimes the stream broadened, often it narrowed; once the sawfish dashed through an overgrown waterway where Dick and the captain crouched to the gunwale to avoid the arching branches that swept over and tore at the sides of the skiff. There was half an hour of this work. Dick's hands were blistered and numb and his brain dizzy with the quick turns and changing courses of the fish, when suddenly he became panic-stricken and called to his companion:

"Captain! Are you perfectly sure you know where you are? Sure you can find Miss Barstow?"

The captain laughed.

157

"Find her? Why she's here within a hundred feet of you now."

And, sure enough, the next turn in the creek showed the girl standing on the bank by the water's edge.

"Can't I get aboard?" she called out as the skiff swept past, and Dick would have said "Yes," but the captain shook his head.

"There's trouble ahead. That fish is just getting ready to fight."

Before they had passed out of sight of the girl, the sawfish turned around and for the first time headed for the skiff.

"Down, quick!" yelled the captain and both Dick and he crouched low in the skiff as a great broad sword, swung with all the power of the tremendous fish, swept over their heads. As the angry creature passed them, a second blow which fell upon the skiff and threatened to wreck it was echoed by a cry from the girl. The attack on the skiff was the last great effort of the fish, and though he still swam strongly he could be controlled. The captain ran the skiff on a shallow bank and helped Dick with the line until sixteen feet of fierceness lay stranded on the bank. As the sawfish is a species of shark, Dick had no hesitancy about killing it, but wanted Molly to first see his captive and have a look at her saw, before it left the place where it grew. The captain brought the girl, and then a rope was made fast to the saw of the fish and tied to a tree, after which the brute's brain was explored with an axe and the saw cut off as a trophy.

"Better wake up," shouted the captain the next morning, before the boys were stirring. "There's a shark outside waiting for you, and I've wired your harpoon line."

The boys omitted their ablutions that morning and must have hurried their devotions, for three minutes after they were called found them aboard the skiff which they drove toward a big fin and a swaying tail, which was cutting the water a hundred yards from the Irene. As they neared the shark, Dick took the harpoon pole and made ready with the harpoon, while Ned sculled quietly in the wake of the ugly fish. Twice the shark heard them and darted away, but on the third approach Dick drove the iron deep in the back of the brute. The shark lashed out with its tail, sending the water flying as the harpoon struck, and then made a straight-away dash for a hundred yards while the boys rode in triumph behind it. Then the maddened creature turned, and rolling up on the line, bit it savagely but vainly.

Again and again the brute dashed away and again and again it turned, biting at the line and attacking the boat with its teeth. Dick held the skiff close to the shark, which lifted its head and seized the gunwale in its huge mouth, when Ned struck the furious creature a powerful blow on its nose with the axe. For a moment the brute seemed paralyzed, but soon returned to the attack, when the boy drove the point of the big gaff through the tough hide of the tiger of the sea.

Ned held on to the handle of the gaff, although almost dragged overboard during the first wild struggles of his captive, and then hauled the head of the brute over the gunwale, where a few blows with the axe ended the trouble.

When the boys got back to the Irene, Ned was happily surprised to find ready a dainty breakfast which his assistant had graciously prepared for all hands and which drew from him the unusual praise:

"A girl on a cruise is a mighty nice thing—sometimes."

The day was to be devoted to crocodile hunting and Dick went in the skiff with the captain, while Molly was put in command of the power boat with Ned as engineer and Mr. Barstow as passenger.

Several crocodile caves were found, but none of the inhabitants were at home. One large crocodile showed itself for an instant, but the river was deep, the overhanging banks offered good hiding places, and the reptile escaped. It was after they had given the hunt up for the day and were on their way to the Irene that Dick, who had stood faithfully at his post in the bow, with his harpoon ready, threw hastily at something he saw crawling on the bottom and found on the end of his line a squirming baby crocodile, scarcely four feet long. The harpoon had barely touched the side of the little reptile and the barb held by a thread-like bit of skin. When the boy saw how lightly the iron was held he dropped the line and grabbed the baby with both hands. His arms were scratched and his clothing torn by the needle-like teeth before he could tie the jaws of the creature, after which he took the baby crocodile in his arms and tucked it away in the bow of the skiff. Before he had time to tie the little reptile in its crib Ned shouted from the power boat:

"There's one under that bank, a big fellow."

The captain sculled the skiff slowly toward the crocodile, which was lying on the water, just under the bank. As they approached, the creature slowly sank beneath the surface of the water, which was shallow, and beneath it a bottom of mud in which the fleeing reptile had left his trail. The captain followed the trail by the furrow-like track of the tail, the spoor of the paws and the roiled water, until Dick got a shot with his harpoon. Then the crocodile towed the skiff into the deeper channels of the river, among logs and snags and under banks, sometimes rolling up on the line and biting at the skiff while Dick vainly tried to get a bight of the harpoon line around the creature's jaw. The reptile was too wary for him, until finally the captain threatened the crocodile with a pole, while Dick got a line around its jaws and took it in the skiff. There was so little room in the skiff that Dick sat on the back of his captive until they reached the Irene. If he had tried this with an alligator he would have gone overboard, pronto, but when a crocodile's jaws are tied he is gentler than most lambs.

As soon as Dick had his new pets safely on the Irene he examined them carefully and then shouted to Ned:

"This is my old crocodile, the very one we turned loose when we were here before. I'd know him in a thousand. Don't you remember the broken point to the tooth that stuck out through his upper jaw, on the right side, too? Why, Crocky, old boy, how are you? I'm mighty glad to see you again."

"Don't you want to set them free to-morrow, Dick?" asked Mr. Barstow.

"I don't, but I've got to."

"Would you rather send them North to be educated?"

"I surely would. I wish I could."

"I think it can be managed. I know of a zoological collection where they will be very welcome. If you think they haven't been injured, I will ship both of them North from Miami."

"They are all right. I know that. I made two bad throws and barely touched both of them. I don't believe you could find where either of them was hit, now."

"Then North they go."

The boys made a box for the little crocodile, gathered a lot of grass for his bed and stowed him away in the hold where he would be safe from the attentions of Tom. There was not enough lumber on board to make a box for the big crocodile and the brute was put overboard to pasture at the end of a hundred-foot line. As soon as the crocodile was overboard Dick drew it beside the boat and untied its jaws. At first it tried to get away, but soon gave it up and thereafter rose to the surface every few minutes and gazed gravely upon its new friends on the boat. When later the Irene was ready to sail, Dick drew his pet up to the side of the boat and tied his jaws without remonstrance from the reptile. It took three of them to haul the creature aboard, where it was fastened to a ringbolt on deck for the first stage of its journey to the Zoo.

"Captain Hull," said Ned, as the whole party were watching the stars from the cabin top and waiting for the moon to rise that night, "we have got back from the Madeira Hammock every thing we lost there, so we will start for Miami to-morrow."

160

"Aye, aye, sir."

"You know you said we might lose a day round here, and now we have got a day to spare."

"You'll be lucky if you don't lose it. There's lots of chances between here and Miami, or between here and anywhere. There isn't six inches between the Irene's bottom and the rocks this minute and we're going to stir the mud a dozen times to-morrow."

"Supposing a storm comes while we are anchored so near the rocks?"

"Anybody who supposes in this country won't ever do anything else."

"Would we make anything by another night run?"

"Make sure to pile up on a bank so high that you'd have time to homestead a farm before you got off."

The Irene stirred the mud a few times the next day, but passed through Blackwater, Barnes and Card sounds and all the cuts and channels to Biscayne Bay without trouble. There a high wind and a heavy sea held her back, so that it was dusk when the anchor was dropped just outside of the mouth of Miami River. During this, their last evening on the cabin roof of the Irene, Mr. Barstow said to Dick:

"Do you feel perfectly well and strong again?"

"Never felt so well before in my life and am getting my strength back fast."

"Then vacation ends for you and Ned to-day. To-morrow morning you will take the train for the North, where you will have about two weeks to spend with your mother. I will wire her from Miami about our arrangement, which I am sure she will approve, and tell her when she may expect you. Very soon you will receive your instructions. You and Ned will be together, work the same, pay the same, and both of you have my perfect confidence that you will justify every hope I have of you."

"Mr. Barstow, I haven't any words—"

"Don't say anything, Dick, I understand it all, my boy. Just go ahead and make good, both for yourself and me."

In the morning Ned and the captain distinguished themselves by waking up a dealer, buying some lumber, hustling it aboard and having the two crocodiles boxed up for transportation North in time for the train of that day. How much of a feat that was requires a residence in South Florida to appreciate.

The Irene was run up the river to the railroad dock, where the crocodiles were put on the cars and the boys took their train for the North. When the good-byes were said, the captain carried Tom

161

across the dock on his shoulder and Dick's last act before leaving was to formally present him to Molly.


THE END